NOT MURDER

NOT MURDER

NO. 4 IN THE MAVIS DAVIS MYSTERY SERIES

SUSAN P. BAKER

REFUGIO PRESS

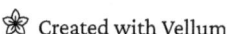 Created with Vellum

PRAISE FOR SUSAN P. BAKER

About *NOT MURDER, No. 4 in the Mavis Davis Mystery Series:*

As always, this has enjoyable characters and an engaging plot. I'm looking forward to the next one in the series!

Meg, an Amazon Verified Reviewer

A fresh and delightful story. Kept me on my toes til the end. So happy to have found Susan P. Baker

Anonymous, an Amazon Verified Reviewer

"Mavis Davis is a great character: smart, funny and stubborn enough to make an efficient P.I." An Amazon Vine ™ Voice Reviewer

"Nothing complicated or flowery – just a good entertaining mystery." Another Amazon Vine ™ Voice Reviewer

––––––––––

About *MY FIRST MURDER, No. 1 in the Mavis Davis Mystery Series:* "I really loved this Texas-based P.I. murder mystery. Mavis Davis is a hoot. She's gutsy and glamorous and fearless. She's determined to get her P.I. agency up and running, and this is her first murder case. She's been handling employment investigations, insurance claims, and other boring jobs, but this is a bonafide murder investigation. It's a bit more dangerous than she expected, but her intuition and instincts are great, and she stirs up more than one hornet's nest on her way to a solution. I'll definitely read more of the series. Fast and fun. Great read." An Amazon Verified Reviewer

"Mavis is a strong and resourceful protagonist, and Baker is a strong and resourceful writer. They make a good team." David Pitt. ALA

ACKNOWLEDGMENTS

Many thanks to the following people:

Mars, editor and virtual marketing assistant; Saralyn Richard, Phyllis Moore, and Gary Hoffman, members of the Galveston Novel and Short Story Writers Group; cover designer, 100 Covers; Maggie and Mike Fuller for inspiration and for hosting me in La Grange; Captain Destin Sims of the Galveston Police Department; and lastly, Tom and Susan Minello, real live people who made a charitable donation to Artist Boat in exchange for being characters in a Mavis Davis novel.

CHAPTER
ONE

Halloween being only a couple of days off, we were decorating the office rather belatedly. Decorating a private investigator's office might be a hokey thing to do, but my able assistant, Margaret, came up with the idea. I always want to keep Margaret happy, since she's the real backbone of Mavis Davis Investigations. So, we were in the middle of decorating for Halloween when my two o'clock appointment showed up fifteen minutes early.

I stood near the top of a ladder, to the right of the front door, reaching for the corner molding to stick on some decorations. I was doing this thing where I was trying to overcome my acrophobia, which had been re-activated recently when I'd been in Galveston on a building rooftop in a dangerous situation.

If you're going to be afraid of something, acrophobia is not the worst fear someone could have according to Margaret. I could have a fear of the walking dead—for which there is no formal name. At least I had been unable to find a name. Margaret is a movie freak and loves watching scary movies at Halloween in addition to teasing me about my one true fear.

So anyway, someone flung open our door, making the cowbell clang, and causing me to wobble on the ladder. I blame Margaret for that, and probably will until we decorate for the next holiday, since she was the one who talked me into getting up on that ladder. My stomach might settle down by then.

A tall, thin, thirties-something female carrying a satchel caused me to immediately wonder if we were going to be served papers. Serving legal documents is something we do at our office besides investigations. I kinda recognize the jaunty, nonchalant way people walk when they don't want you to figure out why they're there, having done that myself.

She wore black boots with stiletto heels, a black pencil skirt with a matching long-sleeved jacket over a pale pink V-necked, chiffon blouse. Her shoulder-length, chestnut-brown hair flipped around when she spotted me clinging to the wall on the other side of the door. Though she looked staid and business formal, her full lips formed a wide smile. Stepping inside and closing the door behind herself, she glanced around the reception area.

Margaret sat before the computer (after roping me into doing the decorating). I was holding orange and black crepe paper with a pumpkin and skeleton print in one hand and a cellophane tape dispenser in the other. I had been trying to stick the decorations to the door frame while doing my best not to lose my balance and land face first on the floor.

"Is one of you Mavis Davis?"

"That would be me." I stuck the crepe paper to the corner of the door frame and held on tight as I picked my way down each step of the ladder until I reached the bottom.

"I'm your two o'clock, Blanche Tellweger." The aroma of gardenias floated in the air. She extended her hand and took my empty one, shaking it, before I even stabilized in front of her.

The adrenaline was settling down, but I still had the queasy gut. Her hand was soft and medium-sized. I always notice people's hands, because mine are large for a woman. People have said my mother should have paid for piano lessons for me. Anyway, the woman had long fake red nails that looked real to unsuspicious eyes, which mine are not. She gave my hand a hard squeeze. "Pleased to meet you. Are you ready for me?"

"Sure, let's go to my office. I hope you didn't have a problem finding us." I led her down the hall. Our offices are in an old house on Westheimer in Houston. My private office would have been the master bedroom or, as realtors call them now, the primary bedroom. The full bath adjacent to the back door has come in handy in the past when I've needed to put myself together before a meeting, but that's another story. My office furnishings consist of an over-sized, light oak desk purchased at an auction a few years ago when I first set up; a couple of chairs that aren't very soft, so the client won't stay long; a sofa, which is a new addition, so I have someplace to think (and sleep); my own executive chair; and a file cabinet that wasn't over-flowing with case files.

Closing the door behind her, I said, "Have a seat, Ms. Tellweger."

I circled around my desk and plopped down. "Delightful to meet you." I picked up a pen and pulled a legal pad within my reach. "When you made the appointment, you told my assistant, Margaret Applebaum, you're from Galveston?"

Ms. Tellweger placed her satchel, and a tiny shoulder bag not much bigger than one which would hold a cell phone, on the client chair next to her. She slid back and crossed her legs. She had sparkling sea green eyes, thick—yet shaped—dark eyebrows, and a clear tan complexion some women would kill for. (Not me, I'm a redhead. I've never thought I looked good in tan. In fact, if I were to lie out in the sun, I'd probably end up a mass of freckles...Okay, I admit it, I surfed in Galveston when I was a girl and was indeed a mass of freckles).

"Would you like some coffee or a bottle of water, or we can make you a cup of tea if you want?"

She shook her head. "No. I won't be long, I hope. My time is valuable. I can't bill for this trip to see you."

"Well, then, let's get down to business." Giving her my best smile, I wrote her name at the top of the first page. "May I have your address and contact information?"

Ms. Tellweger recited everything I needed to know, which I jotted down while my brain raced. What profession was she in that she dressed in more than business casual and took valuable time from her day to visit me?

"And the reason you're here?" I set my pen on the pad and clasped my hands in front of me.

She swallowed and squared her shoulders. "Well, technically, to begin with, to serve this on someone."

She handed me some folded papers, which I recognized as service of process. Someone had inked on them four unsuccessful tries to serve the defendant. "You want me to serve someone another process server has already tried to serve?" Bummer. I was hoping for something meatier.

"Ha! Yes. But I'm sure you won't be successful either, so I want to hire you to track her down. In your line of work, I think you might call it skip tracing?"

Ah, looking for people was one of my best things, digging through physical records if I couldn't find them on the Internet, stalking their homes and workplaces. I was definitely interested in this undertaking, provided she could pay my hourly fee plus expenses. She certainly looked like she could, so I proceeded to extract her information. "Who exactly are you looking for?"

She exhaled loudly and shifted around in the chair, getting comfortable, though I hoped not too comfy, because I couldn't start billing her until she hired me and my time was also valuable, at least to me. "A former client of mine," she said.

"Which gets me to the question of what you do for a living?" I also sat back.

"I'm an attorney in Galveston. Specifically, I'm board certified in family law, though occasionally I do take criminal and civil cases, if they're interesting and pay well."

Ergo, her valuable time. I wanted to find out her hourly fee, though I grew squeamish before remembering she was hiring me. I wasn't hiring her. I'd been in the reverse position not too long ago and had only recently finished making payments to my ex-lawyer. "So you want me to find a former client who owes you money, is that what you're saying?" While we engaged in conversation, my mind wandered to what kind of office she must have. Since attorneys make more than people in my business, my experience has been they have at least richer-looking decor. I hoped she wasn't judging ours.

"Yes. She owes me a great deal. I worked my tail off for this woman, and she stiffed me on a chunk of my fee."

"Don't you lawyers generally get your money up front?" I realized immediately I shouldn't have voiced that thought.

She gave me a sharp look. "Yes, and I did, but it turned out her divorce and her ex were a lot more complicated than I'd been led to believe. She made regular payments on my bill right up until trial, but nothing that week, and nothing thereafter, saying she would pay the remainder when she received her settlement. By that time, I was stuck with her, too late to withdraw, and had to go through with the trial."

"She never got her settlement?"

"Oh, yeah, she got it. The judge also awarded me attorneys' fees so my client wouldn't have to pay me, which her husband was supposed to pay, but her husband sent the check to her instead of to me. She never handed it over."

I was thinking of the expletives which would come out of my mouth had one of my clients failed to pay me a sum big enough for me to go searching for him or her. I was eager to hear just how big the check was Ms. Tellweger's client didn't remit.

"I understand." How bad could it possibly be? Five thousand, ten? "So, she owes you roughly how much?"

Frowning, she said, "Upwards of sixty thousand dollars."

I winced. My body tensed. My hands grew cold, so I pulled them down under the desk and warmed them on my pants legs. "Oh holy cow."

"Exactly. It's not that I can't live without it, I can. It's the principle of the thing. I worked hard for her. We had become almost friends. I don't understand how she could do such a thing."

Surely, she knew where money was concerned there were few limits on what people would do. Of course, I wouldn't say that. I'd never say that. Not if I wanted to be hired. I shook my head. "Let me get the business side of this thing out of the way, all right?"

"Yes, let's. I need to get back to Galveston, back to my office to try to log some billable hours today."

I proceeded to tell her what I'd charge if she wanted me to go out immediately and serve her former client, at which she laughed. Then we went on to discuss what my daily rate was for skip tracing (which we preferred to call investigating), what my hourly rate was if I worked only half a day or less on any given day, and that I charged for expenses. Lawyers were used to that kind of thing, except I think they charge by the minute. She agreed.

"Do you have some sort of contract you'd like me to sign?" She gave me a faux smile.

"My assistant, Margaret, will have it prepared for your signature when you're ready to leave. Excuse me a moment."

I hurried out, seeking Margaret, who was in the kitchen whipping up something in a mixing bowl. I was glad we had that bell on the front door, so we could hear when someone came in. Margaret spent a lot of time in the kitchen of late, especially around holidays. Not that my stomach complained, most of the time. "Hey, I need you to print out a contract for Ms. Tellweger to sign before she leaves. She's hiring us to find someone." The counters were covered with ingredients I hoped would be cookies, only the type I like to eat, not the kind she sometimes made with strange, though healthy, ingredients. "Can Candy finish whatever you're making while you do the contract?"

Margaret shot me a dark look. Seldom did she allow anyone to touch her concoctions, especially Candy or me. She knew we'd probably add a ton of white sugar. Margaret untied her apron and tossed it on the counter next to the bowl. "Candy texted. She's at the courthouse filing the returns on those two services she did this morning."

Candy Finklestein was the third female in our office. We'd practically raised her. She had worked half a day when she was in high school. Now that she'd graduated, she was a full-time employee, which was why I was happy Ms. Tellweger had come in that morning. As always, we needed to keep the money flowing.

"Okay. It'll be a few minutes before Lawyer Tellweger will be ready to leave, but don't wait too long. She's in a hurry." Before I went back to my office, I reminded Margaret, "Be sure to collect a check from her before she departs."

Margaret rolled her eyes in a long-suffering victim look. "I will, Mavis. God, how long have we been in business?"

I hurried back to Blanche Tellweger, eager to find out the details of her former client and where I might begin my search. This case was not murder but was my second favorite kind to be hired on. Now for the sordid details.

"Miss Tellweger, just for my information, may I ask who referred you to me?" I drew a line under her personal info and made ready to write the name of the person I needed to thank.

"Of course, Lauren Smith. She's a retired court reporter who lives down on the island." She smiled for real for the first time. "I believe y'all are friends?"

"Lauren. Sure." We became friends on the case of the murdered cruise ship captain I worked on down there. "How's she doing?" I made a quick note.

"She became bored, so she's subbing sometimes in the courts. That's how I know her." She clicked on her cell phone and gave it a quick look. I was sure it was to check the time.

I flipped to a second page of my legal pad. "I'm ready now if you want to tell me the name of your former client, her address, and whatever else you think might be helpful. Also, what efforts you've made to locate her and the response."

She pulled two pieces of stapled-together paper out of her satchel and handed them across my desk. "Everything you need to know is written out here. If something else comes up, you can always call or text me."

I gave the first page a once-over. The woman's name was Gina Collins. She lived in Houston, used to live on Tiki Island in Galveston County. Her ex-husband's name was Dewey Collins. He was awarded the Tiki Island home. She was awarded the home in Houston and also her separate property interest in two antiques shops. One shop was in La Grange, and one was in Galveston. He got the Range Rover. She got the Mercedes sedan. And on it went.

"Is there anything you need that might be missing?"

I scanned the second page. Probably more details that an attorney might want to know, but I doubted I would. "I think I have everything I need, Miss Tellweger."

"Please call me Blanche. All right if I call you Mavis?"

"Yes, ma'am." I gestured toward the door. "I'll tackle this right away and report my progress to you each evening, if that's acceptable."

She took a business card from the holder on my desk. "I see your cell is on here. I already have your office number. So I guess that's it." She walked into the hall.

I followed her. "Margaret will have the contract ready for you. You can give her a check or a credit card if you want." I hated taking credit cards, because they took a percentage, but these days that's how a lot of people did business. "We also take PayPal."

We shook hands when I left her with Margaret. "Oh, and Blanche, if you run into Lauren, tell her hi, please."

If I couldn't locate Gina Collins in Houston and had to drive down to Galveston to the antiques shop in my search for her, I'd be sure to meet with Lauren for lunch or dinner. She'd been a great help to me in the past. I wanted to maintain our relationship. Besides, if I needed something, Lauren might just be the one to have the skinny. Yes, if I was going to continue to have cases with ties to Galveston, I would have to maintain all my contacts there.

I thought of another person I looked forward to seeing again, in addition to Lauren. If possible, I wanted to reestablish my connection to one Sheriff's Deputy, Andy Crider, regardless of whether Ben, my life partner, (i.e. boyfriend) liked it. You never knew when a contact with someone in law enforcement might come in handy. Deputy Crider had helped me in the past and left me with the impression he'd always be available to assist me in the future. That worked for me.

CHAPTER
TWO

In deciding where to start my search for Gina Collins, I reviewed the pages Blanche had given me. Of course the most obvious place to start would be the Internet, at which Margaret was a whiz. She's a member of some groups I had never heard of, like Web Sleuths. She's talked to me about them (sometimes *ad nauseam*). Other groups I've tried not to learn anything about. She has her life, and I have mine.

After the Internet search, I'd go to the woman's Houston home and see if I could catch her there. I should be so lucky. Or I should say, Blanche should be so lucky, because if I found Gina Collins within twenty-four hours, Blanche would get a refund of my unearned fee. I asked Siri for a map to Gina Collins' home. What she spit out showed the house stood in a decent neighborhood and not more than a twenty-minute drive from my office, depending on traffic. I printed it. I like to have a visual in addition to Siri's directions, if it's possible.

On my way to the front of the office to pick up the map from the network printer Margaret had set up, I passed her in the kitchen. "I'll be right back." Like I said, Margaret is a whiz at computer stuff. If I didn't say that, I meant to. I retrieved the map and put it and the service papers in the file with Blanche's name on it lying on Margaret's desk. I had to love Margaret. Under the folder were Blanche's checks and a deposit slip.

Back in the kitchen, I breathed deeply. Something was in the oven. I was still praying it was edible. My definition of edible, not Margaret's. "Margaret, thanks for opening the file already."

Margaret had the apron tied around her waist again, covering her blouse and slacks, and flour up to her elbows. "You're welcome. Did you find the checks? She wrote one to pay us for her petition being served and a second one as a retainer for the investigation. I called her bank, and there's no problem with them. You should deposit them right away anyhow."

"Why do you say that?"

"For one thing, we have payroll coming up. For another, a bird in the hand and all that."

I looked in the oven window and spied cookies. "Was there something about her that caused you to suspect she might not make good on the checks?"

"Not really. Since I joined Web Sleuths, I've gotten to where I realize anyone can be guilty of anything. I don't trust lawyers any more than I trust anyone else. She looked fine. Pricey clothes. When she wrote out the checks, she pulled an expensive pen from her little purse. One neither you nor I would ever waste money on."

Margaret could be parsimonious. With good reason since she'd never had any money. This was an asset since we ran the office on a more than tight budget. And cookies.

"What kind of cookies are you baking?"

"Sugar cookies. The kind you and Candy like, not the healthy ones." She smirked. "And I'm going to decorate them like pumpkins, carved pumpkins. Are you even listening to me?"

"Yes, Margaret, dear. I'll deposit the checks as soon as possible. I'd hate to think someone who has been stiffed out of $60,000 would stiff us out of a few thousand."

"Sixty thousand dollars? Jiminy Christmas, what kind of case did she have that someone would owe her sixty thousand dollars? Whew!" Margaret was using a cookie cutter to cut out a second batch of Halloween cookies.

"Family law. Crazy, isn't it? I'm not aware there were children, either. I think they fought over property, her antiques stores and his royalties from his books."

"Sixty thousand dollars." She shook her head. "I could do a lot with sixty thousand dollars."

"Me, too, and you can quit saying sixty thousand dollars before it influences me to apply to law school."

Margaret laughed. "I can't see you as a lawyer."

"That hurts my feelings."

"Yeah, right.

Margaret could always tell when I was kidding. "Anyway, as soon as you get that first batch of cookies out of the oven and the second batch in, could you start an Internet search on Gina Collins? That's the name of her client. I put the service Blanche gave me into the folder. See what you can find, beginning with her divorce records in Galveston County."

"Okey-dokey." She turned back to her baking.

I turned back to my office. I had to make a few notes on a case we'd completed, then I could finish the Halloween decorating. By the time I was through, Margaret should have gotten a basic search on Collins done, as well as the cookies, and I'd know where I needed to go after making the deposit. A big part of me was hoping I didn't find Gina Collins quickly. We always needed money.

The bell on the front door rang. A moment later, Candy yelled, "It's only me!"

She came into my office. I hadn't seen her that day, since she left straight from her home to get the service of process done for two Houston lawyers. She'd really grown up since we first took her in. She used to have different colored hair every so often, blues, purples, etcetera. And odd clothing. Odd to me in that I didn't think it matched, but she did. And lots of earrings. Now, she didn't change her hair color as frequently. Today it was platinum blonde. Margaret had bleached her hair that color in the past. That could have influenced Candy. I hoped it would be short-lived. It could put my eyes out if the sun hit it in the right (or wrong) way. These days, I mostly refrained from commenting on any of her attire, unless we had a reason for her to dress in a certain way. That morning, she wore her school uniform again even though she'd graduated high school last spring.

"I got those two people served and filed the returns at the clerk's office," Candy said. "You want me to text the clients and let them know?"

"Well, good morning."

She grinned. "Good morning, boss lady."

"You're getting so efficient. Did the school uniform serve its purpose? You'd think the recipients might be suspicious and wonder why you weren't in class."

"Well, they didn't, but I'll rethink that for morning attire, as you call it. I could keep my uniform in the closet here and wear it when I do late afternoon and evening service."

"Excellent idea. So, yes, if you wouldn't mind. Text the clients for me."

"Okay. Hey, what's Margaret baking? Anything I'd want to eat?"

"I'm hoping so. She said she's baking sugar cookies for us."

"I'm hungry. I overslept and didn't eat breakfast."

"That's not good."

"I stayed up late studying for an exam I have tonight."

Candy had enrolled in community college. She was taking three classes. One class on Mondays, Wednesdays, and Fridays during the day. We made allowances for her schedule. Her other two classes were one each on Tuesday and Thursday nights. I thought three classes plus work was ambitious, but she's a ball of energy and wants to get her associates degree ASAP.

"Do you need to take off this afternoon so you can study some more?"

She shook her head. "I'm going to bother Margaret for a cookie and text those clients and then one of you can find something else for me to do." She grinned. She'd been so happy since graduation the previous spring. Her happiness was contagious. The atmosphere in the office was decidedly cheerful every day.

"Bring me one, please."

She scooted down the hall to the kitchen. Margaret squawked, so I knew Candy had met with success. She flew back to my office and handed me a cookie, undecorated, in a paper napkin. "I'll be in my office."

Our office had two "offices" which were originally bedrooms. The smaller one was a kind of workroom containing a lot of odds and ends, our safe, supplies and the like. After she became full-time, Candy had cleaned out the space, hung curtains, (in young-person taste, not mine), put up some posters and furnished it with an old wooden desk she'd found in a garage sale, ergo, her calling the room her office. I didn't care since the public never went in there.

In the front of "our suite of offices" is our reception area, which holds a desk Margaret homesteads, the big computer, the all-in-one printer, copier etcetera, a lateral file cabinet—the bottom drawer of which is filled with a lesser amount of supplies—those Margaret would need every day, so she didn't have to get up and down constantly. In the top drawer, Margaret had a book with lawyer info, a dictionary even though our software had one—she didn't think it contained enough words—current files if they're not in my office, and I didn't want to know what else. Margaret's stuff.

I worked on my notes on the previous case for a few minutes while munching my cookie. The sugar cookie was made of white flour and white sugar, about as healthy as taking a spoonful of sugar every day, way to go Margaret. I made an attempt to eat healthy eighty percent of the time. At holidays, and that's every conceivable one on the calendar, I indulged. Luckily, I had one of those bodies that didn't bulge.

Not waiting for the Internet search that Margaret would conduct, I went ahead and telephoned Gina Collins at what Blanche had listed as her home number. Some people still had home telephones—landlines. No answer. I left a message that I had a personal matter to discuss with her if she'd call me back. I then tried her cell number. Voicemail. I didn't leave a message. After that, I rang the number for the La Grange antiques store. Again, an answering machine where I left a message. Finally, I called the Galveston antiques store.

"Beachy Antiques," a scratchy male voice said.

"Hi, my name's Mavis Davis. May I speak with Gina Collins?"

"I'm sorry. She's not in. Is there something I can help you with?" His tone was friendly, as any salesperson's should be.

"No, thank you. It's a personal matter. Would you know how I could get in touch with her?"

"We have another store in La Grange. She might be there, though since it's Tuesday she'd only be there by appointment."

"No answer there. I already tried. And her cell and her home."

I could almost see his head shake. "Then I'm sorry. I can't think where she'd be. I haven't spoken to her since last Friday. May I take a message?"

"No, that's okay."

"Are you sure I can't help you with something?"

"I'm sure. What's your name, please?"

"Tom Minello. I'm Gina's cousin."

"Thank you, Tom. You said 'we have another store.' You're a part owner in the Galveston store?" I already knew that, having seen his name on the paperwork Blanche had left me.

"Yes, and I generally run it. Gina is our buyer, if you want to call her that. She might be somewhere I'm not aware of, looking at an estate if she's not in La Grange. Nobody answered at that store?"

"No. She runs that one?"

"Since her divorce, she spends more time there than here, seems like. Oh my gosh, I shouldn't have said that. You're a stranger. You don't need to know all that stuff."

"It's okay. I knew she was divorced. Thanks for your help. I'll try again." I hung up and sat back in my chair. I needed to decide where to start searching. The closest place was her house. I saw a possible stakeout in my future.

CHAPTER

THREE

I deposited Blanche's check and headed for the first home address I had for Gina. There were two on the list of places Blanche had given me. The first one was in a residential neighborhood in Bellaire, a respectable part of Houston. I found the house, an upscale-looking one with a manicured front yard with a Sold sign pasted across a For Sale sign. I banged on the door, but no one answered. The grass needed cutting and, though the windows were covered from the inside, the house felt empty. Turned out the second place was closer to my office than I realized, but with Houston traffic, the trip still took twenty minutes. I probably should have gone there first.

The address was a gated community of condos, with a guard box, which alerted me I'd have to study its ingress and egress in case I had to return for a stakeout. I didn't want to climb over a fence, but I would if I had to. At that time, though, the gate was open, and no one was in the little guard house. It could be there for show except at night, the neighborhood looking like a safe one.

I found Gina's condo, which was a straight shot from the front gate, a few buildings back, and parked in an almost vacant parking area. The condo was a townhouse design, two stories, which signaled to me that probably Gina wasn't too old to climb stairs. Another stereotype I engage in. There are probably a lot of old people who do it every day. If I ever got old, I wouldn't want to. Actually, I wouldn't have to because I own a one-story house.

The front of the place was well-manicured with mulch around the hedges. Undoubtedly there was a condo association with a monthly fee I probably couldn't afford. The parking lot and curbs were all in tip-top shape. No trash in the street or anywhere. A few small trees adorned the place every hundred yards or so. Pumpkins and autumn foliage arrangements decorated the front stoops of most of the units. Some of them had tame Halloween decor. No skeletons hung from windows. No plastic blow-ups graced the grass. I rang the bell.

After about thirty seconds, I rang the bell again. I put my ear to the door but couldn't hear whether the doorbell chimed. I didn't hear any movement either, or a telephone or radio playing. After a third try, I knocked. Okay, banged with the heel of my fist. Again nothing. I didn't expect her to be there since she hadn't answered her home phone or a cell phone, but you never know. She was probably aware Blanche wanted her money. Gina, more than likely, was avoiding Blanche.

So what to do, what to do? No one being around, I tried to peek inside every window. Unfortunately, the blinds were closed. I wasn't really frustrated. I didn't really expect to find her that easily. I'd had to start my search somewhere and had chosen the Houston places first.

As I stood out front and contemplated my options, including walking around to back of Gina's place, a woman came out from next door. "You look lost," she called. "Can I help you with something, or somebody?"

She was an older woman, perhaps old enough for Social Security, but stairs couldn't have been an issue for her, or she wouldn't be living there. She looked physically fit, like one of those yoga mavens, thin, clothed in black leggings and a black short-sleeved stretchy top. She had to be a member of the neighborhood watch, whether official or unofficial.

"Yes, ma'am. I'm looking for Gina Collins. I was told she lived in this condo."

"She does." She came closer. I could smell cinnamon or cardamom. Nutmeg? Some smell I associated with fall. She wore sunglasses. It being October in Houston, the sun still shone like summertime, only the temperature was marginally cooler. "Gina moved in about six months ago. It's a rental." She frowned when she said that, as though unhappy any condos in their well-to-do area would be leased.

"Oh, I didn't know that. I was under the impression she was the owner."

She shook her head. "No, the couple who own the unit have taken up residence in Germany for the next year, but Gina's been an all right neighbor, so far as I know."

"Do you know her well?"

Again she shook her head. "No. At first, she kept to herself, but I'm getting to know her. Lately she's seemed to come out of her shell."

"She went through a bad divorce."

"I did know that. I persuaded her to come over for coffee a couple of weeks ago. So when she returns, can I tell her who's looking for her?"

I didn't see the harm of giving her my name. "Mavis Davis. And your name?"

"Nancy Harmon. I live next door."

"I got that. And I bet you're an owner." I gave her my best smile hoping to indicate I understood the importance of home ownership.

She nodded and smiled back, showing deep dimples. "Yes. I've lived here since these were built. My late husband and I retired here from Iowa."

That explained the non-Texas accent. "Oh. I'm sorry for your loss. Have you lived alone for a long time?"

She stepped a little closer and said in a confidential tone, "I don't actually live alone most of the time. I have a man friend." She looked over her shoulder like she was afraid someone would overhear.

"Ohhhh. Well good for you." I wasn't going to state my surprise at a Social Security-aged woman having a boyfriend. Old people have lives, too.

"He's not here right now. He plays golf several times a week."

I didn't really care, but I've found that people often know a lot about their neighbors they might share if you're friendly enough. "You said he's here most of the time. Not all the time?"

"Well, we haven't decided if we should live together yet. I'm not sure I want to take care of some old man full-time. I like the benefits of having a boyfriend, though. For a couple of years, after my husband died, I was lonely."

"Yeah. I don't live with my boyfriend either. He can stay with me occasionally, but I never stay at his place."

"I don't stay with Grant either. I like to sleep in my own bed."

"So you're always here."

She nodded. "Okay, Mavis. I don't want to keep you. You're young enough that you're probably still working. Anything I can tell Gina when I see her?"

I shook my head. "I'll come back another time and see if I can catch her."

She started back to her place. "You know, now that I think about it. I haven't seen Gina for several days."

"By that you mean in the daytime?"

"She's not usually here in the daytime but returns in the evenings from wherever she goes. You probably know she owns an antiques shop in Galveston?"

"I do know that. And one in La Grange. So she hasn't been here for several nights?"

"No. I just realized that. Grant's been staying over, so I haven't paid a lot of attention to what's been going on outside my own home."

She probably didn't want to admit that normally she knew the comings and goings of everyone who lived within eyeball distance of her condo. And I wasn't going to mention that I suspected that. "You haven't seen her? What about her car? What does she drive?" I hadn't paid attention to what Blanche had listed for a car in the pages she gave me.

"A Dodge Caravan. A big, old blue one. If you'd known that, you'd have known she wasn't here. You can't miss that ugly vehicle."

"I guess not."

"She uses it to haul stuff she buys for her stores. She can tow a trailer with it. More than once she's had a big U-Haul-type trailer parked in the lot, filled with old furniture she's bought at a sale in Waco or someplace. People get mad when she parks parallel to the sidewalk and takes up a bunch of parking spaces."

That explained why a single woman would drive a van. I wouldn't want to, but these days people drove humongous vehicles, at least in Texas. "Well, thanks, Nancy. You've been a great help. I might come back tonight, to satisfy myself she's not staying here right now, because that's what it sounds like."

"She could be off on a buying trip somewhere—I guess that's what they call it when they're off searching for junk to sell."

"Yeah. Or staying in La Grange. You don't happen to know where she stays up there if she decides to be in that store for several days?"

"No, sorry. Wish I could be more help. By the way, I know it's none of my business, but do you mind telling me why you're trying to find her?"

I weighed how much I should share with Nancy. More than likely whatever I told her wouldn't stay with her but would be known around the condo complex before the sun rose on Wednesday morning. She wore a friendly, if expectant, expression as if hoping I'd share information.

"No, I don't mind. It has to do with her divorce. A property issue remains unresolved. Her attorney wants to discuss it with her but hasn't been able to reach her."

She nodded. "I see. There was a man here last week looking for her as well. I don't think it was her ex-husband. Don't know why I think that. Just an impression I had. I tried to talk to the man, but he wasn't friendly at all."

The previous process server. "I might come back tonight, so perhaps I'll see you later, Nancy. Take care." I hastened to my Mustang. After several tries, it started. I waved at her as I backed out.

I needed to decide how to proceed. If I acted fast, I could make it to La Grange, which was only about an hour and a half away if traffic wasn't too bad.

I phoned Margaret.

"Mavis Davis Investigations," her sweet, high-pitched voice rang out. "How may I help you today?"

Shaking my head, which of course she couldn't see, I proceeded to tell her my plans. I was shaking my head because for years now I had been working with her on simply answering the phone Mavis Davis Investigations. We used to be Mavis Davis Productions, which I'd thought was clever. We were set up to do so many things besides investigate, such as serving papers, letting people use our copier, even letting lawyers who worked for themselves and didn't want to hire a secretary hire us to work up their pleadings. People somehow got the impression we made movies, though, or otherwise produced something, not always things I'd want people to think. Since investigations and serving papers had become our main thing, I changed it to Investigations. We were not averse to accommodating other requests, though, as long as they were reasonable and legal.

So, deciding not to address her manner of answering the phone that day, which was not as bad as it had been many other times, I simply said, "Margaret, it's me. I'm leaving the parking lot at Gina Collins' condo."

"Oh, hey, Mavis. Did you find her?"

"Nope. I think I'm going to take a run up to La Grange, to the antiques shop she owns up there."

"Late in the day for that, isn't it?"

"Not really. I'm going to grab a sandwich and eat it on the way. I could make it back in time for rush hour traffic."

"Funny, Mavis."

"Anything going on there that I need to know about?"

"Ben called."

I glanced at the missed calls on my cell. Oops. Ben had called several times. I had silenced my cell when I got out of my car. "Yeah, I'll call him back. So everything's good there?" I had only been gone for a short while, but with Margaret and Candy, you never knew what might happen.

"Everything's fine. I was thinking you might go to La Grange tomorrow, so I looked up La Grange on the Internet. They have the classic Texas town square and her store is on it."

Margaret could be so thoughtful. I didn't remind her that I'd been to La Grange several times over the years. "So I'll be able to find her store with no problem?"

"Yes. And you could do some shopping while you're there. Looks like some fun places, including a kitchen store."

Ignoring that last statement, I said, "Yeah, I'll consider that. What are you working on?"

"Jeremy came by and asked me to type some motions for him. He'll be back in the morning to pick them up."

Jeremy was one of the solo lawyers we worked for. "Okay. And what's Candy doing?"

"Copying some long depositions in a car wreck case. Well, not exactly a car wreck, this eighteen-wheeler ran over a man who was stopped on the side of the road changing his tire. The eighteen-wheeler was like a steamroller over—"

"TMI, Margaret." Candy had a habit of reading some of the depositions she copied even though what they contained was none of our business. She had it in her head that she might want to be a court reporter or a paralegal or even a lawyer someday, perish the thought. I urged her to just do the copying and keep her nose out of other people's business. Attorneys wouldn't like it if they knew. "Tell Candy to be sure to keep track of her time and the number of copies. We'll talk later."

I disconnected and continued to exit the parking lot. As I drew up next to the guard booth, my cell rang with Ben's special tune, so I stopped. "Hey, Ben, what's up?"

"Just checking in. Are we still on for tonight?"

I'd kind of forgotten he was bringing dinner over later, but I'd never admit that. He didn't like to be forgotten, which was understandable. Who did? "Sure. What time are you thinking?"

"Seven? I don't have anything out of the ordinary going on today, so I should be able to get there by then. What are you up to?"

What he meant was no homicides that required his hands-on attention. I weighed telling him where I was going. I know lots of people who communicate frequently with their partners during workdays, but I had never been one of those. I was getting better, though. I was well aware communication was important in any relationship. Ben and I had a tacit agreement that we would more or less keep in contact as long as it didn't become annoyingly frequent. No chance of that with me. If anything, it was too infrequent for Ben. His being a Lieutenant in the HPD sometimes kept him out of contact with me, so it worked both ways.

"I'm heading to La Grange, but I should easily make it back before seven."

"What's going on in La Grange?"

"I'm trying to find someone to serve papers on, that's all."

"Not a murder case again, is it?"

"Why are you asking? It's not murder. Just service of process." I wasn't going to volunteer that if I couldn't serve Gina Collins quickly, it would be a skip tracing case. I tried to keep our communication on a need-to-know basis.

"La Grange is not normally a place y'all go to serve papers, that's all. The last time you went out of town it was murder. Galveston, remember?"

"I know, but I swear it's not murder. This recipient owns an antiques store in La Grange." No need to mention the store in Galveston, yet. "I've tried her condo here without success. Don't worry. I'll make every effort to be back for dinner. I think it's going to be about a three-hour round trip, except I'll probably get some lunch along the way."

"Okay. Be careful. If you need anything in La Grange, let me know. I have a friend on the force there."

Of course he did. I'd concluded a long time ago Ben knew people all over Texas. His connections had come in handy in the past and probably would in the future. "Yes, dear. You be careful, too." I laughed as I clicked off. We had made a joke out of signing off like an old married couple.

I put my Mustang in gear and headed for La Grange, on the cusp of the Hill Country.

FOUR

H aving battled the Interstate 10 traffic all the way to the turnoff, I was happy to be able to relax a little when reaching the less-traveled road leading to La Grange. By the time I arrived at my destination, it was midafternoon. I parked on the courthouse square near Gina's antiques store, Fayette Antiques, which, to my disappointment, was locked up tight. Only about every third business appeared to be open.

There were posters about a fall pick-your-own pumpkin patch with a photograph of a bale of hay painted to look like a jack-o-lantern. I climbed out of my Mustang and stretched before heading to the bakery next door, whose windows advertised coffee and baked goods. I don't like coffee, but sometimes have a cup in the afternoons when my energy is waning. A cup of hot tea, a glass of iced tea, or even a caffeine-filled soda like Dr Pepper doesn't perk me up.

La Grange has continued to grow more country chic over the years. Ben and I had spent a holiday weekend there a couple of years ago, and people had overflowed the shops. In addition to the bakery and antiques store, I spotted the kitchen store and a cafe.

When I opened the bakery door, the aroma of cinnamon and

vanilla rushed me. My mouth was begging for a taste as I approached the glass display cabinets. An older woman sat on a stool behind the counter. She held a paperback in one hand and an oversized ceramic cup of steaming something in the other. She set them both down when I let the door close behind me. Wearing a flowered granny dress, the woman had silvery gray hair and granny glasses.

"Hi there," she said. "May I help you?"

The dress had to be a costume, an attempt to add to the bakery's ambiance. Vintage art posters and beveled mirrors decorated the walls. Round-topped wooden tables and spindle-backed wooden chairs with cane seats made me feel like I'd stepped into a time-warp.

"Hi. Y'all are advertising coffee, and I need some in the worst way. I drove in from Houston."

"You don't have to tell me. I bet this is your sleepy time. I know it is mine. You want plain coffee? I don't carry more than a few additives, but I can fix it up a little."

"Plain, hot, strong coffee is all I need." Inside the glass cabinets, several things appealed to me—cookies decorated like ghosts, witches' hats, and pumpkins. As far as cookies went, I'd stick with Margaret's. I knew what I'd be getting—most of the time. On the other hand, some of the other goodies would appease my stomach, which was complaining that a mere sandwich hadn't been satisfying. Before I ordered, though, I looked over my shoulder, hoping to spot the ladies room, and shifted from foot-to-foot.

"If you want to use the facilities, they're down that hall," she said, with a knowing smile, and pointed toward the far side of the bakery.

I did, in fact. When I returned, a painted china cup of coffee stood steaming on the counter. My stomach continued communicating with me, begging for something to go with the coffee. I didn't want just a donut, or even a brownie, though they looked yummy. I examined the pastries and pointed to one. "What's that?"

"Bear Claw. Some people call them American Bear Claw. De—li —cious." She pulled the tray out of the cabinet and waved her hand over it, sending the aroma my way.

I could possibly die and go to sugar heaven. "I thought that's what they were, but yours are huge. Never seen them that big."

"You know what they say about Texas...and we pride ourselves on presenting pastries a bit different. Mine are the best in Texas. Try one, you'll see." She put the tray back and pulled a piece of parchment paper from a box on the counter, poised to retrieve a Bear Claw for me.

"I'm afraid it's a bit much."

"I understand. Shall I give you a small sample for future reference?"

I didn't say I didn't plan to be back any time soon. I watched as she carved a chunk and handed it over. The pastry practically melted in my mouth. I was in Bear Claw heaven. After swallowing, I said, "I think you're right. The best in Texas." I stuck the remainder in my mouth. My eyes met hers. Her hand hovered over the tray.

"I could pack up one for you to take home. You have someone to share it with?"

She was persuasive, not that I needed much persuading. "Okay, go ahead and pack up the remainder of that one." I'd share it with Margaret and Candy. Margaret might be able to replicate it. There was a flavor just a bit different from anything I remembered.

She shook her head. "I'll save it to give a sample to the next person." She put a whole one in a white paper bag.

"How are the cream horns?" They were quite a bit smaller and would require a lot less guilt on my part.

"Every bit as tasty. We're famous for our kolaches, too."

I never liked kolaches. Too doughy, even those with sausage in them. I'd never say that aloud in any neighborhood near the Hill Country. I knew how Czech people cherished their creation. "Just a cream horn. I shouldn't even be eating that."

"None of us should, but they're outstanding." She pulled another piece of paper from the box and picked up the top cream horn, handing it to me. She was a short, stocky woman. Her silver-gray hair could be a wig. She could have been anywhere from forty to sixty years old, though her skin looked too smooth to be sixty.

"Thanks. Let me put this down on the table, and I'll pay you."

"Take your time. I'm not exactly busy." Her friendly smile looked genuine. She dragged her stool to the counter and climbed back up.

After paying, I sat at a two-top table set against the wall. The coffee was hot and bitter and yuckier than a kolache, but I hoped it would wake me up. The cream horn was decadent and went down easily. I closed my eyes, enjoying a moment of pure bliss. I didn't usually enter bakeries. I restrained myself from eating most sweets. Okay, that's a lie, but I was getting better at restraining myself. Historically, they never made it inside my house.

My cell rang. Ben Sorensen, again. Since he was a lieutenant in the Houston Police Department, I had a special ring for him. The Dragnet Theme. He didn't know about it, but I could hear it from a mile away. I also had special rings for each of the girls, Peter Gunn Theme for Margaret and a film noir one for Candy. "Hey, Ben. You caught me. What's up?"

"You still in La Grange?"

"I just got here." Sometimes I grew annoyed with Ben. That could have been one of those times if he hadn't explained himself quickly, and I wasn't downing a cream horn. "Is something wrong?"

"Turns out I won't be able to make it tonight."

I was only slightly disappointed. I'd be kind of tired anyway, what with the round-trip drive. "Something came up?"

"Yeah. A case that needs my attention."

I wasn't even going to ask. Not that he'd tell me anyway. "Okay. Want to try for tomorrow?"

"I'll let you know, honey." He rang off.

Honey was one of his apologetic words. I put the phone down and swallowed the last slug of coffee, grimacing, and chased it with the last bite of the cream horn. Brushing off my hands, I patted the cream and crumbs from my mouth and tossed the napkin in the trash. Energized by the caffeine and sugar, I hopped up and slung my bag over my shoulder.

The woman behind the counter had been watching me and, no doubt, listening to my brief conversation. No surprise there.

"Since I'm not doing anything, I wonder whether there's something I can help you with?" Granny got down from her stool again and pushed it out of the way. I debated responding, but every investigator knows pulling information from people is part of the job. The detective rule book must say that somewhere. "I'm looking for Gina Collins. She owns the antiques store next door."

Her body stiffened. Her lips tightened. "I know her. I haven't seen any sign of her today, but she was here over the weekend. They were busy with the fall shopping crowd like I was. People often go out to the pumpkin patch and come back here to shop and eat."

I approached the counter and set my empty cup down. I tried not to look inside the bakery case again. I was no longer hungry, but boy those pastries looked decadent. I could take some of those decorated cookies back to the office, though Margaret might get her feelings hurt. Gifting her and Candy with the Bear Claw would have to be enough. "So she was next door Saturday and Sunday?"

"They were open both days, like they usually are. She and her cousin and one of the other dealers who sometimes shows up on weekends or busy days."

"So you didn't see her?"

"Oh." Her lips rubbed together. "No, I guess not. Sheila came in and got their regular order. Same thing every Saturday and Sunday. You'd think they'd vary their order, but no, every Saturday and Sunday the same three pastries, a Bear Claw for Gina, a sausage kolache for Arnie, and a prune one for Sheila." She made a prune face and laughed.

"Sheila's one of the other dealers?"

"Yes. I think she was the only other one there but could be I didn't see the others. Sheila's here the most often."

"And coffee? Did Sheila buy them coffee?"

"Yes, she did. They have a coffee maker in the back of their store, but it wasn't working that day apparently."

I raised my eyebrows in a go-on-keep-talking expression.

"You're wondering how I know that?"

"No, ma'am. I'm guessing most of y'all know each other's business around here. Am I right?"

"I've been here a long time. Grew up here. I know almost everyone except some newbies when they first move here."

"Do you know where Gina stays if she spends the night here, if she stays over a few days?"

"With her cousin, Arnie, I think. At least she used to. Arnie Saxberg."

That was not a Czech name, but I wasn't there to question anyone's ancestry. "So I guess you're acquainted with both of them?"

"Oh sure. We went to high school together, Arnie and me. Gina was a few years behind us."

"You know both of them well, then?" My tone stayed friendly, not the least bit aggressive or even assertive. I'd taken note of her first reaction to Gina's name and wanted to pump her for more information.

"Arnie, more than Gina. Gina was a bit of a late bloomer. She didn't have a group she hung out with that I remember, but like I said, she was in school behind me."

"Late bloomer?"

"Nerd? She often had her head in a book in the lunchroom. Never saw her in the halls with anyone special."

"But that was years ago."

"Oh, sure. A long time ago. Then she went off to college, to TCU, and I heard she joined a sorority. No one could have been more surprised than me. I remember wondering which one would even have rushed her. Then I found out her mother was a sorority girl when she was young, so Gina was a legacy."

I didn't know what this had to do with the price of eggs in China, as Margaret often misquoted, but I wasn't going to stop the woman when she was on a roll. "That makes sense."

"She had changed by the end of college. She didn't come back here to live. She'd come back to visit and had become—I don't know if I should say it..."

"Like weird or something?"

"Humph. No. Like she thought a lot of herself."

That was the first time I'd heard that. Neither Blanche nor Nancy had described Gina's personality. "If she didn't come back here to live, how'd she end up with the antiques store?"

"Inherited it from her parents. At least their share of it. Arnie inherited the other half from his, well, his father. His mother is still alive but too old to work in the store."

"So Gina did come back here to live?"

"No. She married this man who worked for some big oil company in Houston, so she didn't have to work. Later, that ended in divorce and she married some writer guy. When her mother died—her father had passed a few years earlier—she got involved in the business. Arnie's parents and her mother had run it mostly until then. After his father passed, his mother turned it over to him when she retired."

"Gina started running it with Arnie after her mother died?"

"Partly. He did most of the work, along with the others—the ones who have booths there—until Gina and her latest husband started having problems, and then Gina involved herself more. That's the nicest way of putting it."

Clearly this lady didn't have good feelings about Gina. "By the way, I never asked your name. I'm so sorry."

She stuck her hand out over the counter. "Beth Anne Novak."

"Like Kim Novak the actress?" I shook her hand.

She laughed. "Unfortunately no relation. And your name?"

"Mavis Davis."

She wrinkled her nose and stared at me.

"I can see you don't believe me, but it's true. Wait a minute." I pulled a card from my pocket and handed it to her. "See?"

"Private Investigator?" She cocked her head. I was sure she was wondering like crazy what Gina had done.

"Among other things. You can see my office is in Houston. Also, process server. See the small print on my card?"

"So you're—"

"Trying to serve Gina with some court papers, not investigating her."

I could almost hear her say, *oh darn.*

She raised her eyebrows. "Someone's suing her?"

I wasn't sure what the ethics were of answering that, but I did. "Yes, ma'am. In Galveston."

"Where she has the other store."

"Yes, ma'am. So to be clear, you didn't see her over the weekend, but you saw Arnie?"

Her eyes examined the ceiling as her head wobbled up and down. "Yes, I'm sure I must have seen Arnie and, for sure, Sheila. It's hard to remember when we're busy. You know, you assume people are doing what they're always doing."

"Have you seen him since the weekend?"

She shook her head. "No. Not any of them. They're closed on Mondays, so I never see them on Mondays and often they're closed on Tuesdays during the slow season, like today." She leaned her chin on her fist. "They usually put their hours on their website, and they post them on the door. You can tell if she's here, though, because of that thing she drives."

"Let me guess. An old blue Dodge Caravan?"

Beth Anne nodded. "And she has a trailer. She has a Mercedes sedan, too, but normally she drives the Dodge Caravan. She uses it to pull the trailer. There's space out back for us to park and that's where she usually goes, so they can carry things in and out through that door."

I wasn't sure where "out back" was, but I was going to go look on my way out of town. "So is their shop like an antiques mall? I mean, there are a lot of dealers in spaces the owners lease out to sell their own antiques?"

"I know what you mean. Yes, that's how they work. But not any of them ever open up on Mondays. Sometimes Tuesdays and the other days, too. I don't know for sure who does what, when. They come and go. If it matters, you'd have to ask Gina or Arnie."

"It doesn't. I just need to find Gina."

"Is the case something you can tell me about?" Her body became tense, wooden.

Beth Anne was a solid source of information, but I wasn't going to share any details. "I probably shouldn't."

"I was wondering if something was going on with her. There was a man here last week, or it could have been the week before. He was looking for her, too." She chuckled. "He wouldn't tell me what it was about, either."

Undoubtedly the previous process server. "So, I take it you're good friends with Gina and Arnie?" I didn't think so, but, hey, I was still fishing.

She squinted at me a moment. "I hate to say it, but no. I used to be friends with Arnie, but since Gina's second divorce and her being around more often, he's sort of been keeping me at arm's length. After all these years, I don't know what that's about."

"You know about the divorce, then?"

"Everyone knows about the divorce."

"Well, I need to get on back soon, but I'm wondering whether you can tell me where Arnie lives? I might find Gina there."

"Sure, I don't mind. But I have to draw you a map. Give me a minute." She ran my credit card and then opened a drawer and tore a sheet of paper from a notebook, taking only a few minutes to sketch out directions. "Take the second exit off the square to get started. You can follow my map from there. Your navigation system might be able to find it, but I can't be sure."

"Thanks Beth Anne. I guess I'll get going. You won't call him and warn him I'm coming, will you?"

She ducked her chin and shook her head. "I don't like Gina that much. I hate to say it. And you seem like a nice woman. I don't mind helping you."

"Thanks again. Pleasure meeting you."

"Pleasure meeting you, too, Mavis. Come back if you're ever in town again." As I made for the door, she began dragging her stool back where it had originated, the scraping sound following me as I made my exit.

CHAPTER
FIVE

I drove over the river and through the woods, almost literally, to get to Gina's cousin's house. Traffic was light with only a few vehicles on the winding curves. Some of the oak trees had started to drop their leaves. I don't know one kind of oak from another. All I know is there are five or six hundred varieties, some of which lose leaves in the fall, some in the spring, and some not at all. I like most rural areas of Texas, especially the Hill Country—beginning with La Grange, which I consider to be the foot of the Hill Country. I like its peacefulness, less traffic, more green space, but I wouldn't want to live there. There aren't nearly as many trees in Houston, not much rustic in the twenty-first century city, outside a museum, so a visit to a quiet part of Texas is a welcome respite. But I'm used to, and guess I enjoy, a more hectic everyday life.

Beth Anne had drawn an accurate map, and she was right, my navigation system—which is Siri on my phone—did get a bit confused. Anyway, I found the one story, mid-sized, 1950s ranch-style home up on the bluff with a panoramic view. The owners were clearly holdouts. The area was filled with impressive stone residences, which would have cost multiples of what Arnie's house would go for.

Neither Gina's Dodge Caravan nor her Mercedes, nor any Mercedes, was parked at the house, though the Mercedes could have fit in the one-car garage. There were no windows in the garage door, so I couldn't peek in. Gina probably wasn't there, but since I was, I might as well see if I could glean any information from the occupants.

I pulled onto the shoulder of the narrow two-lane road next to a tree that hadn't lost any leaves. Grabbing my purse, I exited my Mustang and locked it, even though I operated on the assumption that country people were not as inclined toward crime as city people. I'd been accused of being suspicious of everyone, which might be true. Okay. Truth be told, it was true. Several oak trees spread out across the yard, some with and some without leaves. I crunched across the yard to the door.

The place couldn't have been over fifteen-hundred square feet but was well-kept with a low-pitched, gabled tin roof. The shutters and the trim around the windows were painted spruce green, matching the screen door frame, as well as the front door. A shallow porch stretched across the front. The entry had a swing hanging down to the right and a wooden antique rocker next to that. Pie pumpkins and pots of yellow chrysanthemums sat on each side of the opening. A fall wreath hung on the front door.

I rang the doorbell and didn't have to wait over a few seconds before someone answered. A man who looked to be in his fifties stood behind the dark gray screen. He wore a blue-plaid, short-sleeved button-down sports shirt. "You must be Mavis Davis. Would you like to come in?" He pushed the screen door wide.

A spurt of adrenaline pumped into me, and I stepped back. No doubt Beth Anne had called ahead. I'd suspected she'd do that when I asked her not to. "And you're Arnie Saxberg, right?"

"Yes, ma'am." He was medium height, with penetrating corn-flower blue eyes behind clear, vintage-framed glasses. Once my eyes adjusted, I considered his request that I enter and decided if Beth Anne vouched for him, I should be safe. Not that I knew Beth Anne. As I walked inside, I inhaled a citrusy scent with a note of something like licorice. Anise?

Clearly, he shaved his whole head, though not the gray stubble beard on his oblong-shaped face. Further than that, all I can say is that he would have been attractive, if he were younger and taller and not bald. I took a deep breath and told myself to disregard any interest in that stranger. After all, I had Ben to go home to. Ben could be annoying, but he'd be classified as hot, for sure.

I passed by a small coat closet just inside the door and entered a living room furnished with antiques: a sofa, two easy chairs, one of which didn't match the style of the sofa and other chair, two end tables with lamps, and a matching coffee table. No surprise there. A tiny, wrinkly, white-haired woman with a magazine in her lap was sitting in one of the chairs. She nodded at me. I nodded back.

"Would you like to sit down?" Arnie asked. He swept a stack of newspapers off the sofa onto the coffee table.

"Sure. And who is this little lady? I don't want to presume."

"My mother, Cora Saxberg." In a louder voice, he said, "Mother, this is the lady looking for Gina. Remember I told you a little while ago she was coming? Her name is Mavis."

"Hello," the little woman said in a gravelly voice. "Gina's not here."

I walked to her and took her small, soft hand, bending down, so we were almost face-to-face. "Happy to meet you, Mrs. Saxberg." On the other side of her thick glasses were eyes as blue as her son's.

"Gina's not here," she repeated.

"Yes, ma'am. I can see that." I turned to Arnie. "Did Beth Anne tell you why I want to see Gina?"

"Why don't you sit down, and I'll get us some coffee. Or tea? Do you like tea?" In a louder voice, he said, "Mother, are you ready for your tea?"

The little lady rocked in her chair, a glider, which explained it not matching the rest of the decor. "That would be nice, Sonny."

Arnie stood looking at me while I pondered whether I wanted to stay that long. If I did, I'd definitely get back to Houston in time for rush hour traffic. But if I didn't, I'd give up the opportunity of garnering any information from those people. If Gina had skipped out with Blanche's sixty thousand dollars, Arnie and his mother might have a clue as to where she might have gone. Besides, Arnie was fairly easy on the eyes. What's a little bumper-to-bumper traffic? Ben wasn't coming over to my house later anyway.

"I had some coffee a while ago when I was at the bakery, but I wouldn't mind a cup of tea. Doesn't matter what kind."

"Of course. Sit down and visit with Mother. We don't get a lot of company, and she loves having visitors. I'll only be a few minutes." He left, and I sat down.

Mrs. Saxberg folded one corner of a page in the magazine and closed it, laying her hands in her lap on top of the magazine. She peered at me through her glasses. "What did you say your name is?"

"Mavis Davis," I said in a loud voice, having decided that in light of the tone Arnie used with her, she must be at least partially deaf.

"Would I know your parents?"

That surprised me. I laid my purse and sunglasses on top of the newspapers and sat back, getting comfortable. "No, ma'am. I'm not from around here. I'm from Houston."

"Oh, I see." She rocked some more. "And you want to speak to Gina, is that it?"

"Yes, ma'am. She's your niece, correct?"

"By marriage. Her mother was my brother's second wife." She began a low hum as she rocked.

In an effort to be clear about it, I asked, "Gina was your brother's daughter?"

"My brother adopted Gina. Sophie was a widow when Earl married her."

"I see." There might be more people to search out in order to serve Gina than I first imagined.

"Gina was a little thing when Earl and Sophie got married. Earl never had any children of his own, so Gina was precious to him."

"And Earl's first wife?"

Cora cleared her throat and said in a confidential tone, "We don't usually mention Hattie around here."

Hattie probably didn't matter to what I was hired to do anyway. "Oh. I'm wondering, Mrs. Saxberg, why is Tom's last name Minello and Arnie's is Saxberg? I hope it doesn't offend you that I'm butting my nose into y'all's lives."

"Oh, no dear. It's fine. Anyway, Tom's not related to us."

"Tom Minello isn't Gina's cousin?" I was past being dizzy from all the characters in that family. I only hoped to get them straight by the end of the day.

"He's Gina's cousin, but he's not related to us. He's not Arnie's cousin."

I wanted to laugh at my confusion. The conversation reminded me of a riddle. In my line of work, a lot of things were like riddles. My job entailed figuring them out. I might need a pen and notebook to draw a diagram of their family connections. "So he's not the child of another of your brothers or of a sister?"

"I don't have any other brothers still living. My baby brother, Carter, was killed in Viet Nam. There were just the three of us."

I was getting into territory I didn't need to know about and would consider off-limits if it had been my family. "Oh, I'm so sorry."

"It was a long time ago. Anyway, he never got married. He was only nineteen when he went into the army."

We stared at each other for a bit. I glanced toward the kitchen, wishing Arnie would return soon. At that moment, the tea kettle began to whistle. Since we were getting far afield, I directed the conversation back to Tom. "So Mrs. Saxberg, who is Tom Minello, and how is he related to Gina if he's not also Arnie's cousin?"

Was there a hint of a smile dancing on her lips? "Tom is Gina's biological father's sister's son. He's a doctor, you know."

"No, I didn't know. I thought he was a part owner of the antiques store in Galveston."

"He is, but he's also a doctor."

Carrying a tray and laughing, Arnie entered through the kitchen swing door. His laugh was a deep bellied one. He set the tray with a teapot, cups, and saucers, and all the fixings for a cup of tea, together with a small plate of cookies, on the coffee table. His eyes twinkled.

I hoped he'd let me in on the joke I felt I'd been the butt of. Cora chuckled. Arnie poured a cup of tea, added a little milk from the creamer, two full spoons of sugar, put two cookies on the edge of the saucer, and took it to her. "Bad girl."

"Thank you, Sonny." She smiled up at him and took the cup and saucer, leaning back but no longer rocking.

Arnie looked at me. "I overheard your conversation. Mother was having fun at your expense, Mavis. She likes to do that." He snickered. "I should have warned you. She's a big tease."

I laughed myself. "Well, at least a small tease."

He poured and handed me a cup of tea and a spoon. "Help yourself." He poured another cup. "Want a cookie?"

"No, thanks." I fixed my tea and sat back again.

"Mother, shame on you for treating our guest that way." He pretended to scowl.

She chuckled again before taking a sip of her tea.

"Okay, Mavis, Beth Anne told me what's going on. You're wanting to serve Gina with some legal papers." He eased down into the other chair, a cup in one hand and some cookies in the other.

"Correct. I called the store in Galveston, but she wasn't there. At least that's what Tom said. I've been to her home in Houston. She wasn't there, either." I sipped some tea. It was flowery tasting, hibiscus perhaps. Though my eyes kept darting toward the cookies, I continued to restrain myself. "I drove up here and saw the store was closed, so I knew she wasn't there. I spoke to Beth Anne who told me y'all usually don't open on Tuesdays except by appointment or if one of your lessees, if that's what you call them, wants to be there." I didn't mention that after I left the bakery, I'd driven around to the back of the store to be sure Gina's Dodge Caravan or Mercedes weren't there.

"And none of them usually want to be except in the summer when we're super busy or over holidays when people do a lot of shopping, like Black Friday," Arnie said and bit into a cookie.

"Do you know where she is?" I studied his face for any sign of what he was thinking.

"If I'm going to betray my cousin, which is what I'd be doing if I help you, I guess I'm going to have to know what she's being sued for." He stared at me; his eyebrows raised.

I glanced at Cora and back to Arnie. Might as well tell them. "In her divorce, her lawyer was awarded a great deal of money for attorney's fees."

"We know about the divorce, of course," Cora said. "But that was finished a while back."

"Here's the deal. Gina's ex-husband, Mr. Collins—I guess that's his name. She kept her married name?"

"Yes," Arnie said. "She didn't want to go to the trouble of changing so many documents back to her maiden name."

"Understandable. Mr. Collins, apparently in an effort to get back at Gina's lawyer, sent the check for the attorney's fees to Gina. Gina didn't turn it over to the lawyer."

"How much money are we talking about?" Cora asked.

"In excess of sixty thousand dollars."

Arnie whistled. "She never mentioned that."

"She wouldn't, would she?" Cora said.

"She got a big settlement," Arnie said. "I don't understand why she'd do that."

"Be that as it may," I said, "Blanche Tellweger wants her money."

"I should say so," Cora said. She had inched forward in her glider and now, shaking her head, she took a big swallow from her cup and scooted back.

"The lawyer is suing her?" Arnie asked.

"Yes. I'm the second process server. The first one didn't have any luck. Did he come out here?"

"If he did, it might have been when we weren't home. Mother goes to the senior center some days and her caregiver, the lady who comes to her for half a day when I can't be here, takes Mother to the store and the salon and such."

More than I needed to know, but, anyway, I had him talking. I said, "So Ms. Tellweger thinks either Gina is hiding out, that she somehow cashed that check, and if she isn't hiding out locally then she could have left the area, even Texas." My hand involuntarily snatched a cookie off the plate. "Sounds like a TV show, I know." I bit down. Had to be full of real sugar. Kill me now. "What kind of cookie is this? It's so yummy."

Arnie smiled, clearly pleased. "Mother and I made them. They're almond and pecan." Cora scooted around in her chair and put her shoulders back, proud to be complimented.

I thought about getting the recipe for Margaret, but if there was real sugar, Margaret would be sure to substitute something, and the cookie would never taste that scrumptious. I wanted to swallow it whole but continued munching to get the full flavor while I waited for Arnie to answer.

"I can't see Gina leaving the area. That doesn't sound like her," Arnie said. "She doesn't need the money. She could have been angry at her lawyer for some reason."

Cora said, "Gina can be ornery when she wants to be."

"You don't know where she is then?"

"She's not in Galveston?" Arnie asked.

He didn't answer my question, like Beth Anne had not committed to not calling Arnie. "Tom says no, at least not at the store. Does she have friends around there she could be staying with?

And why would she do that? Could she stay with Tom if she didn't want to drive back to Houston?"

"So many questions," Arnie said. "Well, she and Dewey lived on Tiki Island. It's before you get on the causeway bridge."

"I know where it is. He was awarded that house."

Arnie nodded. "She got the Houston house and sold it. She's been looking at condos to buy in Houston. But she could have some friends on Tiki. And she could have made friends with people in Galveston. I don't know, but Tom might know."

"Would Tom give me that information if he knew?"

"I don't see why not. He and Gina are partners in that store like she and I are here, but that doesn't mean he'd hide her out or anything. He'd think she should do what's right." His eyes were on me over the top of his cup as he took a sip.

"So you know him?"

"We know him," Cora said. "Before Earl adopted her, he and Sophie talked to Sophie's dead husband's family to make sure they didn't have a problem with it."

One big happy family. I was glad Blanche had given me a sizable retainer. I was going to need it. Shoot, I was already earning it. Glancing at my watch, I realized it would be getting dark around the time I hit the hectic, heavy traffic on the outskirts of Houston. "So neither of you knows where Gina is?"

They both shook their heads. When they did that, they looked astoundingly alike. As well, I realized Arnie had some of the same mannerisms as his mother. Sweet. "She was here over the weekend, right? She worked at the store with you?"

"We were open both days, but I haven't seen her since the end of the day on Sunday."

"Does she stay with you when she's working up here?"

"She's not often here overnight since Houston is so close. You said you know she sold the house and has bought a condo in Houston?"

"Rented a condo from what the neighbor says."

"Rented—I thought she was going to buy one," Cora said.

"That would make sense, I guess. She'd be almost halfway between here and Galveston."

"Would you know anything else that might be helpful to me in finding her?" I finished my cookie and set my cup and saucer down on the coffee table.

"You don't have to leave yet, do you?" Cora wore a wistful expression I took to mean she longed to have an extended visit.

"I do. Let me leave a card with y'all and if you see her or hear anything, I'd appreciate a call." I took a card from my purse and handed it to Arnie. He laid it on the table and shook my hand with his warm one. I'll admit to a tiny shiver at the back of my neck.

"Goodbye, Mrs. Saxberg. I hope to see you again sometime." I headed to the door with Arnie right behind me.

"You take care now," Arnie said when he opened the door. "Enjoyed meeting you."

"And I, you." I wasn't quite sure how I felt about him, them, though I generally thought country people were trustworthy. I hoped my instincts were right.

CHAPTER

SIX

Again, my Mustang decided to give me a hard time in starting
up. There had been a number of incidents over the last few
weeks, but the increase in frequency gave me pause. The
time to cause problems was not when I needed to be on the highway.
As soon as I got a few minutes, I'd take it to my trusty neighborhood
mechanic. I was holding out hope that all would be well until I could
do that.

Back on the scenic road to Interstate 10, I again passed landscape
dotted by bales of hay and trees whose leaves had changed to gold
and orange. After merging into horrific traffic, I passed Columbus, a
sweet little historical town on the Colorado River with a wonderful
restaurant where I'd often lunched alone or with Ben when we traveled together. Although tempting, I didn't veer there for an early
dinner. Not much time had passed since I'd had those snacks, and I
had miles to go before I slept.

Two hours or so later, I landed back at the gate to Gina's condo
complex. The time was a few minutes before seven—right at sunset.
A uniformed guard stepped out from the little hut at the entrance.

He looked retirement age but not incapable in any way. His uniform was standard long-sleeved, tan security guard attire. He wore a black duty belt with no gun but with a long, black baton hanging from it. White plastic zip ties looped around his belt and hung by his side.

Pulling in, I rolled down my window. "Hey there, sir. How are you doing tonight? Okay if I enter? I'm here to see Gina Collins."

"Good evening, ma'am. Let me check for you." He made a call from a phone inside the hut.

Since she didn't know me, if she was there, she probably would deny me entrance. I waited a moment and cast my eyes toward the black wrought-iron fence surrounding the complex. Not more than six feet high, it appeared to be mostly for simple discouragement. Aluminum or steel should hold me if I attempted to scale it, something I wasn't eager to do. If I had any luck, Gina would have returned home, and I'd be able to serve her and go about my business.

The guard draped one arm along the top of my car and leaned down, sharing the air with me, which could have been unpleasant. Thankfully, he hadn't eaten garlic or onions recently. "She doesn't answer, ma'am. I haven't seen her come in or out either in one of her vehicles or anyone else's. Did you have an express invitation to meet her tonight?" He glanced at his watch. "At seven or something?"

I weighed whether to tell him I merely wanted to execute service upon her. Some security guards were helpful about such things. "No, sir. Just a moment." I grabbed a card from my purse and handed it to him. "I'm trying to serve her, that's all."

His eyes went from my card to my face. I hoped he wasn't acquainted with my history. I had been involved in a case that had received an untoward amount of scrutiny and publicity, but that had been a while back.

"Well, I don't know what to tell you. Of course, I can't accept it for her."

"Of course. Now you know my name, do you mind telling me yours, sir?"

"Ira. Ira Showman."

"Nice to meet you, Ira." Looking between the gate bars, I could see far enough that I knew her Dodge Caravan wasn't there, no large SUVs were. I couldn't tell the make of the cars in the dimming light. I could barely make out the colors. "You know her car?"

His eyes lit up. "That sweet little Mercedes? Yes, ma'am. It's definitely not where she usually parks."

"Do you work every weeknight? I mean, I'm wondering whether you were here last night, and how about the weekend?"

"You're wondering when I last seen her, right? Yeah, I was here last night. I didn't work last weekend, but I'll be here next weekend beginning on Thursday."

"So you'll be here Thursday through next Sunday?"

"Yes, ma'am. Our schedule gets switched around every so often, but that's mine for now."

At least if I returned in the next few evenings, he'd know me. Not that his knowing me would necessarily be of any help, but you never know. People often acted in surprising ways. "If you don't mind my asking, when was the last time you saw Ms. Collins?"

He searched the sky for an answer, then the parking lot. "I'm trying to remember. I think I saw her last week, but like I said, I wasn't here over the weekend. You'd have to ask the other guard."

"All right. I'll return another time. Thanks for your help. May I circle around your guardhouse?"

He stepped away. "I'll open the gate so you can do that."

"By the way, I don't suppose you'd give me a call if she comes in, would you?"

With a small frown, he said, "I could lose my job over that, Miss Davis."

"I understand. Just thought I'd ask. You take care." I edged forward. As soon as the gate opened enough, I U-turned and departed. I wanted to defy him and race in and see if I could talk to additional people, but I'd hold off on that until another time if I had no success elsewhere.

BACK AT THE OFFICE, I was alone. Margaret had left several pink-slipped messages on my desk with a small plate of cookies. Candy had left a note telling me she'd finished her assignment. She was going to class to take her exam. I left the Bear Claw on Margaret's desk with a note asking whether she could try making them, with normal people's ingredients, and not with those weird flours she often experiments with.

In my office proper, I put my things down and called Blanche on her cell. "Reporting in," I said when she answered.

"You find her?" Her voice sounded hopeful.

"Sorry, no. I called the store in Galveston, but her cousin Tom said she wasn't there."

"I'm not sure I knew she had a cousin Tom. Wait, he could be one of the owners of that antiques store."

"He is. So I went to her house, which you indicated she'd placed on the market. There's a sold sign, and it looked vacant. Then I went to her condo address. Found out it's a rental, but she does live there, the neighbor said. She just wasn't there today."

Blanche made a noise similar to a groan, if someone like her would actually demonstrate her feelings like that.

"Blanche, I'm going to have to charge you for a day plus mileage."

"Because?"

"I drove to La Grange, to the store there."

"You couldn't call first?"

"No one answered."

"O—kay." She drew the word out.

"No luck at that store either, but I did talk to a lady with a shop next-door. Looks like Gina had been there over the weekend. The antiques store was closed today. That lady gave me information about a cousin of Gina's, an Arnie Saxberg, so I drove out to a bluff, with a beautiful view by the way, and met with him and his mother."

"I take it Gina wasn't there either."

"No, but I did get a little information out of them that might be helpful. Information about the family. There might be other people she could be staying with, though I'm not ready to track them down just yet."

She huffed. Another sign she had emotions.

You know La Grange is about two hours from here. With the heavy traffic, it took two hours, at least, each way."

She didn't respond.

"I went back by her condo complex on my return, but she wasn't there again. The security guard called her place. He said he hadn't seen her or her car today, though he apparently doesn't come on until late afternoon because no one was in the booth when I went there this morning." I picked up a cookie and studied it. Did I want to ruin my dinner? That was my mother's voice in my head, but I did plan to have dinner sometime before I went to bed. I broke off a tiny piece and popped it in my mouth. The sugar and almond butter melted on my tongue. My stomach asked for more.

"And this took all day?"

"Well, I started not long after you left and, considering what time it is now, that is a full day."

"I'm not going to try to do you out of your fee, Mavis. I'm sure you're doing a thorough job. Just keep track of everything and itemize, so I can use it for tax purposes at the end of the year."

She could write me off. Was that figuratively speaking or literally? I'd have to think about that. "Anyway, I thought I'd take a run down to the island tomorrow. And also, what do you think about me contacting her ex-husband? To look for her at her former house?"

"They despise each other, but if there's one thing I've learned in family law, you never know what people are going to do. If you call him, though, you'll be alerting him you're coming. Might be better to just show up."

"Okay, I'll do that tomorrow."

"He's there all day. He's a writer, a very successful one, which is how he can afford to live on Tiki Island."

"So he might be there any time of the day or night? Great. I'll definitely stop by there."

"If you do, be careful. He hates me. If he finds out you're working for me, it may not go well."

"You're saying you think he'd hurt me?"

"Don't know. Also, you need to know that he lives behind a tall wooden fence with a gate. You'll have to call him over an intercom system once you get there. If he'll see you, he'll give you a code you can punch in and the gate will open."

"Sounds fancy."

"Ever been on Tiki Island? Many of the houses go for the high sixes, if not the sevens."

"I'll keep that in mind in case I ever win the lottery." To win, though, I'd have to buy a ticket.

"I guess we're past the service of process part and now at the skip-tracing part of your job."

"Looks like it. Before I go down there tomorrow, I'll put Margaret onto seeing if she can discover anything about Gina on the Internet. Margaret's a wonder at finding things, plus, between you and me and the fence post, I think she has some kind of connection with someone somewhere who helps her sometimes."

"I think I followed that."

"Yeah. TMI, right? We all know we'd get in trouble if the person was a hacker and someone found out."

"Found out what, Mavis?"

"Nothing, Blanche. So I'll head to the island tomorrow."

"Thank you. I suspect you're much more thorough than the last person I hired. I appreciate that."

We disconnected. I put the big part of the cookie into my mouth and plopped back in my chair while enjoying it. Closing my eyes, I sat in silence while I pondered my plans for Blanche's case. The hour was late. I was tired and hungry and didn't see what else I could accomplish that evening. I reviewed the messages and wrote a note to Margaret about how to handle some things that had come up. On my way home, I stopped for Chinese carryout and made plans for the morning in Galveston. Catching Mr. Collins early might be my best bet. I'd have the energy to deal with a hostile individual.

CHAPTER

SEVEN

After a quick, early breakfast of scrambled eggs and toast, I headed south to Tiki Island, which is on the way to Galveston. I would have a brief stop-off with Gina's ex-husband, author Dewey Collins, before I went onto the island. I wanted to arrive early enough that if he had planned to run errands, I'd catch him before he left. Otherwise, I expected he'd be there.

Tiki Island is a lick of land that has Galveston Bay on one side and West Bay on the other. Technically, it's an island. There's a tiny bridge that has to be crossed just before the entry to the ginormous Mitchell Causeway bridge. If I'd blinked, I'd have missed the exit.

Every house faced the water. The charm of living on Tiki outweighed the risks, like hurricanes, for some brave people. I wended my way around various roads and past high-raised houses with boats and RVs in the driveways, until I finally found where Dewey Collins lived.

The Collins house was not, strictly speaking, surrounded by a fence with a gate as Blanche had led me to believe. An eight-foot cedar fence on each side from the water's edge enclosed whatever the owner didn't want anyone to see. I stepped back enough to view the north side. The fence surrounded the staircase and had a gate with a keypad. Stairs ran up the side of the house to a landing for each floor. The house must have also had some kind of entry from inside the three-car garage—another set of stairs, or an elevator. All three windowless garage doors were closed.

As far as I could tell, no one was about when I parked in front of one of the garage doors, though vehicles sat in front of many of the other houses. I stood my ground for a minute and let the salty breeze sweep over me, blowing my hair across my face. The aroma brought back memories of when I was a surfer and the first fall cold fronts would blow in making the weather a bit too cool to surf without a wetsuit. While the temperature wasn't really cold, that morning the wind had a bit of a chill. I pulled my windbreaker closed across my chest and zipped it up.

Collins' house had a small, plain keypad on a post between the garage doors, but the keypad on the gate had an intercom and a call button, which I pressed. While waiting for a response, I continued to examine the neighborhood, as any PI would. There was no house I could ever dream of owning. Even some of the smaller ones, the less spectacular ones, fronted on the water, which was what would make them out of reach for the average citizen, meaning me. Even if Ben and I were married and combined our incomes, we still wouldn't be able to afford to live on the water. Not that I was thinking of getting married. When Ben had mentioned it in the past, I changed the subject fast.

After about sixty seconds, I pushed the call button again. There was no way of telling whether Collins was home. I'd wait a few more minutes before going on to Galveston.

"What is it?" A male voice came from the speaker.

Startled, I leaped and sucked in a breath before I spoke. "Mr. Collins? My name is Mavis Davis. I'm a private investigator from Houston and would like to speak with you."

After about thirty seconds, which led me to believe he enjoyed making people wait, he said, "About what?"

I weighed how much I should say before we came face-to-face. He definitely had the advantage. "About Gina."

"Oh, her. I have nothing to say to you about my ex-wife."

"Sir, I'm trying to locate her. If I could speak to you for a few minutes, it would be most helpful."

"We're talking already."

"The damp breeze out here is uncomfortable though, sir. I promise I won't be but a few minutes."

Another thirty seconds elapsed. "Jab the numbers nine two three, but you only get a couple of minutes."

With a person as angry as he sounded, I wouldn't want more than that. I punched in the numbers and pushed the gate open.

"Hey, pick up my newspapers, will you, and bring them up? Come to the second door, the one at the top of the stairs."

The papers were probably the real reason he'd granted me access. The house was a two-story, if you count from the first high-raised floor, so the flight of stairs was two flights of stairs. Sweeping up the newspapers and keeping to the inside arm rail, I tried to keep my vertigo from kicking in by focusing on the railing. I proceeded to climb and climb, passing a wooden exterior door with glass panes on either side. Continuing upward, I reached the top, a wide deck that I was not at all comfortable standing on. Whatever was holding it up, I hoped was reliable. I clutched the porch railing, refusing to look out on what I'm sure must have been a fantastic view. Vertigo was a new thing for me. Not until the previous year when I'd grabbed a woman who was being thrown off a rooftop, did I have it, and then it was a delayed reaction, surprising me the first time I experienced it.

Using my ring, I tapped on a glass patio door and drew a deep breath, trying to calm myself and overcome my dizziness. I wanted to peer out into the bay, where the sky met the water, but I'd wait until he let me inside.

A sweaty, muscle-bound man, wearing a white wife-beater shirt and a pair of blue gym shorts, jerked the door open. "Hey." His appearance looked threatening, as did his frown. He snatched the newspapers out of my grasp and gestured for me to enter. I did, though my dizziness was replaced with a fast-beating heart.

I wore my usual running shoes, sneakers if you will, so I could run fast if necessary. In this particular case, I'd have to run down two flights, which was almost as unappealing as jumping over the side. Of course, I'd never jump. I was hoping if he threw me out after a few minutes, that it would be figuratively, not literally.

He was about as tall as me, five-foot ten, but his girth was twice as thick, a lot of it muscle. When I passed by his hairy bod, his odor filled my nose. I forced myself not to make any kind of face in distaste. He closed the door behind me. I scanned the glassed-in room, which reminded me of a cruise ship gym. A treadmill stood directly in the center, with a view of the bay as wonderful as I knew it would be. Also, there was one of those expensive spinning bicycles— a machine that could have been used to torture people—and a weight bench together with rows of weights of various sizes. Clearly, Dewey had been in the middle of his exercise routine when I arrived on the scene.

He wasn't a bad-looking man in the sense that he had that chiseled look—sculpted nose and jaw—and thick black eyebrows and lashes as long as fake ones over deep-set hazel eyes.

I offered my hand. "Mavis Davis."

"Dewey Collins. I'd shake with you, but my hands are slick with sweat." His voice was deeper, richer than the tinny sound I'd heard on the intercom. "An attractive woman like you wouldn't want to touch that."

I dropped my hand. At least he didn't say *A pretty little lady.* "I won't take up much of your time, Mr. Collins. I can see I interrupted your workout."

He shrugged. "I can pick it up again. You need to sit down after that climb? Here, sit on the bench."

I weighed whether to take him up on that offer, since it probably had sweat on it too, but I was wearing my washable slacks, so no problem. I hoped not to be very long. My legs were a little wobbly and not just from the climb. His tone of voice had become friendlier than when I'd been downstairs. So I did walk over and sit, facing across the room from a huge poster of a book. Turned out every wall had framed posters of his book covers.

Each book cover bore pictures of various boats or ships in dark water, some with fire coming out of them. Across the top of each cover was splashed the name DEWEY COLLINS. I realized then that he was the famous, if not infamous, men's adventure novel writer. I'd seen some of his books on Ben's nightstand. No wonder he could afford a pricey house on the water. His books had been bestsellers for years.

He stood not far away and watched me. I imagine surprise was written all over my face. Finally, he smiled, showing sparkling white teeth.

I grinned back at him. "I didn't realize who Gina Collins had been married to."

He nodded. "You've heard of me?"

"Oh, yeah, well, I don't read your books but my, uh, boyfriend does. He's quite a fan."

"Always what an author wants to hear. Thanks. So anyway, Miss Davis, what can I do for you now that you've come all the way up here?"

"Right. Okay. I'm looking for Gina." I thought I ought to be open with him, if not completely forthcoming. "I'm a process server as well as a private investigator." I handed him a card.

He glanced at my card and leaned against the workout machine. "Someone is suing her?"

"Yes, sir. And before you ask, I was provided with several addresses in addition to yours, since this was her previous address. I've been to y'all's former house in Houston."

"She's already sold it." It was a statement, not a question.

I nodded. "Also, the condo where she's currently living, the antiques store in La Grange, and to see her cousin Arnie."

"And couldn't find her anywhere, obviously."

"Or I wouldn't be here, sir."

"Not sir, just Dewey." He gestured at the poster across from me. "Everyone calls me that."

I wondered whether he had a first name that he'd abbreviated to Dewey but didn't ask.

"Have you been to the Galveston store?"

"No, sir—Dewey, that's next on my list. Your address is on the way from Houston. I thought I'd stop here and then see Tom Minello."

"Sure. Well, I don't know what to tell you. I haven't seen her since the day she came with the constable." His voice had deepened. "She brought him when she took the stuff she was awarded from this house."

"And that was when?"

His frown revealed deep marks in his face. "Oh, wow, a month or so? I can't be sure. Is that important?"

I shook my head. She'd been seen since then. I chewed on my lower lip and pondered what else to ask.

"Who's suing her? I know it's none of my business."

"I don't suppose it would hurt to tell you. Blanche Tellweger."

"That b—witch. What does she want? The judge gave her a load of money."

"That's just it. She didn't get the money."

He ducked his head, having the grace to look sheepish. He turned away from me for a moment. Hands on his hips, he turned back. "My bad, I guess. I sent the check to Gina."

"Do you mind my asking why you did that? Gina didn't give it to Blanche."

"The judge screwed me on the amount of attorney's fees she ordered me to pay to Blanche."

It wasn't like he couldn't afford it, as far I could see. I opened my mouth to say so but stopped before any words escaped.

As if he could read my mind, he gave me a sharp glance, one eyebrow raised. "I can't say I was taken to the cleaners, but Gina did get a heck of a lot of money and property in the divorce. I had to buy her out of this house, and she got the Houston house. And her interest in both her stores."

"So Blanche did well for Gina."

He snorted. "Yeah."

"Well, we're getting far afield." I started counting on my fingers. "You sent Blanche's check to Gina. Gina didn't turn it over to Blanche. Gina is avoiding Blanche. Now Blanche is suing her for the money. And I'm looking for Gina, so I can serve her with the court papers."

"Blanche can't sue me for the money, can she? I didn't think about that."

"I'm not a lawyer. I don't know whether she'd have grounds to do that." I wasn't about to ask him if the judge had made a written order instructing him in exactly how to make the payment. None of my business if he went to jail for contempt of court.

He paced back and forth and then stopped. "I was going to make the check to her and Gina but decided to send it to Gina with a note to give it to Blanche."

I'm afraid I made a face at that. "Because..."

He shrugged. "To give her a hard time. She'd have to wait for Gina to mail it to her or make a trip to Houston to get it from Gina. I just thought..."

"You'd get back at her a little." Nothing new under the sun in divorce cases from what I knew. "Let me ask you this, has the check cleared your bank?"

"It wasn't in my last statement. Are you thinking Gina forged Blanche's signature?"

"She could have. She could have taken the money from the sale of y'all's Houston house and the sixty or so thousand from the check and headed to the hills, so to speak." Didn't account for her having been at the La Grange store the previous weekend, but still, it was a possibility.

He grimaced and clenched his jaw. "Blanche probably *could* sue me, huh?" His face had turned pink.

"Like I said, I'm not an attorney. I'm thinking you should call yours. Anyway, I'll get out of your hair. You're saying you haven't seen Gina and don't know where she is."

His jaw flexed. "She wouldn't come here." He paced some more.

"Blanche thought there might be a possibility y'all—"

"No. No way. I'd never get back with her. Gina'd be crazy to show up here for any reason."

"And you don't know where she'd go if she were to take off?"

"Nope." His body stiffened. "I don't think she'd do that, though."

"But you'd tell me if you knew."

"I'm kinda getting tired of your questions." His eyebrows crouched over his eyes. "You need to go. I've got stuff to do."

The talk of money hadn't gone well. He probably wanted to call his lawyer. His change of tone was abrupt, but I didn't need to be told twice. I made haste to the door. Grabbing the knob, I opened the door and turned back to him. "I hope you'll give me a call if you hear from her." I didn't wait for an answer. I went out on the deck and started down the stairs. The door crashed closed behind me.

When I reached the ground and the gate, I realized there was no handle on the locking mechanism that I could use to make my exit. There was, however, another speaker and a call button. I pushed the button but received no response. I looked up the stairs to see if he was coming after me. Not that I thought there was any reason for him to come after me, though his change in tone—in mood—had happened fast. I had frequently been accused of being paranoid.

He wasn't there, at least not on the stairs. He could have gone down from inside or taken the elevator, assuming there was one, which he'd be crazy not to have with all his money. Who wanted to make trips back and forth carrying bags of groceries up the stairs? My imagination ran wild. I pushed the button again. Enough time had passed that even if he'd gone to the john he could be out and available to buzz me through, since that's what I'd concluded needed to happen. Still no response.

Could the guy be a Dr. Jekyll and Mr. Hyde? Could he be contemplating doing something to me for no real reason? I did carry his newspapers up to him, after all. And now that I thought of it, could he have done something to Gina? Is that why I couldn't find her to serve her? He had a three-car garage. Was a boat in one of the bays? Could he have put her in his boat and carried her body out to sea and dumped her? I recalled hearing once about a Florida judge and his wife being taken out to sea in a small boat and drowned.

I was giving myself the creeps. Without waiting any longer for the gate to be buzzed open, I jumped up but couldn't reach the top of the fence. I backed up a number of steps and took a running leap, grabbing the top and getting a foothold, glad the fence was not higher than eight feet. I tugged and dragged my body over, not quite falling to the ground on the other side. Without any further ado, I backed out and drove away while watching for him in my rearview mirror. I'd pull the splinters out of my hands later.

CHAPTER

EIGHT

Crossing the Mitchell Causeway, I wasn't so shaken from being at Dewey's that I couldn't enjoy the glistening water view. It took my breath away every bit as much as it had the first time my mother had brought me to Galveston when I was a kid. Being at the apex of the bridge was better than sitting at the top of a Ferris wheel. I could see for miles, though I tried to keep my mind on my driving.

After exiting at the bottom of the causeway on Harborside Drive and cruising to downtown Galveston, I found the business district was waking up. Plenty of parking spaces were available near Beachy Antiques which, as I'd anticipated, was not yet open. I walked a couple of blocks to Mod Coffee House for a snack and a chai tea.

A few students populated the tables inside. A couple of people sat reading the newspaper at tables outside. I placed my order for tea and a slice of pumpkin bread, my favorite thing every autumn. After receiving both, I people-watched from a tall stool at a narrow counter in front of a window facing Postoffice Street.

I was familiar with the area since I'd spent a number of days roaming around Galveston not too long ago when I'd been trying to figure out who'd axed a ship's captain to death. I'd met some interesting characters. One of the people with whom I'd become friends was the court reporter who had referred Blanche Tellweger to me. Pulling out my cell, I punched in her number. I'd meant to call her the night before to tell her I'd be down but hadn't gotten around to it.

"Mavis!" Lauren said in her raspy voice.

"Hey, Lauren. Glad you answered. I'm in Galveston for the day. Are you subbing or anything?"

"You just caught me. I'm in a DWI trial. We're on a break for another few minutes. What are you up to?"

"Blanche Tellweger hired me. I'm down here looking for her defendant. I can wait around this morning if you want to have lunch. Does that judge give y'all much time?"

"I can't wait to see you. Meet me at that Mexican restaurant on 50th and Broadway at twelve-fifteen. Looking forward to it. Gotta go!"

That was short and sweet. I knew exactly which restaurant she was talking about, having lunched there once with a hot deputy sheriff, Andy Crider, when I was working that ax case. Andy was a friend of Ben's. I could think of no reason to see Andy on my current case, though I wouldn't have minded.

Savoring each sip of tea and bite of pumpkin bread, I waited for ten o'clock to roll around when the antiques store would open. The business owners on Postoffice Street had decorated for Halloween, with jack-o-lanterns carved with goofy faces and scary creatures hanging around doorways. Foot traffic on the street began to pick up. Galveston, being a beach town—an island—was inhabited by an eclectic bunch of people. Not your usual professionals, but fishermen, shrimpers, writers, artists—there was an art gallery a few steps out the front door of the coffee shop and another across the street. Galveston was one of those places I would have liked to live if I didn't have to earn a living. I wouldn't mind being a beach bum or owning a little shop selling touristy stuff.

At precisely ten, I bused my table and left. Time to see what was doing at Beachy Antiques.

A few blocks west, past still another art gallery and a boutique, the store sat on a corner across from a bank. Clearly the building had had a prior life, but then almost every building in Galveston had had a prior life, many of them dating to before the 1900 hurricane that killed six to eight thousand people. But I digress.

A shiny black baby grand piano stood between me and a glass counter, its case full of bits—bits of jewelry, smaller collector items, shiny objects. On top of the counter were an aromatic pumpkin-pie smelling candle and more collector's items I took to be ones the proprietor would want to keep an eye on, though at that moment, no one was present.

I could take the aisle to the right or to the left. To the right was a folding table partially covered with an antique-looking lace table-cloth, a platter of what smelled like freshly baked cookies, and a container I assumed contained coffee, together with cardboard cups and the fixings next to it. Though I wondered what kind of cookies, I'd just finished a slice of pumpkin bread, and Mexican food was on the menu in the near future. I chose the aisle to the left, skirting between racks, tables and chairs, sofas and chaise lounges, and old windows decorated with flowers. Faint guitar music came from somewhere at the back of the store, not a song really, but some strumming, some chords. When I made it halfway through the store, a tall man holding a guitar came through a doorway. He didn't see me at first. He was examining something on the guitar's neck. The man was deeply tanned and had thick silver hair. When he spotted me, he grinned. His sea-blue eyes sparkled in the fluorescent light.

"I didn't hear you come in."

"Sorry about that. I hope I didn't startle you."

"Nope. Should have been up front. Are you looking for anything in particular, or window shopping?" His tone was so much friendlier than Dewey's had been when we'd parted company. The man came toward me, guitar in hand. "Let me find a place to set this down."

I followed him. "I'm not looking for anything. I'm looking for a person."

He turned. "Oh. Okay." He moved some relics around and laid the guitar on the top of a wide shelf. I wondered whether it was for sale. I'd had a few guitar lessons when I was sixteen and didn't have time to learn now, but the thought skimmed my mind.

"Gina Collins?" He must have been around six-two, because I had to look up to see his face. He didn't register surprise. I wondered whether he remembered my phone call.

"She's not here. Is there something I can help you with?"

"You wouldn't, by any chance, be her cousin Tom Minello, the doctor? The retired doctor?"

He laughed. "I don't know who you've been talking to, but I'm not a doctor, though my wife is a nurse practitioner."

"Cora Saxberg?"

"That explains it. Arnie's mother. She's a character. I have a PhD, not an MD." He had deep smile wrinkles at the edges of his eyes.

I barely held back a chuckle. "Funny."

"Yeah, she likes to tell people her cousin is a doctor. We're not cousins, either."

"I figured that out yesterday. She was doing her best to confuse me when we were talking."

"She's like that. I'm guessing you're the one who called yesterday morning looking for Gina?"

I nodded. "Still haven't located her."

"You want to come up front, so I can be near the door? I have a couple of stools behind the counter where we can sit down, if you're not in a hurry."

"Sure."

"You want some coffee or a cookie? My wife Susan baked the cookies. They're from a recipe of Cora's and made from almond flour."

"I'll take a pass, thanks." My mouth remembered the yummy almond cookie I had eaten almost involuntarily at Arnie and Cora's house the day before. Did I look like I needed a cookie? Or were people in that family just really hospitable? He beckoned at me to follow him behind the counter, where I perched on a stool next to him.

"Arnie called and said you might come down sometime."

"Oh, he did? I'm not surprised. Did he tell you why I'm looking for Gina?"

"Her lawyer is suing her, right? Blanche Tellweger?" He raised his eyebrows.

"You know her?"

"Not really, but she was here last month chasing after Gina. Not very happy to say the least." He began sorting through some paperwork.

"Obviously Gina wasn't here then either."

"No. She's been busy since the divorce, getting her life in order. I don't think she's deliberately avoiding Blanche."

"Blanche thinks so."

"I get that. Gina's had a lot to do, though. She's so stressed out." He scooted his stool closer to the counter and laid the papers in two piles.

"Everyone is stressed out after a divorce. But, anyway, do you know where she might be today? Or even tomorrow?"

"She could be meeting with a Realtor about buying a condo."

I didn't need speculation. I needed a firm answer. "So you don't know."

"I guess not." He paper-clipped papers together and slid them in a drawer.

"When's the last time you saw her?"

"Friday." A pair of women pushed through the entry door, and Tom stood. "Good morning, ladies."

"Hey," one of them said. "We're just looking."

"Okay. Let me know if I can help you with anything or answer any questions. Help yourselves to coffee and cookies."

After sitting back down, Tom said, "A man and a woman came in

Friday afternoon. They were looking for a chest. They'd sold their Galveston home and were moving to a much smaller one in La Grange. Apparently, they'd been in the La Grange store and Arnie had referred them to this store. Since they were still coming back and forth every week, they decided to look here."

And he would get to the point, when? I nodded and smiled and couldn't help myself, I looked at my watch. I still had plenty of time to drive to the restaurant.

He saw me. I smiled again when our eyes met. "Anyway," he continued, "they found an old chest, an antique hope chest painted with a Japanese garden scene but with an odd-shaped, yellow pagoda painted on the top."

"Sounds unique." I wasn't into old chests or Japanese art, but the description did sound rather unusual.

"I was happy to get it sold. We'd had it in this store for quite a spell."

"I imagine there's not a lot of demand for chests with pagodas painted on them." Or much demand for chests at all, but what did I know?

"It was too long for their little truck. They didn't want it exposed to the weather, hanging off the back of their truck with a red flag affixed to the end. Gina, in an effort to make the sale, told them she'd take it up there. She was going anyway, for the weekend. She has a Dodge Caravan and a trailer."

Now we were getting somewhere. "So if I understand, you're saying you last saw her last Friday?"

"Correct. That couple purchased the chest. She told them she'd meet them up there when she was able to make it and took down their La Grange contact information."

"She wasn't going right then."

"Oh, no, it was still morning, and she'd agreed to be here Friday afternoon, while I had some time off. She was going to take some other things in the trailer after a trip to the storage unit. She told them she'd call them when she was there."

"Are y'all the only two who work here?"

"You can't really tell, but we have ten booths. The owners are required to work one day a month for each space they have. Some have two spaces or more. One of the owners was scheduled to come in later Friday afternoon. We try to keep two people here at all times, though it doesn't always work out that way." He glanced at a half dome safety mirror high in the corner near the door. He could watch customers as they roamed the store.

"If I understand correctly, the last time you actually laid eyes on her was Friday morning?"

He held his hands in his lap. "Yeah, that would be right. I left after lunch, and Conrad was supposed to be here around one-thirty."

"Conrad being one of the other owners?"

"Booth owner. Gina and I are the owners of the shop."

I took out my phone. "Do you mind if I make a few notes?" There was a lot I had to learn about antiques-selling.

He gave me a brief smile. "No, go ahead."

I thought a moment about what he'd said. "Y'all own the building?" I put Conrad's name in the little notepad.

"Oh, no, no. It's part of a big family estate. Gina probably couldn't even afford the building with what she got in the divorce. Galveston real estate is not cheap."

"Do you mind if I ask if this is your only job? I mean, you said you're a PhD. In what, if you don't mind telling me?"

"Marine biology." He stood and moved a little to the left, as if to get a better view of the two ladies.

"So that nautical stuff I spied in the back of the store?"

"Mine." He cast his eyes back at me. "Here's the thing. I retired, but my wife, Susan, wasn't ready to give up working at the University of Texas Medical Branch. She retired but went back part-time."

"Oh, that's pretty cool. Where'd you retire from?"

"NOAA—National Marine Fisheries Service. I was there thirty-six years." He grinned, his pride showing. "So anyway, Gina owned this store, but money was tight when she and Dewey started getting

NOT MURDER

their divorce. She sold me part ownership. I had to do something in retirement, and I like old stuff like you saw back there, old marine, ship stuff."

"I thought they got divorced recently."

"They did, but they separated and filed for divorce several times over the years. Every time they got back together, the suit would be dropped. Then when they'd separate again, she'd have to hire another lawyer. It got expensive. And Dewey has so much money, he dragged it out and cost her as much money as he could."

"I met Dewey. Delightful fellow."

"I get what you're saying. He wasn't bad years ago, before he got so famous. We used to hang out, go fishing. He's had some great boats over the years and knows a lot of people."

"Y'all speak now?"

"Rarely. I'm hoping when things settle down, he and I might get together...if Gina wouldn't blow a gasket."

"I'm sorry. We're getting far afield."

"That's okay. I talk too much sometimes and get lonely. I've been known to talk people's ears off."

"So, Tom, I know from Arnie that Gina has some distant relatives, and then locally, I mean here in Texas, she has you and Arnie. And she sold her house in Houston."

"Yes and rented a condo. I helped her move."

"Okay, well, I went to the condo twice yesterday, and she hasn't been there recently. I drove to La Grange, and she wasn't there."

"That shop is closed on Tuesdays except by appointment."

"Yes, but I went to Arnie and Cora's house, and she wasn't there. He didn't know where she was. Do you know where she might be?"

He looked at me sideways. "You could be like two ships passing in the night."

"Funny, but Blanche is paying me by the day. I need to overtake Gina's ship."

"The only other place you might be able to catch her is at our— her storage unit up Highway Six, but only if she's loading or

69

unloading something. There are two units. One belongs to this shop, and she has one just for her." He picked up a pen and began twirling it. "Hers is where she keeps the Mercedes when she's driving the Dodge. They let her leave the van and trailer there when she wants to, in the back, inside the fence. People with big trucks park back there, too. Her unit is one of the big ones you can park your car in."

I'd heard of people putting cars in storage units when they had no other place to park them safely. I was appreciating that I only had my house and office to worry about. Gina's life was way too complicated. "If I go up there, she's not likely to be there, is she?"

"Not really. But the office might be able to tell you if they've seen her and what she was doing—loading or unloading. And if the van and trailer are there, you'd at least know what she's driving."

"I could call, right? Are they the kind of people who would give me information over the phone?"

He looked at me, his head barely shaking.

"Could you call them, Tom?"

Three people entered the store at the same time he reached for his cell phone. He glanced at me. "If you want to wait awhile." He whispered, "I don't want to be too tied up with five people in here." He greeted the potential customers.

I needed to meet Lauren. I'd just have to run up there after lunch. "Could you give me the address? And is there a storage unit in La Grange that Arnie omitted telling me about?"

He chuckled. "No. Just the one. Cora might conceal information, but not Arnie. I'm sure he was straight with you. That's who he is."

"I appreciate your helping me find her. I don't know why you're doing it."

"I'd like her to get all this behind her and get started with her new life. She'll never be able to do that if she keeps dodging Blanche and you or other process servers."

"That makes sense. And you probably don't like people showing up in your store either."

He shrugged. "You could say that."

"If you wouldn't mind giving me the address of the storage unit, I'll get out of your hair. By the way, do you have any other ideas on where I might find her?"

His face turned solemn. "I don't see her fleeing to any distant relatives to get out of paying her lawyer. To be perfectly honest, I have no idea what Gina might be up to, unless she has some secret life I know nothing about."

CHAPTER
NINE

Cooler weather makes me hungry. Okay, let's face it, almost everything makes me hungry. I arrived before Lauren and was shown to a well-worn booth. The place looked like a dive, but the food was genuine, family-owned Mexican, not chain-restaurant Mexican, and the employees, friendly. The smell of sautéed garlic and cumin and onions floated through the air. My mouth watered. A waitress dressed in an embroidered peasant blouse and gathered skirt, a dishtowel tucked into her waistband, brought me a basket of warm, salty-smelling corn chips and two containers of salsa—one red, one green. Despite the chill outside, I ordered iced tea. The spicy Mexican food would keep me warm.

Lauren arrived about five minutes after I did and caught me with a chip halfway to my mouth. I knew it was rude to start before her and was guilty as charged. When she spotted me, a grin spread across her face. Lauren is one of those people who smiles all the time and laughs a lot. She wore a jacket and slacks and low heels, the courthouse-professional court reporter look. Her hair shone in the fluorescent light.

We hugged, and she plopped into the opposite side of the booth.

"So great to see you, Mavis." She shook out her napkin and dropped it on her lap and placed her order with the waitress.

"I guess Blanche went ahead and hired you then?" She bit down on a chip.

"Yep, and I've been trying to find her client to serve her ever since. Do you know Gina Collins?"

She shook her head and dipped another chip. "I only know Blanche because I've been subbing a little in family court. The reporter they ordinarily use for subbing went to work full-time in Houston and shared my contact info before she left."

"That's good, I guess. Isn't it?"

"Gives me something to do. Retirement was okay at first, but now it's gotten old."

The waitress returned with Lauren's tea and both of our plates. I had ordered cheese enchiladas with rice and beans. Lauren got a platter with *especial nachos:* chips layered with beef, beans, cheese, and *jalapeños.* Where she planned to put all that, I didn't know.

"Doing any more spying for the cops or the DA's office?" She had spied on me when I was working on the ax murder case. I didn't find out until it was all over.

"You don't hold that against me, do you?" Her eyes danced as she bit into a heavily-filled chip, the stretchy cheese extending back to the platter.

"Not really. Surprised me, though."

She took a moment to swallow. "So how do you like Blanche?"

"Are you close friends with her? Are you going to tell her anything I say?"

She was sipping her tea and snorted with laughter. After wiping her mouth, she said, "No. I swear."

I studied her. She was my friend, but I wasn't sure how far that friendship extended. She did refer the case to me, but I couldn't help wondering if there was some ulterior motive behind it. Yes, I'm suspicious of everyone, as people who know me well understand.

"Let's just say she's an interesting character." As I cut into my enchiladas, I watched her for a reaction.

"She's a killer in the courtroom."

I was hoping she wasn't a killer elsewhere.

"She'll be questioning someone, sounding sweet, but luring them into a trap and then pounce! Kinda fun to watch, but I wouldn't want to be on the other side of a case from her."

"That's what Dewey Collins said."

"He was the husband in the case you're working on, right?"

"The writer—the rich writer of adventure novels, like deep sea stuff."

"Yeah. Blanche said it was a knock-down drag-out battle over their property—their money. Gina wanted him to give her a lot of money, but she didn't want him to get any interest in her shops. Dewey didn't want to give her anything, according to Blanche."

"But we're a community property state whether he likes it or not."

She stuffed a big bite into her mouth and nodded.

"I met him this morning. Sweet guy."

"Not from what I hear."

"Kidding. He was kind of weird, not-friendly, then friendly, then not-friendly all in a matter of a few minutes. I think I teed him off during our conversation about money." Clearly he'd read my face even if I hadn't said what I'd been thinking.

She gave a belly laugh. "You kill me."

"I was worrying about him killing me when his demeanor changed so fast. He wouldn't buzz me out of the gate, either, so I had to climb over the fence." I showed her my hands. I had, by then, picked out the splinters, but my palms had tiny nicks in them.

"Blanche didn't warn you that he might be, um, unfriendly?"

"Well, I thought I needed to at least ask him where he thought Gina might be. But Blanche could have been more specific. I mean, I got the impression Dewey held Blanche in contempt."

"Ha. Ha. Like a judge. Good one. Yeah, she told me he hated her."

"Okay, hated her. She may have told me, and I didn't comprehend."

"Didn't you find her a bit—"

"Stiff? Full of herself?"

"Yeah. I guess so. But...well, you probably didn't see a side of her I've heard about."

I didn't like the sound of that. "What aren't you telling me?"

Lauren hesitated. "I haven't seen it. She's always been friendly to me, but—"

My stomach started feeling queasy, but the enchiladas had never affected me that way before. "What? What?"

She rubbed her arms and glanced around. "They say she has a temper."

"Oh, lovely."

"I heard she actually went off on a judge one time in the middle of a trial—with the jury in the box."

"And you referred her to me? Thanks a lot."

"There's no reason for her to get angry with you, though, Mavis. You're trying to help her."

"Yeah, but what if I can't help her get her sixty thousand dollars?"

Lauren shrugged. "I shouldn't have said anything. I just thought you should know."

I couldn't help it. I rolled my eyes. "Out of curiosity, did that judge put her in jail?"

Lauren had taken an enormous bite of food. She had to cover her mouth when she laughed. I waited for her to swallow. "No, but he threatened to hold her in contempt..." she made a wry face "and throw her in jail if she ever did something like that again. At least that's what I heard."

I whistled. "She's lucky. I hope she never goes off on me. I hate to be around toxic people."

"I can't stand them, either. She could be in that category, or she could have been off her meds that day." She chuckled again. "Courthouse joke. Supposedly everyone at the courthouse, including in the legal profession, are on some kind of medication."

"Understandable. Anyway, let's talk about something else. What else have you been up to besides substituting? Have y'all gone on any trips or anything?"

"And then you can tell me how things have been going with Ben."

We both took bites of our meal and launched into catch-up before Lauren had to go back to work.

AFTER WE PARTED, I drove to the other side of the causeway bridge and up Highway Six to the storage unit place, following the directions Tom had given me. I could see why someone would want to park their vehicle there. The elevation was at least four feet higher than the road. A hurricane would have to push a lot of water a long way to flood that property.

I parked in the small lot that bordered the gated units. Razor wire ran across the top of the black, metal fence all the way around, as far as I could see. A small office, probably no larger than ten by twenty, was adjacent to the six-space parking lot. Inside, the air-conditioned air smelled stale, or it could have been the man in a gray wrinkled work shirt who sat at a small gray metal desk. Were they supposed to match? A black landline telephone stood at his elbow. You didn't see that every day.

The man looked up as I entered. "Can I help you?" He didn't stand, but I could see he was hefty, not anyone most people would want to get physical with. A short stack of letter-size papers lay in front of him.

I held out my hand. "Mavis Davis."

He ignored my hand. "Zebulon Jones. You looking to rent a unit? We have a few available, though not any with air-conditioning." He rummaged in a tray on the desk and came up with a printed sheet bearing sizes and prices of units.

I waved the price list away. "I'm only here for some information about one of your customers, if you don't mind. I was referred here by her business partner."

"And who is that?"

"The owners of Beachy Antiques. Tom Minello sent me here. Gina Collins, his partner, is who I'm seeking information about."

He stared, resting his elbows on the desk. "We don't usually give out information on our customers."

"I understand. You can call Tom, if you want. He should be at the store. He said I might find Gina here."

"If you show me some ID, I'll see if I can answer your questions."

Pulling out my identification from the inside pocket of my purse, I flashed it at him.

"Guess it's okay to tell you. What do you want to know?"

"Have you seen her in the last few days?"

"Haven't seen her today." He looked back down at the papers on his desk as if he thought his answer would make me go away.

Not quite yet. His answer was, at least, helpful. "What about since last Friday?"

He shook his head. "Nope."

"Could you tell me if her van and trailer are here? Obviously, I can't see the area behind your units from the road."

"No, ma'am."

I let the ma'am pass. I wouldn't get acquainted enough with this man to tell him calling me ma'am made me feel old. I preferred to think of myself as ageless. "'No, ma'am' you can't tell me, or 'no, ma'am' the Dodge Caravan and trailer aren't here?"

"They aren't here. I walk the premises when I arrive every day just to know what's going on, if anything."

"Did you see her yesterday?"

He shook his head. "I said no. Didn't see the van and trailer yesterday either."

"So that means her Mercedes is in her storage unit?"

"That would be my guess."

"No way you could check on that?" I suspected not, otherwise people wouldn't rent units. People were entitled to their privacy.

He merely looked at me, one eyebrow raised, and shook his head.

He never did ask me to sit down. No Southern gentleman, he. At least I knew Gina was out and about somewhere, in the huge state of Texas, with a painted cabinet in tow that was destined to be delivered to La Grange. Beyond that, I remained stymied.

ON MY RETURN TO HOUSTON, I entered my office by the back door. I hadn't been at my desk five minutes before Margaret came in carrying two saucers with a hunk of chocolate cake on each. I became suspicious when I saw only one fork and napkin.

"What's up with the cake?" The sweet aroma of chocolate filled my nose. My mouth watered, as usual. Margaret knew me so well, knew I'd be ready for a snack when I returned from my travels.

"Taste test." Her eyes beamed, but a worry-line crossed her forehead.

"Aw, no, couldn't you for once gift me with something normal? Like a Bear Claw?"

"Your definition of normal or my definition of normal?" She set the saucers in front of me and backed away.

"Betty Crocker's definition of normal. Good old standard recipes."

"Try both of them. I don't even know which is which. I taped a number to the bottom of each saucer correlating to the recipe for each cake. Then I shuffled them around with my eyes closed, so I wouldn't know one from the other."

"Why are they shaped like little rolls?"

"They're actually in the shape of the insides of cups, now turned on their sides. They're cupcakes."

"Oh, I get it. Little cakes baked in a cup. Cute."

"Microwaved for one minute."

My mouth had ceased watering, dried up like a west Texas creek bed in the middle of summer. She was going to press me into judging another of her experiments. I still wished she'd tried making a Bear Claw. I forked a taste of the first one into my mouth. I could barely stop myself from spitting the bite back out into the napkin. Through a mouth almost gagging on the concoction purporting to be cake, I asked Margaret, "Cup of water to clean my palate, please?"

She made haste from my office. I spit out the cake. As soon as she returned, I guzzled the glass of water. Tissuing off my eyes and hoping she didn't notice the disappearance of the paper napkin, I cleared my throat, readying myself for the next taste test. The second one had to be the winner, if there was a winner. I steeled myself. She stood over me again as I took a bite. Ah, yes, Betty Crocker would have been proud to serve the second one. After swallowing, I nodded to Margaret. "This one. Definitely this one is your *piece de resistance*, though I do detect a similar flavor in both."

The disappointment on her face clued me in that Margaret did know which cake was which. "*Pièce de résistance*. If you're going to use French phrases, at least you can pronounce them correctly." Margaret had taken French in high school, so her accent wasn't half bad, at least to an American. Without further ado, she picked up both saucers. "They both have almond flour in them as a base."

"Speaking of almond flour, you should have tasted the cookies Cora Saxberg made. I mean, Margaret, they were..." I didn't want to say *to die for*, "most excellent."

"Yeah. Yeah. Like the Bear Claw." She flipped her hair as she departed my office, saying over her shoulder, "I will make you some Bear Claws. And you will like them."

One could always hope. My cell rang with Ben's special ringtone. His face popped up on the screen. "Hi, Ben. It seems like ages since I've seen or talked to you."

"I feel the same way. Listen, I was wondering, since I'll still be wrapping up some things for several hours, whether you want to grab some Pad Thai and meet me at my place tonight?"

His offer was most appealing. We both adored Pad Thai and a particular restaurant where they packaged take-out, so it stayed as warm as any take-out could. "Sounds like an offer I can't refuse. Got a disgustingly bad case today?"

"Still the one from yesterday. In addition to the millions already in the works."

I was happy to hear from him. His voice made my insides squirm, in a good way. Ben had been really busy lately. Homicides never stopped. He was often too tired to be enjoyable company. I wasn't always available either, though my schedule couldn't match his. "What time are you thinking?"

"My best guess is seven, give or take."

"Okay. I'll swing by the store for some wine and then the restaurant and meet you at seven. All right if I let myself in?"

"Sure, but don't buy any wine. The subscription to the wine club has started arriving. We'll have several choices. I've been putting the whites in the wine fridge and, now that I've been properly educated, storing the reds as instructed." His laugh was welcome to my ears.

He was such a love sometimes, really making an effort. Over the last year, well, now that I think about it, after I'd been down in Galveston and met his friend Andy Crider, Ben had been more attentive. But to give myself credit, I did buy him that wine refrigerator for his birthday after we discussed how much fun it might be to join one of those online wine clubs. And he did get on YouTube and watch some videos about wine. Anyway, we had our ups and downs. Currently, things were better between us. He'd mostly learned not to mention marriage, too.

"Sounds good. I always have things to do here. So I'll see you at seven at your place, and we'll have a feast."

"Looking forward to it, honey." If a voice could have a smile in it, his did. He disconnected.

Glancing at my watch, I calculated how much time there was

before I had to pick up the take-out. I might be able to squeeze in a shower and change my clothes into something more, shall I say, comfortable. I'd worn my casual detecting outfit all day, that being sneakers, slacks, blouse, and windbreaker.

For the rest of the afternoon, which was only a couple of hours, I busied myself with paperwork, writing up Blanche's case as well as reviewing some of our other cases. Candy returned after having served some papers. Serving papers had become a solid source of income for us, helping to pay Candy's now full-time salary.

"How'd your exam go last night?" I asked Candy when she stuck her head in my office.

"Think I aced it!" Her eyes flared with pleasure. She wore jeans and a University of Houston sweatshirt. She aspired to transfer there after community college.

"That's great. I knew you could do it. Are you enjoying all your classes? Any problems with any of them?"

"Not so far, but I'm not sure I'll take as many hours next semester if they're going to keep piling on the homework." She ran her fingers through her hair. "I'm tired a lot, Mavis."

"Understandable. Well, it's your decision. Have you discussed it with your mother?"

"I don't discuss school with my mother." Her expression grew dark, her eyes half-closed. "All she cares about is that I give her money every time you pay me." She edged toward the hallway, as if to head to her office.

"Would it help if I talked with her about how well you're doing? How important school is?"

"No!"

I jumped, surprised at her vehemence. "Sorry. Have things gotten that bad? None of my business, but if you want to tell me..."

Candy turned her back and took a step before spinning around. "She wants me to find another job that pays more." She looked sideways at me. "Not that I'm asking you for more money, I'm not. Or, she says, I could get a second job. She says if I quit school, she's sure I could find another job."

My stomach burned with anger at Candy's mother. I'd always maintained distance between myself and her family, not delving into her business unless she mentioned it. From the little she'd told me, I thought her mother would be happy Candy was making a full-time salary now instead of the half-time she made when she was in high school. I didn't reply, just waited for her to share more, or not.

"If it wasn't for my little brother, I'd get out and find a room somewhere, you know what I mean?"

"I'm sorry, Candy." I wished I could be some help.

"I shouldn't have brought it up. Most of the time I let her crap roll off my back."

"Language..."

She smirked. "Anyway, I've got some copying to do, and then I'll run to the courthouse—if I can make it by five—and file the returns."

"Okay, sweetie. You know I'm here for you."

"I know, Mavis. You and Margaret, both. By the way, did you taste those cupcakes she baked?" Her face screwed up, and she stuck out her tongue before glancing over her shoulder.

"I wish she'd stick with those cookies shaped like pumpkins." I refrained from mirroring the yucky expression on her face.

"I almost threw up on the spot. Ha!" Candy's face had changed into a smile as she left my office.

I couldn't help chuckling. She'd bounced back fast. Resilience was that girl's middle name. Everything I'd learned over the last few years told me she'd make it no matter what was thrown at her. And a lot had been thrown at her from an unreliable mother.

Before heading out, I straightened the files on my desk while I tallied up the information I'd gleaned about Gina Collins over the last two days. What I had learned was not in any particular order, chronologically or otherwise.

Tom said Gina was supposed to have left Galveston Friday with a chest that she was taking to the La Grange store. He has not spoken to her since. The man at the storage place said her van and trailer weren't there but didn't know anything more. She was supposedly at the La Grange store over the weekend, but her cousin there made no mention of the chest. Of course, since the store was closed, I couldn't see whether the chest was there, though I don't know why it would have been if the customers had taken delivery of it over the weekend. Neither the neighbor nor the security guard had seen her at the condo lately. Was I forgetting anything?

CHAPTER
TEN

While heading home in the Houston traffic in a car that had been increasingly giving me trouble, I had a few minutes to consider my mode of transportation. My old yellow Mustang had been a trusty friend for many years. I'd tried to ignore the fact she'd felt more and more sluggish, that she didn't have the pickup-and-go current vehicles had. And the air conditioning system wasn't that great, either. There had been periods when I'd suffered the Houston heat over the previous summer when the erratic system decided not to work, but we'd made it to fall.

Now, the car had started but chugged along, making an unrecognizable noise. Thank goodness it hadn't begun on my trip to La Grange. As soon as my calendar permitted, we'd be headed to the local garage where I'd become almost bosom buddies with the owner/mechanic.

I'd been thinking of getting another car, though I wouldn't mention that aloud in case my old yellow dog overheard. But the time may have come to purchase something more reliable. I could keep my Mustang and drive her occasionally around town when traffic was light, whenever that would be, and only risk the hazardous traffic on trips to Galveston to cruise Seawall Boulevard.

A down payment had to come from somewhere. I had faith that my income, now that the business had been up and running for a while, would be enough for a monthly payment. Candy also needed something more reliable. She deserved it. She worked hard. And I didn't like the idea of her being out in her clunker in some of the places where process had to be served, heck, even in her own neighborhood. Would I care what her mother might say to my helping Candy get a better mode of transportation? Uh, no.

Reaching my house in good time, not long after five, I took a brief respite and actually dozed for about ten minutes. Afterward, I showered and dressed in a pair of kitten heel pumps, tan slacks, a flowered blouse, and bone-colored jacket, knowing it would be chilly later.

The sun had cleared the sky by the time I arrived at the Thai restaurant to pick up our shrimp appetizers and Pad Thai. The strong scent of pepper and shrimp made my stomach plead to be satisfied. When I had climbed back behind the wheel to drive to Ben's, my cell rang with a number I didn't recognize. I answered it anyway. You never know, a rich potential client could be on the other end of the line.

A vaguely familiar voice said, "Miss Davis?"

"Yes. How may I help you?"

"It's Ira. The security guard at Miss Collins' condo complex. I've been meaning to call you, but I got busy with a lot of people coming and going today."

"Well, hi, Ira." Excitement tickled my insides. "Do you have some news?"

"Yes, ma'am. I'm trusting you not to tell anyone I called, though. Her van is here."

"Gina's Dodge Caravan?" I looked at the take-out on the seat beside me, weighing my options. Cold Pad Thai is not appealing. Cold Ben wasn't either. On the other hand, I couldn't pass up a chance to serve process on Gina Collins. "Thanks so much for calling, Ira. I won't say a word."

I phoned Ben to let him know I might be a few minutes late. Voicemail came on, which was okay with me. I didn't have to explain.

Almost giddy, I drove as fast as my dear car could safely go to Gina's condo complex, where Ira sat on a high stool in the booth. Rather than speak to me, he opened the gate and waved me in, giving me a thumbs up.

My cell rang, lighting up with Ben's picture again. "Hey, babe, glad you're going to be late. I will be, too. Go on inside, and I'll get there A-sap."

"No problem. See you later." The Dodge Caravan was backed into a space in front of the sidewalk. The trailer wasn't anywhere around. I stopped a couple of spaces down and jumped out, service papers in hand. Ira stood outside the booth, watching me, so I waved. He nodded and stepped back inside.

On my way to the condo's front door, I glanced through the vehicle's dirty windows. The rear seats had been removed. The old hope chest was squeezed between the front seats and the back doors. Though night had fallen, the bit of moon gave off enough light for me to make out the yellow pagoda painted right smack dab in the middle of the lid. Why hadn't she unloaded the chest when she'd been in La Grange over the weekend? Of course, I checked all the doors. They were locked, not that it mattered. I was only there to get the papers served.

I practically skipped up the sidewalk to Gina's front door, eager to complete my job and have dinner with Ben. Though no light shone from inside or above the stoop, she had to be in there somewhere. Perhaps in a room with the door closed? I rang and rang. I banged and banged. I pounded and pounded on the windows. Nothing. I tried the doorknob, no result. Casually strolling around the side, when I came to the shrubs, I climbed over to reach the rear door. Banged some more. Still no answer. That door was locked tight, too, as was the window next to it. She could be in the shower but not in bed asleep. It was way too early to go to bed. I'd give it a few more minutes.

Back to the front and Gina's van, I perched on the curb on the passenger side and called the number Blanche had given me for Gina. No answer. What were my options? I wanted to serve Gina and go on to my next task, but could there be a clue in the van as to where she'd been and/or where she was? I'd also been hired to trace her, to find her whereabouts. And, though it would be a long shot, could she have left the check in the van, intending on taking it to Blanche? If I found the check, I wouldn't have to serve Gina.

The least I could do before I left was search her vehicle. I wanted to be able to tell Blanche I'd done as thorough a job as possible. Besides, people leave the strangest things in their cars even though experts keep warning them not to, including, weirdly enough for this day and age, the keys. I looked, but the keys were not in the ignition.

No one was in or around the parking lot. Stomach churning, I opened the passenger door of my Mustang and threw the service papers on the front seat. Then to my trunk for my trusty slim Jim, hidden under the carpet, one of several tools of the trade that were part of my stockpile. I also popped on a pair of plastic disposable gloves and pocketed some smaller tools in case I needed them. Never let it be said I was stupid enough to leave fingerprints. Fingerprints on the outside weren't against the law. On the inside of a vehicle, well, yeah.

Approaching Gina's van on the passenger side, out of Ira's view, and still seeing no one else in the area, I went to work. Moments later, when I got the door open, a strong mothball odor enveloped me. Inside, the odor not only grew worse but turned out to be closer to rotten eggs. The second smell could be in addition to the first. That didn't bode well. Something uncomfortable was under me on the passenger seat. I hoped I wasn't sitting on the odoriferous item. Putting on my phone flashlight, I discovered a quart-sized plastic bag of cookies—now, somewhat crushed cookies—clearly not the source of the stench. Pulling my sleeve over my nose, I rummaged around the front seat area, hurrying. I didn't know how long I could stand to remain inside. Finding a shoulder bag, I searched inside but didn't turn up the check. A checkbook and check register didn't reflect a deposit. Wouldn't have been the first time someone forged someone else's signature for a substantial amount of money. Phooey. The check wasn't in the glove box, either.

That left me with the rest of the vehicle to search. Twisting in the seat, I ran my light over the chest. Thankfully, Gina'd had all the rear seats removed. There was plenty of space for the chest and would only be a little tight for me. Nothing else except a few pieces of trash were on a sheet of plywood cut to fit over the cargo space in the very back all the way up to the front seats. I climbed over the console and crouched down. The Japanese garden scene that had once been painted on the chest had faded, the paint flaked off in several places, but the pagoda still stood out, almost like it had been touched up. The stench was now unbearable. My eyes watered. I knew without looking that something I didn't want to see was inside the chest.

The chest was almost as long as a casket. Not knowing how tall Gina was, I had no way of knowing whether it was her coffin, but based on the smell, I concluded it was someone's.

Breathing through my sleeve, I lifted the lid, my flashlight revealing a fully clothed woman who, even though her face was already distorted by the beginnings of decay, matched Gina's description. I dropped the lid.

After a few moments of shock and ugh, the realization of where I was and under what circumstances struck me. I couldn't serve a dead body with process and didn't want to be caught in the van. I'd searched the Dodge, but now I wasn't sure what I should do except call Blanche. Climbing back out of the van, I almost vomited when fresh air hit me. Swallowing several times in quick succession, realizing my vomit could be used as evidence that I might have been inside the van, I headed for the back stoop of Gina's condo again to place a call to Blanche.

She answered after one ring. "Mavis, what do you have for me? Did you find her?"

I licked my lips and swallowed, trying to wet my dry mouth and throat. "Uh. Yes. I was unable to serve her though."

"What? Why not?"

I pulled the phone away from my ear and crouched on the back steps. I still wanted to upchuck but held it.

"What happened? Did she get away from you?"

After a quick mental debate on how many details she needed to know about how I found Gina, and whether I could trust this allegedly toxic woman, which I doubted, I said, "She's dead."

"What the f—"

"I was more or less sitting next to her—her body—a few minutes ago." My haunches were wearing thin—okay, not thin, but aching to the point that I needed to stand up or sit down before I fell over. It didn't help that I felt weak-kneed.

"Explain, please." Her voice still hadn't lowered to normal, but the phone could remain closer to my head.

"Okay, well, uh, to give it to you in twenty-five words or less, she's in a chest in the back of her Dodge Caravan, which is parked in front of her condo. I was inside the vehicle, where I could have gotten into a lot of trouble if I'd been caught."

"That's more than twenty-five words."

She chose now to exercise a sense of humor? "Not funny."

"So you didn't find the check, I guess."

That was what she was worried about when I'd just informed her about a dead former client? "You're assuming I searched for it. All right, I did, even her purse, but no."

"What about her condo? Have you searched it?"

"Look, Blanche, it's one thing for me to get caught inside a vehicle. That's a misdemeanor. But you want me to burglarize her condo? Are you going to get me out of jail if I get arrested? Are you going to represent me for free? I've seen the inside of the jail in the not too distant past and only recently paid off my lawyer."

"Who knows where you are right now?"

Had she heard me? "The security guard knows I'm trying to serve Gina, but other than him, no one. And I've been here way too long just to serve someone."

"If she can't be served, I need that check, Mavis."

"Why can't you call Dewey and ask him to make out another one to you?"

"Because I know him. It would be a wasted call."

"Well, take him back to court then. Didn't you say the judge ordered him to pay you directly?"

"You know how long that would take?"

Not as long a time as I would be in prison if I got convicted of burglary of a habitation. Even if it never ended in a conviction, my life would be a nightmare for years from court appearances and all the procedural stuff, not to mention having to see the inside of the jail again.

"I would have to file a motion for contempt, get a hearing set, which could take a considerable amount of time even though it's not supposed to, then serve him, go to court, and then *if* the judge held him in contempt, it still wouldn't get me the money unless Dewey decided to turn it over, so as to not go to jail. *If* the judge would jail him, which this particular judge is wont to do. He is already enamored by Dewey's fame."

That was more than twenty-five words, too. Having met Blanche, I had a hard time believing she needed that sixty thousand desperately. I'd ask her about it, but where would that get me?

"Blanche, it's not worth the risk." I'd been inside the condo grounds way too long and hoped Ira wasn't getting suspicious. It wasn't likely that a person being served with process would invite the process server in for tea and crumpets. Ira would know how long it would take.

"Tell you what, I'll give you a finder's fee of five percent."

A lousy three thousand dollars? And she still hadn't said she'd bail me out of jail and represent me for free if I got caught. If not, that pittance wouldn't come close to what I'd be paying in this day and age. "That's not much of an enticement."

"Okay, ten percent. I'll represent you if you get arrested. That would be in my best interest anyway."

"You bet it would. What about making my bail?"

"Yes, sure. So you'll do it? I'm assuming you know how to get into someone's house."

I ignored that last comment. If she gave me six thousand dollars, that would go a long way toward a down payment of a newer vehicle for me and/or Candy. But on the other hand...seventy-five hundred would go further. "What do I get if I go in there and don't find it and still get arrested? You still going to take care of me?"

"Oh, come on, Mavis!"

I held the phone away from my ear again. "Well?"

"Yes. Yes, yes, yes."

"Seventy-five hundred and you agree to protect me."

She huffed into the phone almost as loudly as she had screamed into it. I still had doubts about whether I could trust her. I was about to find out, that is, if she agreed.

"Okay. Just get to it. And call me right away if you find it." The phone went silent, and my icons reappeared.

If I hurried, I could be in and out and away from the condo complex before anyone else discovered the body. After a few minutes, I gained access to the condo. My plastic gloves were a little worn by then, but not so eroded my fingertips would be exposed.

Continuing to use the flashlight on my phone, I proceeded posthaste to search the condo, careful to put things back so the place wouldn't appear ransacked. The condo was clean, neat, and like new. Gina probably had stored most of her stuff after the divorce until she figured out where she'd be permanently. A fresh paint smell permeated the kitchen.

Gina could have had no reason to hide the check, no reason to think anyone would get inside her condo and look for it. However, in an abundance of caution, and knowing from TV shows that people hid things in the freezer, I examined it, which was easy, as there were only a few packages of frozen vegetables and one of chicken breasts. I searched the living room, the bathroom where I looked, among other places, down the back of the toilet for a plastic bag, and continued into the bedrooms.

One bedroom was set up as an office with a desk, office chair, easy chair, lamp, and file cabinet. The other, a regular bedroom, was neat and clean and appeared to be unoccupied recently. Making short shrift of the bedroom, I moved on to the office. After a thorough search, I found nothing in or on the desk. The file cabinet, however, had far too many files for a quick search, but since Gina would have no reason to hide the check, I figured she'd put it someplace logical. Her divorce file? Nope. Her bank and credit union files? Nope. If it had been my home office, those are the places I would have stashed it.

Not knowing Gina, I couldn't begin to imagine what her thinking was in not forwarding it to Blanche. Had Blanche gone off on her? Could Gina have been withholding it out of pure belligerence? From what I'd heard, yes. There was no safe. Both closets were full of clothes. I couldn't take the time to search the pockets of every garment. I gave up.

After I exited and locked the door behind me, I walked back through the hedges to the front of the condo. Flashing lights came through the gate toward my location. Peeling off the gloves, I stuffed them in one pocket, my little set of tools in the other. At the same time I reached the sidewalk leading from the front door, a Houston Police Department sedan raced up, lights flashing, and stopped perpendicular to Gina's van.

Two uniformed cops climbed out of the police unit. I recognized the one coming my way. Stomach bulging in his blue uniform, Lon Tyler or Lumpy Lon as I often thought of him, if I thought of him at all—approached me. I didn't need this...the worst of Houston's finest reappearing in my life.

"Mavis Davis. Not you again."

CHAPTER

ELEVEN

Confronted with my nemesis, Lon Tyler, I put my hands in my jacket pockets and kept them there, praying Lumpy hadn't spotted me coming from behind the condo.

"What are you doing here?" we said at the same time.

Thumbs hooked in his gun belt, Lon said, "Dispatch sent us to this address in response to a phone call about a body. Why are you here?"

My brain raced as I wondered who could have called. Even if he knew, Lon wouldn't tell me. "Why am I here? Trying to serve process on someone. You do know what process is, don't you?"

"Ha. Ha. Ha. And you was looking for that person in the back of their house? Or what?"

The other cop—the driver and person unfortunate enough to be partnered with Lon—stood next to the police cruiser. Across the parking lot, two people came out of their condos. An unmarked sedan flew up and stopped behind the first vehicle, distracting Lon.

Ben, dressed in plain clothes, as per usual, jumped out of the sedan. Another man climbed out from the drivers' side. He wore a

Houston Police Department uniform and, as best I could tell in faint light, had sergeant stripes. I sucked air.

Ben stalked up to me. "So this is what delayed you?"

"I'm here to serve papers for my client. What are y'all doing here?"

He considered me before answering. "Responding to an anonymous call about a body in a chest in a Dodge Caravan at this address."

"That Dodge Caravan?" I pointed at Gina's SUV. "Oh holy..."

"You recognize that van? That vehicle wouldn't belong to the defendant in the lawsuit you're working on by any chance?"

I put my hand back in my jacket pocket and voluntarily shivered as though I were cold. The air wasn't exactly warm. "It could. It matches the description of the vehicle my client's former client often drives."

His stare, in the glare of his vehicle's headlights, would have melted some people, but not me. I'd seen it before.

"So you're not sure?"

"Well...I haven't matched the plate to the information in my file. My file is at the office. I came out here to serve her."

He glanced at my hands. "Where's the process? The paperwork?"

"In my car."

"In your car?"

Lon said, "How can you serve someone if the papers are in your car?"

"All right, Officer Tyler," Ben said, giving Lon *the look.* "I'll handle this. You and your partner keep people away from that vehicle." Several more residents had come out of their condos and were milling about.

"Okay, Lieutenant. But while you're at it, ask her what she's hiding in her pockets." He trod down the sidewalk toward the lot.

"Well?"

"Well, what?" I asked.

"Are you hiding anything in your pockets?"

"My hands." I pulled my hands out. "I'm cold." For a moment, I thought he was going to ask me to assume the position and search me. I'd seen the expression that telegraphed that message on more than one cop's face.

"I thought you said your case was not a murder."

"Well, first of all, you don't yet know there was a murder."

"If there's someone in a chest in that vehicle, I don't think he or she climbed in there voluntarily." He glanced over his shoulder. "Though I suppose it could be a suicide."

Suicide hadn't occurred to me. She could have done something to herself and climbed into the chest to die. "You can't be sure there is a body. There could be another Dodge Caravan on the condo grounds, in one of the other sections."

"Good point." Ben's eyes swept the parking area. He walked to Lon and engaged in conversation, whereupon Lon got into the cruiser, leaving his partner standing next to Gina's vehicle. Lon apparently put the car in meander and coasted toward the next section of condos.

When Ben came back toward me, I asked. "Do y'all know who made the phone call?"

Ignoring that, Ben said, "Okay, so tell me what's going on, about this person you've been trying to serve since that *could* be her van."

Since civil lawsuits were a matter of public record, and I'd already spoken to several people about it in my effort to serve Gina, I didn't need the grief I'd get for avoiding the question. I was also hoping to distract him from thinking about the possibility of my having something in my pockets he might want to know about.

"It's not complicated, except that I haven't been able to find her. The person I'm working for is a Galveston lawyer. She's suing her former client for a sum in excess of sixty thousand dollars for attorney's fees the ex-husband was ordered to pay directly to the lawyer. To mess around with the lawyer, the husband sent the check to his ex-wife." I drew a deep breath. "By the way, the ex-husband is Dewey Collins, that author whose books you love so much."

He disregarded that last sentence and crossed his arms, his stare beginning to penetrate. I held up my hand to stop him from saying anything, so I could finish. "The ex-wife didn't give the check to her lawyer, so the lawyer, after not being able to reach her client for a while, filed the lawsuit. The first process server couldn't locate the woman, and a court reporter friend of mine in Galveston recommended me."

Ben's eyebrows had drawn together like a long, black caterpillar, but he nodded like he understood. "And the name of the woman you're trying to serve is?"

"Gina Collins." I pointed to the door of the condo. "This is the condo she's renting. The Dodge Caravan does fit the description of the vehicle she often drives, but, like I said, I haven't verified that it's hers from my file. The name of the lawyer is Blanche Tellweger."

"You've been here before."

At that point, Nancy Harmon, the neighbor with whom I'd spoken initially, came out of her condo, followed by a man. I could see him by the light from the front door fixture. He was tall and older, though not geriatric-type old. Her boyfriend, Grant, I assumed. Not bad looking, for his age, and knew it by the way he held himself. Full head of graying hair. Clean shaven. Dressed in khakis and a crisp sport shirt. Smooth. A little too smooth.

"What's going on?" Nancy called to me as they grew near.

Ben halted them with his hand. Across the parking lot, a small crowd had formed. Behind us, another condo door opened, and a man took a few steps out onto the pathway to the sidewalk and stopped. From what I could see from the sliver of light from the moon and their front door lights, everyone looked like upper middle class and probably upright citizens. At least that's the appearance they gave, neat and well-dressed, respectable, though one never knew what truly went on with people.

Ben said to Nancy and Grant, in a voice loud enough for almost everyone on this side of Houston to hear him, "Folks, we received a call regarding a possible incident in a vehicle in your complex. We're investigating. Y'all can go back inside."

No one moved. The cop who'd been riding with Ben stood on the sidewalk between the van and the people on the opposite side of the parking lot, prohibiting them from getting close.

"Nancy, this is Lieutenant Ben Sorensen," I said. My mother had sent me to charm school where they taught us to always introduce the woman first. "Ben, this is Nancy Harmon. And Grant?" They shook hands with Ben.

"Mavis, are you still looking for Gina?" Nancy asked. "That's her van, but I haven't seen her."

"When did you first notice it?" I stepped nearer to Nancy and so did Ben, who shot me a warning look.

Grant said, "This afternoon when I returned from golf." His voice sounded as smooth as his appearance.

Nancy said, "You didn't mention it when you came in."

"Oh? No reason to." His eyes shifted to mine then to Ben's. He shrugged.

"You didn't see Gina?" I looked from Grant to Nancy. "Neither of you?"

"No." Nancy glanced at Grant. "No, we didn't. I heard some banging a little while ago, but that's all."

I didn't admit that banging had been caused by me.

"I'm going to speak to the other neighbor," Ben said, pointing at the man who stood on the walkway behind us. "Be right back."

I stuck my hand out toward Grant. "We haven't been properly introduced. I'm Mavis Davis. I assumed you're Grant?"

He shook my hand, his handshake being almost bone-crushing. As I pulled my hand away, I noticed his highly buffed fingernails reflected the light. Anyway, he said, "Yes. Grant Westbrook."

"While we're waiting on that police lieutenant to return, I'd like to ask y'all a few questions, if you don't mind."

"Fine." Nancy stood with her arms crossed.

"Okay, well, are you sure that's Gina's Dodge Caravan? Could it be someone else's?" Like I didn't know.

"I'm sure," Nancy said. "But it's kind of strange that she'd be driving the van without the trailer attached. I mean, if she's not hauling stuff, why isn't she driving her Mercedes?"

"She is hauling something. There's a chest inside. Her cousin down in Galveston told me she was supposed to deliver it to the La Grange store. You didn't see anything when you came in from golf, Grant?"

"I haven't looked in the windows," Grant said. "No reason any of us would. But Nancy's right. We're used to seeing a trailer attached. Especially if she's been off at some estate sale."

Nancy glanced at Gina's condo and frowned. "Don't you think it's odd there are no lights on in her condo?" She looked at Grant. "Gina usually left a light on in the back of the condo somewhere. If it's the same layout as mine or even the mirror image, it probably comes from the kitchen. At night, you can see a faint light inside. But it's not on right now."

I was sure there was no light on when I went inside. Of course, I didn't say so. What did it mean that there was no light on when normally she left one on? Possibly the bulb had burned out, though not very likely in the days of LED bulbs that lasted forever. Could someone else have turned out the light? Why would they do that?

Feeling a chill for real, I rubbed my hands together. I asked Grant, "You didn't see anyone else coming or going to or from her condo when you returned from golfing?"

He shook his head. "Haven't seen anyone other than residents at their own places."

"You, Nancy?"

"No." She dropped her arms and took hold of one of Grant's. "Well, we were kind of in the middle of something before we came out here. Time for us to return inside."

Was she trying to communicate something with that comment? Who knows?

"I hope Gina's okay. I do." She tugged on his arm.

Grant saluted me and smiled, a light in his eyes that somehow, I didn't find attractive. "Great meeting you, Mavis. See you later."

Ben strode up then. "Where are they going?"

I didn't give a flip reply like *going to see a man about a dog*. I merely said, "They were in the middle of something when they came out and said they had to go back inside to finish it. What did the other neighbor say?"

"I got his contact information." He pointed at a police cruiser in the lot. "There's Lon. Let me see what he's found."

He left me on the sidewalk. I walked back to my car. I wanted to get out of there as soon as possible. When I opened the door, the Pad Thai aroma accosted me. My stomach growled. Oh crud, as my mother used to say. I had been looking forward not only to the food but a fun evening with Ben. Now I wanted to get as far away from him and the scene as soon as possible before he started quizzing me again.

Lon crawled out of his cruiser and approached Ben while giving me the stink eye. "Ain't no other Dodge Caravan or even a big SUV in the rest of the complex," Lon said in a voice loud enough that I could overhear.

"Okay, stay with your partner and help him discourage the crowd. At the least, keep them back. Hey Roker," Ben called to the cop who'd arrived with him. "We're going to need a search warrant. After you call that in, see if you can raise anyone inside this condo."

As far as I was concerned, that was my cue to make a quick exit. I took a few steps closer to Ben. "I'm going to head home. If you need me, you know where to find me. I'll save you some dinner."

His don't-leave-town expression wasn't lost on me. "I'm going to have more questions for you, but you can leave now."

Like I needed his permission. On my way past the security booth, I beckoned to Ira. When he stepped out of the booth and up to my window, I said, "You have any idea how long that van has been parked there?"

He shook his head. "I think it was there when I arrived today."

I glanced over my shoulder. Ben's eyes were on us. "Well, Ira, looks like we may have found Gina."

CHAPTER
TWELVE

In the middle of the night, I was awakened by pounding on my bedroom window. Scared the bejesus out of me at first until I decided if someone wanted to do me harm, they'd hardly announce it with banging. Stumbling to the window covered with blackout curtains and stepping to the side just in case, I peeked out and saw Ben was the offender. Once he saw me, he made a motion with his finger that I took to mean unlock the front door.

Pulling on my robe, I hurried and let him in. I couldn't think what was so important that it couldn't wait until morning. Grim-faced and with fatigue written into his demeanor, he was still dressed in the same clothes as earlier.

"You must have been sleeping soundly not to hear the doorbell." He kissed my cheek and walked past me into the living room.

Glancing down at my robe and bare feet and back up at him, I said, with no intention of being a smart aleck, "What do you think?" The wall clock read 1:00 a.m.

"Sorry. We finished up with that van only a few minutes ago."

Thinking only of myself, I was glad I wasn't him, that I'd been able to go home, eat—even if it was cold pad Thai—and go to bed.

"You want to sit down? Or come into the kitchen, and I'll heat up the pad Thai leftovers?"

"Nah. Had enough coffee to stay awake to get myself home and want to hit the hay myself." He yawned and stretched. "Sorry."

"No problem. At least sit a minute." I led him into the living room. "In fact, if you want to crash here, it's fine."

He shook his head and sat.

"So what's going on?" I didn't think I'd left any evidence of what I'd done, but what else could have brought him over at that time of night? "Did you get the warrant? What'd you find?" I sat in a chair opposite him.

"She was there. In the box. At least we're making the assumption the body is Gina Collins."

I feigned a wince and shook my head. "That's terrible. Could you tell what happened to her?"

"The medical examiner will let us know as soon as he can. She looked like any other cadaver laid out in a coffin."

"Was there blood? Was she strangled? Surely you would have seen marks on her neck if she'd been strangled."

He shook his head and yawned again. "No sign of either of those."

That confirmed what I'd barely had time to notice myself. "Are you sure you don't want something? I could make you more coffee."

He ran his fingers through his hair. "Mavis, we need a formal identification and to notify the next of kin. I asked several of her neighbors if they knew of a relative who could do it, but they all said they didn't know her that well." He yawned a third time.

His yawn was contagious and triggered one in me. "Well, I'm not a relative, so I couldn't ID her even if I'd ever met her." My brain was foggy. I still didn't realize why he came over. "What are you telling me this for?"

"No, I know that." He shook his head. "I thought since your client gave you all that information on her, and I think you said you met her cousin, right? You could give it to me, so I could contact them. Does she have kids? Did she?"

I pulled my feet up under me. "Not as far as I know. No kids. There's Dewey Collins, but he's her ex, not related anymore."

"Much as I wouldn't mind meeting him under other circumstances, it wouldn't be appropriate, and a blood relative would be better. What about siblings?"

"No. At least, I wasn't given any info on that. Cousins, only."

"Yeah, you went to La Grange to see one, right?"

"Well, not to see one, to serve Gina, but ended up meeting a cousin. Arnie Saxberg. I met him and his mother the other day."

"No one nearer geographically?"

"Tom Minello in Galveston. You could ask him, but I'm not sure there's a legal relationship between them."

"He's who?"

"This can get confusing. A bio cousin but also her partner in the Galveston antiques store, Beachy Antiques."

"You have his contact info?"

"In my file. But I'm not sure if he's legally her cousin. She was adopted, if what Arnie said is correct. Does that matter?"

He stood and crossed his arms. "Give me the information on both cousins, and I'll figure it out."

"Arnie Saxberg is her cousin, by marriage, also her partner in the La Grange antiques store, but would a cousin by marriage work?"

"Mavis..."

"Okay. Okay. Let me get the file—oh, it's at the office, but you're not going to contact them tonight—this morning—anyway, right? I can text you the info later today."

"For both of them. And while you're at it, give me Dewey's home address. We're going to have to talk to all of them."

"So do you think one of them had something to do with her death?"

"No idea at this point." He walked toward the door.

"Are you sure you don't want to stay for a bit and have something to eat or drink? You look so tired. I'm worried about you driving." I was only being polite. If he stayed very long, unless he went right to sleep, he might get around to asking me questions.

"Headed home. Send me those names and addresses as soon as you get to your office."

"Yes, sir."

He pivoted. "Thanks." He cupped my face and kissed me. "Later."

"Goodnight." I was halfway to breathing a sigh of relief when he stopped on the bottom step and turned back toward me.

"And don't worry, I haven't forgotten we need to talk about what you were doing when Lon Tyler drove up this evening. I hope there won't be any evidence that you were up to your old tricks." He didn't wait for me to answer. "Because, you know, our forensic people will find out if you were." He waved and went to his car.

His leaving without grilling me allowed me time to come up with a reasonable explanation for my behavior earlier. Turning off the lights, I fell back into bed. Before drifting off, I realized it was Halloween.

CHAPTER

THIRTEEN

Halloween was full of surprises, and they weren't candy. I hadn't warmed my office chair before Blanche called, and on my cell, too, not on the office phone. She probably wanted to be sure she caught me wherever I was. With nary a "good morning," she said, "So you didn't find any hint of where my money might be in Gina's house?"

Even if I hadn't recognized her voice, I could see from my phone who was on the other end. "Hello, Blanche. How are you today?" I don't know about her, but I was tired, and wired, too.

"Well?" Plainly *Patience* wasn't her middle name.

"If I'd found anything that resembled a check made out to you, I would have informed you." I'm not sure she trusted me. But then again, she didn't really know me. She had merely trusted Lauren to recommend someone reliable.

Her exhalation was loud. She was the type my mother would have described as a flouncer. Mother had rarely let me get away with that behavior when I was growing up. I wondered if Blanche had ever flounced out of a courtroom, and how that had gone over with the judge. I waited her out.

"How thorough a search did you conduct in her home?" *Anger* might have been her middle name. Her tone made me glad we were on the phone and not speaking in person.

Flexing my fingers and breathing deeply, I answered, "About as well as can be done in the relative dark with the knowledge that I was committing a felony."

"What the hell does that mean?"

"I went through her office—her desk, the desk drawers, file cabinet, closet—just about any place I could get to quickly. I rifled her files. Not knowing Gina, I had no way of knowing if she'd have any reason to hide the check. Some people, if they'd been angry with you and withholding the check out of spite, would have left the check in plain sight where they could see it every day and gloat."

"Not funny."

"I didn't mean to be funny. I searched obvious places and not-so-obvious places and didn't find anything. It's not like I could take my time. At the very least, the security guard at the front gate knew I was there. My car was parked next to Gina's van. Someone would be wondering where I was."

"Okay. Okay." She sighed again. I could picture her shaking her head, face red, steam coming from her ears. But it wasn't me she was angry with; it was Gina and Dewey. I was lucky enough to be the handy recipient of her wrath. "I don't know what to do now."

"Well, I don't either, Blanche. I think I've gone as far as I can for you." And more, I wanted to say. I wanted to be rewarded for the risk I had taken on her behalf, but I had an inkling that wasn't going to happen.

She cleared her throat. "I'm terminating your services, Miss Davis."

I knew we weren't new best friends, but her abruptness surprised me. "I'll send you a final statement, Miss Tellweger."

"Will I be receiving a refund?"

Whoa, what? "As soon as I get a few minutes, I'll go over your file and my time sheets and my mileage book. I'll send you an itemized statement."

"Thank you." She disconnected.

I'd wanted to ask her if she was the one who called the cops, but the animosity between us was already thick. "Margaret," I hollered from my doorway. Margaret appeared from the direction of the kitchen. I wasn't even going to venture a guess of what she was doing in there. So far, I couldn't smell anything cooking. "Blanche wants us to give some of her money back."

Margaret giggled. "Like there's any of her retainer left. As soon as I finish in here, I'll pull her file."

Ben might have said not to, but I called Tom Minello to see if he knew about Gina's demise, in case he hadn't already been informed.

"Beachy Antiques, Susan speaking." Her telephone etiquette was way friendlier than Blanche's.

"May I speak to Mr. Minello?" I wasn't sure who Susan was and had no interest in finding out, at least not at that moment.

"Um, he's tied up right now. May I give him a message?"

"It's rather important. Is there any way you could disturb him? It'll just take a minute."

"I'm sorry. Give me your name, and I'll have him return the call as soon as possible."

Disappointed, because Tom needed to know about Gina, I gave her my name. "Mavis Davis."

The woman on the other end of the conversation said in a whisper, "Oh, Miss Davis. I'm Tom's wife. He told me you'd been looking for Gina. We've had bad news about her, I'm afraid. He's with the police now."

A shiver circled around my neck. "Bad news?"

She continued whispering. "She apparently died yesterday. That's all I know right now. You want Tom to call you when he gets free?"

"Do you mind telling me, if you know, what's the name of the police officer or officers who are speaking with Tom?" I had my suspicions. If it was Ben or Lon, I sure didn't want Susan Minello saying my name aloud. I'd be in big doo-doo.

"I don't know. A lieutenant in a suit."

I didn't know who it could have been if it wasn't my ever-loving beau. Ben wasn't letting any grass grow under his feet. "Thanks, Susan. Y'all have my condolences. Please ask Tom to give me a call when he can."

I clicked off and immediately called Arnie Saxberg. I might be accused of messing in police business, but I didn't care. A phone call from me, someone he'd met, would be gentler than a cop showing up at Arnie's door or at the shop.

"You're too late, Mavis," Arnie said as soon as I identified myself.

"What?"

"If you're calling to tell me Gina has died, you're too late. The police telephoned me early this morning. Someone is coming up here in a little while to talk to me."

Fast work for HPD. Were they, perchance, trying to improve their clearance rate? "I'm so sorry, Arnie. Getting a call from the police must have been quite a shock."

"How did you know about her, anyway?" I got no hint from the inflection of his voice as to what he was thinking.

"I was still trying to serve her. I was at her condo when the police arrived." He didn't need to know any more than that.

"Oh, I see. Well, I appreciate the call. That's very considerate of you."

"That's all right. By the way, does your mother know? How is she taking the news?"

"Not that well. I stayed with her until her caregiver arrived, but I had to come open the store. The police are going to meet me later."

Poor little Cora. At her age, she might not have an extensive circle of friends or relatives still alive and kicking. "Okay. Well, I'll let you go. I'm sure you have better things to do than stay on the phone with me. By the way, do you know the name of the officer or officers who are coming to see you?

"A Sergeant Abernathy. You know him?"

"No. Just wondering. You take care, Arnie. Give my best to your mother." Abernathy was someone with whom I was unacquainted. Ben had been smart enough not to send Lon to La Grange. Not that I was surprised. I would have been shocked if he had.

About one o'clock Halloween afternoon, I received a call on the office line that at first, I thought must be a trick. Margaret came jogging down the hall to my office, "Mavis, it's that famous author on the line."

I'd been trying to see if I could squeeze any more minutes onto Blanche's final bill. I still thought I should get some kind of bonus for risking going to jail. "What famous author?"

"That Mr. Collins. Gina Collins' ex-husband." Margaret's eyes glowed like a jack-o-lantern with a lit candle inside.

"What does he want?" Dewey wasn't anyone I particularly wanted to speak with. I figured he'd want to yell at me for giving the police his contact information.

"Well, I don't know. Get on the line and ask him." She tossed her head as she started back down the hall.

I picked up my extension. "Yes, Mr. Collins. How may I help you?" Glad he couldn't see the expression that had to be on my face.

A guttural sound answered me. Then, "Sorry. I swallowed wrong. So hey, I need you to come down here to my house."

"And why, pray tell, would I do that?" I didn't think I needed to remind him about how I'd had to exit his premises.

"Look, I know you put the cops onto me."

"This isn't one of your adventure novels, Mr. Collins. I merely gave them the information on Gina's contacts I had in my file. Your name and address happened to be one of them."

He huffed into the phone. "Could you come down here? I'll make it worth your while."

"You'll pay my hourly fee?"

"Yeah, whatever. Can you get here this afternoon?"

Another trip to Galveston County so soon was not number one

on my list, but if he was going to pay me, well, that was another matter. I told him how much I charged by the hour and for mileage.

"Yeah. Yeah. So what time will you be here?"

I glanced at my watch and said, "Give me an hour and a half."

"Right. Buzz, and I'll let you in."

"I know the drill." He disconnected, and I opened the notepad on my phone to make a note of the time of the call. I'd also record my mileage and the amount of time I spent with him to be sure I squeezed every penny I could onto his bill.

Margaret appeared in my doorway again. "So what'd he want?" Her eyes still glowed.

"For me to go back down there to see him. And he's going to pay me."

"He didn't say why?" She ventured into my office and sat in one of my client chairs.

Shaking my head, I said, "I can't take you with me."

She straightened up. "I wasn't going to ask you to."

Sure she wasn't. "I'm not going to ask him for an autograph for you either."

"Aw, Mavis, you know they made a couple of movies out of his books."

Margaret was a big movie buff, old movies, new movies, kid movies. If it were the 1950s, she'd be reading movie magazines. As it was, she read *People* cover-to-cover. I could always go to her if I wanted to get the goods on someone famous, which I didn't, though Candy did.

"How unprofessional do think it would be for me to ask a man who is potentially a suspect in a murder case for an autograph?"

She slumped in the chair. "Yeah, I know. Never hurts to ask."

How well I knew her. "This is what you could do, Margaret. Go to his website and look for his calendar of events. He may have a book signing scheduled in this area."

"You don't think he killed his ex-wife, do you? I mean, they're already divorced. The time to kill her would have been before the property settlement."

"I don't care one way or the other. I'll go down there to see what he wants. He said he'll pay me. Why he couldn't tell me over the phone, I have no idea. You've heard of drama queen? He's a drama king."

She headed for the door. "When are you leaving?"

"About five minutes. I told him I'd be an hour and a half. What are you working on?"

"Some pleadings for one of our regulars. And Candy's due back any time from filing some returns." She traipsed to the front with less energy than when she'd come.

A few minutes later, I grabbed my jacket and shoulder bag and went out the back door.

ON THE HIGHWAY on the way to Dewey's, I was entertained by some interesting drivers who easily reminded me what day it was. One person wore a rubber Freddie mask and stared at me as he passed by. I'd have thought those were passé if I'd bothered to think about Halloween costumes at all. Another had one of those arms hanging out of his trunk. A third had a real pumpkin carved into a jack-o-lantern wired onto his grill. That could be a mess.

When I arrived at Dewey's gate, there was a sign that said in all capital letters NO TRICK OR TREATERS. Lovely. He buzzed me in right away and said to go to the door on the first landing. He answered, dressed in a pair of Dockers and a Polo shirt, and beckoned for me to enter. I was grateful he wasn't in costume. "Thank you for coming."

I admit to being wary of him. I'd seen him in workout clothing and knew he was muscular. He could hurt me, though I didn't think that was his intention. After all, he had to know people knew where I was. "I think you're welcome. I'll let you know when I find out what you want."

He closed the door behind me and led me into an impressive living area with a long bar and bar stools to the left, and a conversation pit, reminiscent of something out of Architectural Digest, to my right. I didn't bother being envious of the wealth of people like Collins. I'm a realist, though I can be impressed and have to make an effort to hide my awe sometimes upon seeing such a display.

"Can I fix you a drink?" Dewey asked, walking behind the bar.

I slid onto a bar stool and laid my keys on the bar. "Just some water. On ice, if you have any."

Across the back of the bar were enough bottles of liquor and mixers to give competition to any respectable establishment that served alcohol. He filled a glass with ice from an ice maker at the enclosed end, pulled out a bottle of water with an unpronounceable name on the label, and poured it over the ice. My suspicions of a possible poisoning allayed by his having to twist off the top of the bottle, I received the glass from him with my thanks. The end of October on the Gulf coast made for humid, if not as hot as summer, weather. Humid weather made for lots of perspiration. My throat was parched.

Dewey dragged a bar stool from the end of the bar near the ice maker and sat across from me. Still behind the bar.

Putting the almost-drained glass down on a coaster he'd set out for me, I crossed my arms and waited to find out exactly what was worth him paying me to come all the way to Tiki Island for.

He didn't mince words. "Look, I'm going to be straight with you. I want to hire you. I might have wanted to kill Gina for all she put me through over the years, but I didn't."

CHAPTER

FOURTEEN

Dewey wanted to hire me after the way he'd treated me when I'd been there before? No one could be more surprised than I was. "So who's accused you of murder?" I was eager to hear what he wanted me to do.

"No one yet. But I know enough to know the husband is the first person they look at."

"But you're the ex. Your motive ended when you were divorced." I continued to keep my arms crossed, which, since he was a writer, I'm sure he knew was a defensive position. I hadn't completely forgiven him for the way he'd treated me.

"Unless they think I was out for revenge. I'll pay you for today, and then I want you to find who really killed her. In other words, I'm prepared to write you a second check today as a retainer to see if you can figure this thing out. I don't trust the police."

Admittedly, I was without a client at the moment since Blanche had terminated my services. And he was moneyed. "I shouldn't get involved in an active police investigation." I held out my glass, still thirsty, hoping he'd refill it. He probably would be the worst type of client, a controller. I could visualize him being worse than Blanche, calling me regularly before I'd had time to get anything accomplished.

He leaned in close to me and poured the remaining water from the bottle into my glass. His men's cologne about wiped me out. He said, "Oh, come on. You can't tell me you've never done that."

Which got me to wondering whether he'd done a cursory Google search of me and found something in my past I wasn't especially proud of. Like when I'd spent time in the Harris County jail. It was for an honorable thing, though no Internet search would say that. I drank some more water and stood, poised to depart. "So you want to write me out a check for my time today, or are you paying me in cash?"

He came around the bar but stayed far enough away that I could still breathe. "I'll make it worth your while."

"Why are you so eager to hire me? Why don't you wait to see what the police turn up? They're not accusing you yet. I still think you'll be okay because y'all were divorced." I drained the glass and set it down again.

"I could have said some things publicly..."

I bit the inside of my cheek, positive it was more than likely he'd said some things about Gina publicly, but words never killed anybody. "Surely you have an alibi." I perched on the edge of the bar stool.

"Do you know when she was killed?"

I wasn't sharing anything I knew at that point. "No, but can't you account for your actions over the last few days? Since, like, last Friday?"

He shook his head. "I'm here most of the time alone."

"The neighbors—"

"They can't tell when I'm here. I park my vehicles in the garage. They could only vouch for my comings and goings if they happened to see me pass by."

I noted *vehicles*, plural. "So where and when might you have said some things about your ex-wife?"

"Umm, possibly in a bar or two."

Or three or four. I wondered if he was more than a social drinker. "Out drinking with friends?"

"Yeah, and alone—but where I know the bartender. He's a fan."

"But you weren't at any of those places Friday or thereafter, were you? This was stuff you said right after the divorce?"

"I could have been there Friday night. Maybe even Saturday."

"Could have?"

"If you're not going to represent me, you don't need to know any of this." He strolled toward the desk on the other side of the room under a picture window with a view of the bay. Sunlight sparkled on the water.

"Lawyers represent people. I'm not sure what you'd call a PI. You'd be a client, though, which brings me to the question, why aren't you hiring a lawyer?"

"And that wouldn't make me look guilty of something?"

He had a point. I weighed my options. I didn't have anything else on deck at the moment. I could use the money, especially after the deal I'd had with Blanche fell through and she'd terminated my services. I could do a few things for him on the QT and not tell Ben. I took a few steps toward where he'd headed. "Well, I guess I do understand your concern."

He threw himself into a chair, causing it to roll back on the floor mat, his head cocked toward me. He pulled himself close to the desk and reached into a side drawer, taking out a dark blue check binder and laying it on his desk. "Look, not only will I make it worth your while, but I'll go you one better. Since my check to Blanche hasn't cleared, and I suspect Gina probably burned it or otherwise disposed of it, I'll write another check to Blanche. You can deliver it to her once I'm in the clear."

My brain went into overdrive. Was that incentive or what? At least, that's what my brain was telling me. If I could get Blanche to renew her offer of the night before, and Dewey paid me too, that money would go a long way toward not only a newer car for me, but

Candy also, not to mention the rent, electricity, and water bill. Wasn't it millionaire Robert T. Kiyosaki who said, "Most people have a price"?

"I'm not reading your mind, lady, but something tells me you might be interested."

My body language must have changed while I wasn't looking. "I'm curious about why this is so important to you. Surely the police will clear you if, as you say, you're a suspect and did nothing wrong. So why? What's going on?"

He cleared his throat and took a pen out of the center desk drawer. "Sit down. I don't like anyone standing over me."

I complied. Some of his tone of voice from the previous visit was seeping in.

"You said the other day your boyfriend was a fan. How many fans, i.e. how many sales would I lose if I became a suspect in a murder case, and it went public? Because it would definitely go public." He tapped the pen against his lips.

I could see law-and-order-types like Ben throwing Dewey's books in the trash if he became a suspect. I was familiar with articles about famous people being accused of a crime appearing on the front page and articles exonerating them appearing in small print way in the interior of a newspaper. Nowadays, with the Internet, an exoneration piece wouldn't necessarily pop up as one of the first articles in a search, if anyone bothered to search at all.

"I have a new book coming out. What would the cops think of me leaving the area to go on a book tour?" He raised an eyebrow. "You see my problem?"

"And you want me, rather than someone from a big firm, because I've already been—" I started to say poking around, but he didn't know that. "Because I'm familiar with Gina's uh—family and activities?"

"Right. So what do you say, Miss Davis? Do we have a deal?"

I restated his offer, "You'd give me the money you owe Blanche plus my fee?"

"That's what I said. But you don't get the check for her until...I'm cleared."

"You know, she could take you back to court, ask the judge to hold you in contempt for not paying her directly in the first place."

"Sure. I spoke with my attorney. I don't know why she hasn't already taken me back to court. She might think what she's been doing, having you track down Gina, would get her the money faster, that Gina would be intimidated by a lawsuit and hand over the check. Believe me, not much intimidates—intimidated Gina." He laughed, not a pretty sight at that moment. "Blanche probably knows my lawyer can stall like crazy, anyway."

I was sure she did. He was probably one of those clients who hired only the best long-winded and slow-acting lawyers. I had an uneasy feeling in the pit of my stomach, but I sure could use the money. Darn it. Why wasn't I born to rich parents? "Okay. So how about writing me a retainer for a couple of days, on top of today's visit and mileage." If I found out anything juicy, I could always tell Ben, or not. Telling Ben would implicate me in an investigation I wasn't supposed to be doing because of it being an active police investigation. Well, I'd worry about that later.

"I can do better than a two-day retainer." He opened the binder and wrote out a check, tearing it off and handing it to me.

After glancing at it, anxiety skipped around in my chest and at the base of my throat. I swallowed hard. My knee bounced. I held it down, hoping Dewey didn't notice. My eyes met his. "I meant a nonrefundable retainer." Recently—that being since Blanche had hired me—I had decided nonrefundable retainers were the way to go. I hated refunding money to a client, especially since money didn't stay long in our office account. Our expenses sucked our accounts dry every month.

"You can keep it. Insurance. I want you to do a thorough job for me. Today's costs are included as part of that."

"I uh—"

He held a hand up. "I know you probably don't like me, Miss

Davis, and I'm not trying to buy your approval. But, believe me, I understand what it's like to run your own business. If you're paid well, it's easy to put money concerns out of your head and do your best. Right?"

Our eyes met for a moment. I'd like to say I read trust in his eyes or honesty or something beneficial to the opinion I'd formed of him previously, but *nada*. "Okay, then." I stood again. "I tell you what, I'll pay a visit to Gina's cousin, Tom, before I go back to Houston this evening and see if I can get more details on her planned activities the last time he saw her. In the meantime, write up and send me an email with what you did and where you were from last Friday and include the names and contact information for anyone I should talk to who could alibi you." I realized, then, I was making an assumption that what Tom had told me about Gina, about her supposedly planning on hauling a chest up to La Grange, was true. I hoped it was. There was something about Tom that made him likable and trustworthy. Dewey, on the other hand, not so much.

He walked me to the door, his hand lightly on my back as though guiding me. Like I'd lose my way. "Thank you, really. I think we'll work well together."

I wasn't sure about that but didn't say so. I nodded and when I reached the door, I said, "Also, in the meantime, if the police happen to stop by to see you, please don't tell them about our arrangement." I gave him a *faux* grin.

"No problem. I think you need to go, though, because the cop I talked to said he hoped to be out here sometime this afternoon."

More anxiety filled my chest, flies circling, no doubt looking for an interesting place to light. Ben would kill me if he arrived while I was there, and I couldn't give him a reasonable explanation. I was still anticipating a discussion with him about the night before—dreading it to be more precise. "I'm outta here."

I grasped the handrail closest to the house, glad to be exiting from a lower level than I'd done before, and hurried down the steps.

This time, when I reached the gate, the buzzer went off and kept it up for well more time than I needed to let myself out.

Tiki Island doesn't have a lot of ways to enter and exit from the feeder road near the causeway. My Mustang, if spotted, would give me away. There aren't many yellow Mustangs from the '60s still on the road. Leaving billowing clouds of dust from crushed shells and rocks in my wake, I sped off that island as fast as I could, keeping my eyes peeled for anything that even resembled an HPD unmarked car. I couldn't be sure, but in my rear-view mirror as I climbed the causeway bridge, I thought one entered the island. I prayed I was mistaken.

CHAPTER
FIFTEEN

Midafternoon traffic was fairly light going into and out of Galveston. The speed limit sign of 60 mph on the Mitchell Causeway Bridge appeared to be only a suggestion. I abided by the suggestion and was alarmed by a tailgater wearing a latex clown mask until I remembered it was Halloween. At least I hoped it was a mask. He followed so close I thought he was going to push me over the top. I didn't get a chance to enjoy the view.

Once I made it to the other side, the clown passed me and waved, though it was the middle finger wave. We were on an island. The island was only so long. What could be his hurry? Had the Halloween parties already started?

Anyway, I pointed my Mustang toward Beachy Antiques so as to start working for Dewey right away. Enough time had passed for Ben, or, if it hadn't been Ben, whatever other investigator might have called on the antiques store, to have departed. I cruised down Broadway to Twenty-third Street, and, not seeing any sign of HPD, parked not far from the store. About the time a city marshal grew close to my car, I finally figured out the app for a computerized system of paying for parking. I didn't even want to ask how much a ticket would be.

A fifty-looking lady with reddish hair, though not as red as my own, wearing a green polo shirt with the Beachy antiques insignia on it and a wide smile, stood behind the counter. I thought she might be Tom Minello's wife. "Are you Susan Minello?"

She nodded. "May I help you?"

Sticking out my hand, I said, "Mavis Davis. We spoke on the phone a while ago."

Though her smile faded, her handshake was firm, her hand, warm. She said, "Tough to meet you under these circumstances."

"I'm so sorry for your loss. Is this a bad time for me to speak to Tom?" I hadn't seen anyone else in the store or heard any noise from the door Tom had come through the last time.

"Thank you." She frowned and shrugged. "Tom went down to Mod Coffee Shop. He should be back in a few minutes. You want to wait back here with me? I have an extra stool."

"Thanks, but I'll nose around a little, if that's okay. Y'all have so much interesting stuff in here." The guitar he'd previously put on a shelf near the counter was no longer there, having been replaced with what might have been a mandolin, but what did I know? Just that it wasn't a guitar or a ukulele.

Susan dragged her stool closer to the counter. "Let me know if you're interested in anything in a locked case."

"Okay. By the way, I thought Tom told me you were still working at the University of Texas Medical Branch."

"Part-time. My schedule is flexible, so I help out if he needs me. Today being Halloween, I might be able to help out if some ghouls and goblins show up." She feigned a small smile.

"I noticed your cool Halloween decorations. I guess that's to let shoppers know y'all are in the spirit of things?"

"You never know what brings them in. We want to appear welcoming to everyone."

I moved down the line of displayed items. Fascinating what

some booth owners thought people might buy. Old books with the dust covers in tatters. Some of the old books must be worth something, because they were wrapped in some kind of transparent paper. A set of jacks and a ball. Antique teapots and cookie jars. On one rack hung vintage clothing that might work for costume parties, though I knew some people who wore that stuff every day, like Candy, when she wasn't serving papers.

Working my way around the store, I approached the table where the cookies had been previously. More cookies were laid out but on a different plate, looking and smelling fresh. I glanced at Susan and caught her eye.

"Have some cookies," she said.

Grinning, I took a paper napkin and two cookies. They were the same kind as before. "I think Tom told me Cora, Arnie's mother, gave you the recipe for these?"

"Almond cookies. It's an old family recipe, she said. I don't know anything more except they're very addicting. From the first time Tom came home from La Grange with a batch, I can't leave them alone."

"I found that out." The one I bit into practically melted in my mouth. I love almond and stuff made from almonds, including Amaretto. I was gratified to taste the strong flavor of almonds. Seemed like everyone I'd come into contact with since working for Blanche also liked almonds and/or almond cookies. There had been cookies in Gina's van. Where had they come from and from whom? If Gina didn't love them, that could be why there were still some in the plastic bag. In my car, there wouldn't have been any left.

Susan laughed as she came out from behind the counter and grabbed a cookie for herself. "We've attracted a lot of return customers with these." She chomped down on one. "Here comes Tom with the coffee. I'm sorry we can't offer you any."

I shrugged and, as she turned away, stuffed a couple of napkin-wrapped cookies into my jacket pocket. I couldn't help myself. If I saw Cora again, I'd ask for the original recipe for Margaret.

Tom, also wearing a green polo-style shirt and khakis, burst into a smile when he saw me, then frowned like he remembered his cousin was dead. He handed a cardboard cup of coffee to his wife and walked around behind the counter where he set his own down. "I was expecting you, Mavis. Don't know why, because I can't do anything for you or Blanche. But I figured you'd show up here sooner or later."

"And here I am. I'm so sorry about Gina."

"Thank you. It was a shock. I never thought she might commit suicide."

Adrenaline charged through my body. "What? Who told you that?"

"Well, the police officer who was here said that was a distinct possibility. He asked me about her, of course, and I couldn't think of a reason why she would do that, but on the other hand I couldn't think of a reason why someone would want to harm her."

My head spun like a computer's hard drive. I'd never considered she might have offed herself, that she might take something fatal and climb into the chest to die. But why? Gina'd received a big settlement from Dewey in the divorce. She'd sold their house and had the money to buy whatever she wanted. She owned an interest in two shops. Why would she have done that? I wasn't buying it.

On the other hand, why would someone want to harm her? That, I'd do my best to find out.

"Could we go somewhere private to talk? It's best if we have our conversation where no customers who might come in would over-hear. Do you mind, Susan? He can tell you later if you're interested."

She swallowed from her coffee. "I'll hold down the fort."

"I wanted to talk to you, too, Mavis. I can drag a couple of chairs into the storeroom." I followed him to the back of the store. He set his coffee down on the seat of a pine hall tree before dragging two red brocade Queen Anne chairs from one of the booths and closing the door. The chair wasn't the most comfortable but, it being an antique, the stuffing had to have been way past its sell-by date.

He heaved a huge sigh. "Boy, Gina's death came as such a

surprise." Tom sat opposite me in the matching chair. He shook his head and grimaced. "Maybe it shouldn't have, since you'd been looking for her and couldn't find her. But, then, that doesn't necessarily follow. She hasn't been hard to keep track of in the past. Even when she and Dewey were off someplace, she always kept in touch. Still, I never thought something like this would happen."

I stared at him, waiting for him to finish. I couldn't tell whether he was truly aggrieved, or just stoic as many men were in times like these.

He stood. "I'm running off at the mouth, aren't I? I guess I'm still upset. Sorry."

"No, that's fine. It's understandable. You haven't had a lot of time to process everything."

"Yeah, that police lieutenant who was here hasn't been gone very long. If you'd come earlier, you could have spoken to him."

I didn't exactly conceal the fact that I probably knew, intimately knew, the police lieutenant, but I didn't volunteer the information either. "I talked to the police last night and probably will again." Understatement of the century.

"I told him what I'd told you before, Mavis. She left here last Friday with her van and trailer and the chest she was to deliver to the La Grange Store."

"And you told me there was a booth owner, Conrad something, who worked on Friday afternoon with Gina, right?" It's not that I didn't trust Tom, but I needed to confirm his statement with this Conrad person. I'm sure he understood that.

"Conrad Seahorse."

I laughed. "Be serious. I really need his last name."

"It's true. That is his real name. You can ask him the onomastics of his name. He loves to get into that."

Tom looked earnest. No twinkle in his eyes or smile on his lips. Onomastics might be a thing, but it wasn't a thing I was interested in. "I believe you, but I do need his contact information, phone number, email, etcetera."

"Not a problem. If you stick around here for a few minutes, you can meet him in person. He'll be helping out tonight."

"Because it's Halloween? People come into an antiques store on Halloween? That seems weird to me."

"We're an eclectic bunch, those of us who hang out downtown. A lot of people live around here, downtown, in condos and lofts. You'd be surprised. Usually there's some kind of costume party." He took another slug of coffee.

I knew about condos and lofts and apartments from when I'd had the case of the cruise ship's captain. I didn't see how Tom could actually sell anything if it was only locals who came in. But he and Susan could be in it for the partying. "Do you and your wife dress up?"

He shifted around in his chair, crossing and uncrossing his legs. "We dress in whatever vintage we have on hand. Which reminds me," he stood again. "In a minute either I need to change, or Susan does, and I need to relieve her. Which also brings me to what I wanted to speak to you about." He wore that earnest look again, his eyebrows drawing together.

"Okay." I was curious on so many levels.

He sat back down and leaned toward me. "I want to hire you."

"Not you, too." What was it with them that they couldn't wait for the police to do their job? Had they read the same *Texas Observer* magazine article I had read the previous January that said the murder clearance rate for HPD was forty percent or less?

He stood again. He was way antsier than the last time I'd been there. "Who else? Wait, don't tell me. Dewey?"

I shrugged and nodded.

"Has he hired you?"

"Yeah, a little while ago. Tell me, what is your interest in solving Gina's murder that can't wait?"

He sat down again. "Besides her being my cousin?"

My cheeks grew warm. I admittedly was being a little brusque. "Well, let's back up a minute. I want to get y'all's relationship straight. Cora said you were Gina's biological cousin, is that correct?"

"Yes. She was adopted by her stepfather. I'll tell you a little more about that in a minute."

"This whole family situation could be relevant to her case, so I'm trying to understand."

"First tell me, why is Dewey hiring you? Does he think he'll be a suspect if they decide it wasn't suicide?"

"Everyone will be a suspect." I explained the rationale Dewey had given. "So see, he's trying to protect his reputation. Why do you want to hire me?"

"Besides her being a blood relation, I really did like her."

"So your motive in wanting me to investigate for you is what? Don't tell me that police officer said you could be a suspect."

He nodded. "Said if it's a murder case, everyone is a suspect. Just what you said."

"You explained to the cop you haven't seen her since last Friday morning or so, right?"

"Yes, and he's going to verify that I left hours before she left, but that doesn't mean anything. He said there was plenty of time between last Friday and yesterday for anyone at all to harm her."

"Yeah, he's right. So explain the bio relative thing."

"Gina was adopted by her step-father after my uncle died and her mother remarried. Since her father had died, her rights to inherit were never cut off. Back then, they used to cut off inheritance rights in adoptions, the lawyer said, but since her father had died, they didn't even consider it."

Lawyer? Hmmm.

"Anyway, it stands to reason that if her right to inherit from her biological father was not cut off then wouldn't it also be true that her right to inherit through him would also not be cut off?"

My eyes were about to roll up in the back of my head. "And..."

"I don't mean to confuse you. I'm just quoting what the lawyer said. So, wouldn't that work both ways? If she could inherit through my family, couldn't we inherit through her if she didn't have a will?"

"I have no idea. And anyway, if you bought into the shop, wouldn't you have had some legal clause that says if something happens to one of you the other gets the shop? Or right of first refusal? Or something similar?"

"That would be another reason for me to be a suspect. I think. I have an appointment to go over our paperwork with him, the lawyer, because no one ever thinks they're going to die, right? We may have agreed that the other party had a right of first refusal to buy the heirs out. I'm not sure. Or if we didn't have a will leaving our half to our heirs, like our kids, or if we didn't have any, then the co-owner would inherit. She didn't have any children or sisters, or brothers and her parents are dead, so I'm thinking the court would look to aunts, uncles, cousins..."

I hoped my eyes weren't crossing at having to listen to all that technical, legal stuff. "So if I understand, you, as a blood relation, would have the legal right to inherit?"

"Precisely. I saw something like this on TV once. But if the person who is supposed to inherit murdered the relative, they would forfeit their right to inherit."

Oh what a mess. "Tom, I'm not a lawyer. I'm a PI. You and your lawyer will need to untangle this, not me."

"Yeah, Mavis, but look, if Gina's murder becomes one of the sixty percent or more that is unsolved, how would the inheritance be resolved? What would my rights be to this store that I invested so much money in?"

"You read that *Texas Observer* article, too?"

"I mentioned it to that officer, but he didn't take too kindly to what I told him the article said."

I could well imagine Ben, especially an exhausted Ben, not taking too kindly to most everything, but especially to someone reciting facts and figures to him about the subpar HPD homicide clearance rate. "Tom, I'm beginning to understand your concern, but I'm already retained by Dewey. I can't work for both of you."

"Dewey could back off, and you could work for me."

Even if Dewey would, and I didn't think he would, I wouldn't go for it after the deal that Dewey made with me. I was still hoping to get some kind of contingent fee out of Blanche if I could come up with the money Dewey was supposed to have paid to her. I shook my head. "It doesn't work that way."

He stood over me. I imagined his knees were getting awfully tired of working like hinges, popping up and down every minute or two. He frowned. Not an angry frown, but with a look of frustration in his eyes. "I don't guess you could keep me posted on what you find?"

"You could call Dewey."

He let out a big sigh. "Okay, well, I need to get out front. Thanks anyway."

I followed him out. A very short, tow-headed man was speaking with Susan at the counter. He wore a rubber monster mask pushed down under his chin and thin, ragged black strips of fabric dangled around his shoulders. A Frankenstein's monster? The mask was scrunched up, but spikes protruded from each side of the temple.

"Conrad," Tom called as we approached. They shook hands. "This is Mavis, a private investigator uh—"

"I told him about Gina," Susan said. "I'm going to leave y'all for a few minutes while I change." She made a quick getaway.

"I'm so sorry, Tom," Conrad said, shaking his head. "She was so young."

"Anyway, Mavis is helping the police figure out who killed Gina," Tom said. "Isn't that right, Mavis?" He stepped behind the counter and leaned against it.

I didn't exactly disabuse Tom of that notion. Okay, I didn't correct Tom at all. But as long as the police didn't know I was poking around, I'd be all right.

Conrad stepped forward and took my outstretched hand. "Conrad

Seahorse." He was a shrimp of a man. Five-one, if not only five feet tall. But his grip was strong. I towered over him, but he didn't appear the least bit ruffled. "Have we met before? Seems like I've seen that red hair."

"You could have seen me at Mod. I was down here some a year or so ago."

"That's possible, I guess." He stepped back and took a long up and down look at me. It wasn't sexual, more like he was taking my measure.

"Could I speak with you a minute, Conrad? And Tom, could I use your storeroom back there for a few more minutes? You won't mind if I talk to Conrad privately, will you?"

"You have to wait until Susan's out, but sure. She'll only be a minute. I can change my shirt and put on the vintage stuff out here, so long as no customers come in." There were some clothes on hangers near the far end of the counter section. He began removing them and unbuttoning his shirt.

"Thanks." I walked toward the back, taking baby steps. Conrad joined me.

"So what do you want to talk to me about, Mavis? Okay if I call you Mavis, or do you prefer your last name, which is?"

"Davis. And if you laugh at my name, I'll laugh at yours."

"Fair enough." He smirked, scrunching his avocado-green eyes. "So, Mavis it is, and I'm Conrad."

The toilet in the storeroom flushed and moments later, Susan came out dressed in layers of thin white flowing fabric and a white wig. A stuffed bird sat on her shoulder. "All yours."

Conrad said, "She's supposed to be a character out of a historical novel." He clapped his hand to his forehead. "I can't even remember the name of it right now."

I wondered if the news about Gina had shaken him up more than he let on. I touched his shoulder. "That's understandable. You've had such a shock. Let's go in here, okay?"

He gestured for me to go ahead of him and closed the door

behind us. After we were seated, he said in a sugary voice, "I'll tell you something and if you repeat it to Tom, I'll call you a liar."

That caused me to sit up.

"I couldn't stand Gina. She was a real B, if you know what I mean."

I was taken aback.

"You look surprised. Well, don't be. She was syrupy around Tom, most of the time. She did go off on him once a while back but begged his forgiveness and attributed it to her divorce."

"He hasn't said a bad thing about her."

"He wouldn't. He's too much of a gentleman, too polite. Susan, too, though Susan may have seen more of Gina's rude side. She never would have said anything. Tom loved Gina too much. He doesn't have a lot of other relatives."

Things often aren't what they appear to be. So what else is new? My job was to figure out what was real.

"Is that what you wanted to know?" Conrad pulled his mask up.

I laughed and covered his hand with mine. "Not so fast, if you don't mind. Could you tell me about the last time you saw Gina?"

"Sure, that's easy. Last Friday. Tom probably already told you that."

"He did, but I'd like to hear the details from you."

He pulled one leg up and crossed it over the other at the knee. "Not much to tell. I showed up here much like today, only earlier. Tom took off. Susan normally isn't here and wasn't that day. She works part-time at UTMB."

"So only you and Gina were here?"

"Yeah, and only a few customers wandering in and out that day, unfortunately."

"Did y'all talk about anything specific?"

"She and I didn't talk a whole lot. I didn't like her, and she didn't like me. She told me about the chest she was going to deliver to her shop in La Grange. Before the end of the day, I helped her load it onto her trailer and came back inside. After a few minutes, she came back inside. She'd had to cover it with a waterproof tarp, you see. She'd tied it down."

"What happened after that?"

"Nothing, really. It was already late. She packed up a few things and left. We hadn't had much business. I locked up."

"And that was the last time you saw her?"

Shrugging, he said, "Honest to God." He pulled his mask down and leered. "And I guess I'll never have to see her again."

I didn't respond to that other than to thank him for the information. He put his mask back up. He was the shortest Frankenstein's monster I'd ever seen outside of children wandering the streets trick-or-treating.

We left the storeroom and walked to the front. Tom had changed into some kind of clothes that were allegedly vintage. I couldn't tell whether they were, or who or what he was supposed to be. I told them goodbye and left. On my way out of town, I stopped at a convenience store for a soda and a few quiet moments before I hit the Interstate 45 traffic. Sitting for a moment in the parking lot, I gave some thought to what Conrad, and Tom earlier, had said about the van and the trailer. The questions in my mind became: when was Gina put into the chest? Who put Gina into the chest? Or did she crawl into the chest to die? When did the chest get moved from the trailer to the back of her van? And again, by whom? If she couldn't move it by herself, and she wanted to commit suicide, who assisted her?

CHAPTER

SIXTEEN

By late Thursday night, I had called and checked in with Margaret and Candy at the office, making sure everything was as it should be. You never knew with those two. And it was. Without revealing what was going on to Blanche, I phoned to tell her I still had a line on her money. She sounded skeptical but agreed we still had a deal on my receiving a percentage if I recovered it. She also made it clear she was no longer paying me for my services, which I already knew from our earlier conversation, though the bill wasn't in the mail yet. I didn't tell her I was currently employed by Dewey.

I drove straight to my house from Galveston, hoping for a respite. The last few days had finally taken their toll. I needed to decompress. Luckily, in my older neighborhood of mostly ranch-style and craftsman homes owned by people with few or no children, ghouls and goblins were in short supply. Only one or two trick-or-treaters showed up each year. When I went inside, I made sure the automatic front door light was turned off, so if anyone came looking for candy, they'd bypass my place, though I did leave out a small bowl of treats in case any of them actually made it up on my porch. Laying my purse and keys on the kitchen counter, I opened the refrigerator door to see what was available for dinner.

Cooking wasn't my best thing, but when I did it, I usually cooked batches, so I'd have leftovers that could be reheated and frozen meals that could be quickly thawed out. Leftover meatballs and spaghetti were on the menu that night. The sauce and meatballs went into a microwavable bowl, ready to warm up, and I put a pot of water on the lowest setting so it would be about to boil when I returned from the shower. All I wanted to do was clean up, eat, and go to bed.

Afterward, clothed in my most comfortable old ratty bathrobe and with my hair wrapped in a towel, I went to the kitchen to cook the noodles. Comfort food was what I was looking forward to. A few minutes later, I sat at the dining table with a glass of red wine, my plate of spaghetti, and a hunk of garlic bread. All was right in my world, at least temporarily. That is, until someone banged on my front door and inserted a key in the lock.

I peeked through the peephole and couldn't see much with the lights off, but Ben was the only person I'd given a key to, so it had to be him. Having a key to the front door meant he could come and go at will. That's why I'd given him one. Plus, he had to know I was home since my car was in the driveway. Pulling open the door, and in spite of a moment of freaking out because of how I appeared, I said, "Hey, babe. I wish you'd called first, so I could at least have combed my hair."

He looked dead tired, his face gray tinged. He said hello and cupped my cheeks between his hands, planting a big kiss on me. When we came up for air, he said, "Did I taste garlic? And your special spaghetti sauce? I could smell both from outside." He was in his shirt sleeves and a rumpled pair of slacks and smelled like he could use a shower himself. Lucky for me I was attracted to his scent, as opposed to some other people's whose names I won't mention.

Ben loved my spaghetti and meatballs. It was almost as if the aroma had somehow lured him to my house. "Are you off duty? Can you stay if I fix you a plate?"

"If you have enough." His eyes danced. He knew I always made a big batch, which both of us would eat from for several days.

He followed me into the kitchen and stood close behind me while I prepared his plate. At one point, he even nuzzled my neck. I was glad he apparently was in a good mood, though my guess was he was more worn out than I was.

I held out the plate, and he said, "Throw some of that garlic bread on top, would you please, while I pour myself a glass of wine?" He plucked a wine glass from the cupboard.

We exchanged only a few words for a while, both of us focusing on our meal, our wine, and occasional glances at the other. I was kind of waiting for the other shoe to drop, but to do that, I'd have to know what the first shoe did. If that made any sense.

After he cleaned his plate, Ben pushed back from the table. "So what have you been doing?"

"You mean other than showering and washing my hair?" The towel unwrapped itself and fell to the floor. "You mind putting the dishes in the sink while I comb my hair before it gets too dry?" As my mother would say, I probably looked like the wreck of the Hesperus but wanted to make an attempt at remedying that. "If I'd known you were coming, I'd have—"

"Yeah, yeah." He grinned. "Go on."

When I returned, Ben had put everything in the dishwasher and wiped down the stove, which made me wonder whether he was buttering me up for something.

He wrapped his arms around me, enveloping me like a giant sloth. Boy, did it feel good. I dragged him into my bathroom and started the water for him. "I'll be waiting for you when you get out." I laid out my largest bath towel and a washcloth for him and closed the door behind me. Admittedly, I liked him to drop by, for him to feel comfortable enough to know it was okay. We'd been exclusive for a long time, though I still refused to get married whenever he brought it up. A long-term relationship was enough for me.

When he came out with the towel wrapped around his waist, I expected to see a light in his eyes, a light that communicated he wanted to have an intimate moment, but instead, he sat back against the headboard, his sign he wanted to talk. Darn. Then he yawned, and I realized how weary he was.

I had slipped into something more comfortable and more presentable, though still what my mother-voice called decent. "You've been tied up with the Gina Collins case all day?"

He shifted so his face, at least, was toward me. "Most of the day. Sanchez won't have anything to report any time soon."

"The ME?"

"Or someone on his staff. They're overloaded. Nothing new about that."

"Whoever came out last night didn't attempt a guess about how she died?"

He shook his head. "You know in a situation where there's nothing obvious, they're not going to do that. They could tell she'd been in that position for several days with the way the blood had pooled."

Not wanting to reveal what I'd heard from Gina's cousin, Tom Minello, I picked my words carefully. "We haven't talked much since last night. Were you able to learn anything today? Mind telling me what's going on? What do *you* think happened to Gina?"

He studied my face for a moment. Ben was not stupid. He knew I'd be beyond curious. Since it was an active case, he was limited in what he could share with me. Though I've never seen it in writing, cops have some kind of code of ethics and Ben, for one, did his level best to follow the rules.

He closed his eyes. For a moment I thought he was going to doze off right then and there, until he spoke. "I shouldn't tell you anything. You still need to account for your actions, but I'm not going to grill you right now. I'm too tired. I can tell you this. She looked like she was sleeping. There was no blood evident anywhere, even in that box after they removed the body."

I was surprised he didn't describe how decomposed her body was, but again I couldn't say anything, or I'd get myself in hot water. "So there's no way to know what someone did to get her in that chest?"

"*If* somebody did. *If* somebody put her in it." He yawned again.

"What do you mean? *If?*"

"She could have climbed inside by herself." His eyes opened a fraction and cut toward me.

"You mean suicide?" As if I didn't already know. "You think she committed suicide?"

He shrugged. "Could have, Mavis. We don't know. Me? I have serious doubts that anyone would do that. Why not just lie down on your bed?" His eyes closed again. His face relaxed. I wasn't sure how much more I'd be able to get out of him.

"Lon said someone called dispatch. And didn't he or you say someone reported a body in a box? How would anyone know she was in there if they didn't put her in there—or maybe help her climb inside which doesn't make sense. Maybe it was assisted suicide. But nobody—"

"Assisted suicide?" His face wrinkled with skepticism. "Who have you been talking to?" Ben had been slowly sliding down from the headboard and scooted back up.

The conversation was warming up. "The people I talked to when I was trying to serve her with Blanche's petition. Nobody said anything about her being sick or anything and people who engage in suicide—assisted suicide—have a reason to, like terminal cancer or something."

"No. No one mentioned that. We spoke to several of the neighbors. They didn't know anything. In fact, they barely knew her at all. She was a new resident, and that unit is a rental with a somewhat frequent turnover."

I wasn't going to admit I already knew that. "So if it wasn't assisted suicide or whatever it's called, if someone put her in the chest, it would have to be murder, right? I mean, if she dropped dead of a heart attack, why would they put her in the chest? But, if she committed suicide for other reasons, like she was depressed or something, she could have staged it so her body would be found pretty quickly." I was babbling but wanted to get as much information out of him as I could while he was tired and had his defenses down.

"No. It would have taken several days since it was parked in a parking lot. Anyway, who would have called dispatch and reported a body?"

"So you don't think it was a suicide?"

"I'm not guessing, Mavis. How about you tell me what you were doing there? I know you said you were trying to serve her, but Tyler said he saw you coming from the back of that condo."

So much for hoping he wasn't going to give me the third degree. At least he wasn't stretching my legs out between two chairs and jumping on my knees like police have been reputed to do, at least in the movies. I needed to be careful. "You want another glass of wine?"

He gave me the side-eye.

"I guess not." I yawned and stretched. "I'm exhausted, and I know you are. I can tell from looking at you."

"Mavis—"

"Okay. All right."

"And don't tell me you were inside that dead woman's condo."

I wasn't going to tell him that.

"Or her van."

I wasn't going to tell him that, either. "How could I have been inside her van when it was locked?"

"So you admit you tried to get inside it."

"I'm sure y'all had someone take fingerprints from the outside of the van. You'll find out I was there. I looked through several windows, checked to see if it was locked. I don't think it's a crime to look in the windows of a vehicle."

137

"Attempted burglary of a vehicle."

"No way. Why, did someone say they saw me try to get inside her van?"

"What about her condo? Lon saw you stuff something in your jacket pockets. What was that?"

"Okay, so you won't get all in an uproar, get mad, threaten to take me downtown, I'm going to give you a rundown on what's happened since Blanche hired me, even if it's confidential between me and my client." Not that I'd kept it confidential. Everyone and their cousin knew what I'd been doing.

"You'd have to testify to what you know if you were called to court."

"Yeah, well, my bedroom is about the farthest thing from a court of law there is."

"You're stalling."

His eyes were drifting closed again. "Okay, this is what transpired since I was hired on Tuesday. After I deposited Blanche's check, I began working for her." I launched into a blow-by-blow of what I did on Tuesday, where I went, who I spoke with. Ben's eyes stayed closed. Then I went into Wednesday, again where I went and who I spoke with. His eyes continued to stay closed. Next, I began with that morning, intending on giving him as sketchy a rundown as possible, but by then he was sound asleep. I knew that, because he let out a loud snort.

Walking around to the other side of the bed, I eased the covers out from under him. Magically, I was able to remove the towel from around his waist and blanket him with the duvet in one accomplished move. Not my first rodeo. Ben had slept at my house many times before, including falling asleep on me in the middle of things. A dedicated public servant, he definitely was.

He was too large and too heavy for me to move down from the top of the bed, from the headboard, so I left him sleeping. I knew in the middle of the night he'd probably scoot down on his own or face a stiff neck in the morning.

Turning off the light, I left Ben snoring away. Knowing I'd be unable to get any shuteye because of the volume of his snoring if I climbed into bed beside him, I took a coverlet and pillow from my hall closet and headed to the sofa, relieved I wouldn't be facing any more interrogation that night.

CHAPTER

SEVENTEEN

T he following morning at the office, Margaret said, "So how do you think you're going to figure out who killed her— that is, if she was killed." We were in the kitchen, me, in my favorite jeans and jacket, poring over the Houston newspaper and sipping a cup of hot English breakfast tea. Margaret, trying to decide what she should take to alleviate her hangover. According to her, she and Stan, her newest significant other, had gone to a Halloween party the night before. She'd looked better. Her clothes, though clean, could have been slept in. Maybe it was the wrinkles. I wasn't going to mention it, but her earrings didn't match. I doubted that was by design.

I'd explained a lot of what had transpired in the past few days without implicating myself in any criminal activities—like burglary. The less Margaret knew about some things, the better. I'd keep it on a need-to-know basis. That way, if Ben dropped by, Margaret couldn't tell him what she didn't know. Ben was good at questioning my staff when I wasn't around.

"You have any acetaminophen in your purse? The aspirin I took isn't working, and I guess we've used up what was in the bathroom cabinet."

"Sure. You know where I keep it." I was somewhat envious of her —that she'd been to a party. I would've liked to have gone to a party. I'd decided I worked too much and so did Ben. We hadn't been anywhere lately. The last time I remember the two of us going some-place was when we were in Galveston together after the case involving the cruise ship captain, and that trip started out being work-related.

"I'll be right back, and then I want to hear what you're thinking about that Gina person." She eased around me and left the kitchen, so I had a few minutes to myself. Ben had been called out in the wee hours of the morning, so we hadn't continued our conversation about the case. An interrogation by him might still be in my future, in spite of the fact he had way more than me to worry about. He was constantly stressed over the number of homicides in Houston he had to deal with. I was hoping he wouldn't have time to drop by the office for a while, though I admit I was missing him.

The bell over the front door jingled. "Mavis," Candy called as she jogged down the hall. "They cancelled my class today, so I came on in." Breathless, she threw herself into a chair. She wore white jeans, sandals, and a Hunter Green sweater, like she couldn't decide what season to dress for.

"Hey, good morning. How was Halloween for you?" I folded the paper and put it to one side of the table.

She pulled the newspaper toward her. "I took my little brother around the neighborhood, but you know, where I live you don't get quality candy." She shrugged and opened the paper. "Plus, like I had to go through his bag. You know. Can't trust anyone nowadays."

"Yeah. I know." I took a final swallow of my tea. "Since you're here, I need you to cover the front for Margaret. She's not feeling great, and I need to discuss some things with her."

"Like what things if I may ask?" Her eyes widened in anticipation.

"Like since Dewey Collins hired me, I'd better figure out what I need to do next."

"Yeah, you started in Galveston yesterday? Now where?"

"That's what we're going to talk about. Who, what, where, when, and why."

"And how?"

I grinned at her, knowing she'd love to be in on the conversation. Sometimes I let her. Others, I didn't. We were often stretched thin with there being only three of us. "Yes, how she was killed."

"You think there'll be anything in the paper about her? Maybe it'll say how she died." She paged through the thick newspaper until she found the crime section.

"They won't know anything we don't already know. You can take the paper up to Margaret's desk."

She folded it and stuck it under her arm. "Okay, Mavis. I'm sensing you don't want to discuss the case with me. Am I right?"

She'd been able to peg me for a while. A stupid young woman, she wasn't. "I'll tell you when there's something you need to know."

"Oh all right." She took the paper and disappeared around the corner. "Hi Margaret."

Margaret returned, holding the bottle of acetaminophen, a bottle of aspirin, and a bottle of ibuprofen. "I'm going to keep these nearby." She plopped down in the chair Candy had vacated.

"I know it's too soon to ask if you're feeling any better yet."

Margaret gave me a look and shook her head. She might want me to send her home, but she was going to have to ask, which she wouldn't do. Having been friends since elementary school, I knew her better than that. She thought she should tough things out unless she was in the hospital or unless someone forced her to do the alternative. Our mothers had raised us that way. For many years in our youth, each of us had won perfect attendance certificates. Our mothers wouldn't let us stay home unless we had one foot in the grave.

"Okay, Mavis. So you can continue your story."

"Forgot where I was." I didn't feel exactly overwhelmed, but I was getting there. I wasn't sure I had enough information or how I'd be able to get more.

"Dewey hired you, then Tom wanted to hire you. So have you ruled both of them out?"

"Well, first, I've been thinking how I'm one step ahead of the police. I've met a bunch of people who were acquainted with or married to or related to the decedent. That saves me a lot of time. I don't have to start from scratch."

"You have a point." She closed her eyes and rolled her head around as if to loosen her neck.

"I haven't ruled anyone out, yet, but those people—the ones she was closest to—should obviously be on the top of any list of suspects. Of course, if she was, in fact, murdered, the killer or killers could be people I—we—are not even aware of, people who had a motive no one is aware of. We're going to focus in the beginning on those closest to her. After they're ruled out, we can look at other people with possible motives."

"You implied Ben thinks she was murdered, right? And from what her cousins told you, it sounds like she didn't have much of a life outside of the two antiques shops. Has anyone said she did?"

"They said her life was mostly going from shop to shop and to estate sales and to her condo or the storage units. No one has even implied she had much of a life after the divorce, not seeing anyone, not dating." She might have had a secret life, but I didn't think so. She had so much going on, trying to find a place to settle and dealing with both stores. "She rented that condo after she sold her house, so she hasn't—hadn't been there long. Maybe not long enough to give anyone there a motive."

Margaret massaged her temples. "So no one connected with the condo rental would have had a motive. I wish you'd had more time yesterday to bring me up to date. I miss when I used to get to go with you sometimes."

"I know." I hadn't wanted to tell her about some of the things I'd done this time. I'd been tired the day before and needed to go home. "So I don't think anyone connected with the sale of her house should have anything against her. But no way of knowing that. Even though money is a factor with her ex and her lawyer, a Realtor wouldn't have an issue with her like that. Or a buyer. The Realtor would have been paid at the closing."

"So we can rule out anything to do with the house or the condo."

"I don't know about the condo. The condo rental, yes, but I had a feeling at least one of her neighbors at the condo complex wasn't that fond of her."

"Who was that?"

"The woman who came out and talked to me the first time I went by to serve Gina. Nancy Harmon. And Nancy has a boyfriend, Grant."

"Huh. Did Gina live there long enough to try to get between Grant and Nancy?"

"Nancy could have thought so. I'm not clear on that."

A small rumble came from the hallway. "Thought y'all might need this," Candy said, wheeling our whiteboard in from her office, where we stored it, in addition to supplies.

Margaret left the kitchen abruptly and returned almost immediately with the eraser and a couple of markers. She wrote *Nancy and Grant* on the board.

"You're welcome," Candy said with a smug smile as she departed again.

"Thank you, Candy," I called after her.

Margaret busied herself with writing down the names she knew.

"That supposed to be a list of suspects? If so, cross out Grant for now," I said. "I can't think why he'd want Gina dead."

Margaret drew a line through Grant's name. She looked at me and wrote *Dewey Collins*.

"I hope it's not Dewey. I'm counting on him laying a lot more money on me and helping me get a bonus from Blanche."

"Still…" Margaret wrote *Blanche*. "I ought to put them in order of your meeting them." She erased the names and started the list over.

"I'll make this prettier on the computer later, so we can put it in the file." She wrote *Blanche* again. "First, you met Blanche last Tuesday."

"Second would be Nancy—Nancy Harmon, the neighbor who I met when I went to Gina's condo."

"Then those people you met in La Grange. What are their names?"

I thought a moment. "The bakery woman—Beth Anne." I referred to the little notepad on my phone. "Novak. Beth Anne Novak. I got the impression she didn't like Gina, though I can't think of a motive for murder."

After writing that, Margaret said, "And the cousin and his mother? Their names?"

"Arnie Saxberg and Cora."

"Cora of the cookies?"

"Right."

"And that Beth Anne is the one who makes those big Bear Claws?"

"Correct. The ones you're hoping to successfully reproduce."

"*You're* hoping I'll successfully reproduce them."

"Anyway, once you accomplish that, keep them for a special treat, or they'll contribute to an expanded rear end for all of us. Let's move on. Dewey, the ex-husband and my current client."

"I don't see a motive for him, really, Mavis. I mean, they were already divorced. You said he's rich even though he had to give her a lot of his money. He's got another book coming out."

"I don't think so, either. I hope not. Their case was over. Would he want to risk everything out of revenge? Then there's Tom Minello, the other cousin. The biological cousin. His wife's name is Susan. You know, most of these people are so nice, I hate to think any of them could have killed Gina. I'm hoping it was suicide, though that seems improbable."

"Yeah, right." She held the marker at the ready. "I know you don't believe it was suicide, but you haven't told me why. Next?"

"Conrad Seahorse."

Margaret laughed. "No way."

"Yes way. But let's not get into a discussion about names. Conrad, who I met, is a little guy who has a booth in Tom's antiques shop. Conrad was the last person to see her alive."

"I thought she went to La Grange from there."

"Yeah. Okay. Last person to see her alive in Galveston. And it was last Friday afternoon when he helped her load up that chest—the chest that ended up being her coffin."

"So she went to La Grange and was there on Saturday?" She wrote Galveston on the board and made a column and wrote La Grange. Then she put the names of the people Mavis had met under the cities' names.

"Beth Anne said Gina was there. And there's a woman who is also a booth owner in the La Grange store. Beth Anne said the woman came and got pastries from her on Saturday. Her name is Sheila. I haven't met her."

"That's nine if we rule out people who didn't have significant contact—that we know of—with Gina. You also went to the storage place and talked to a man there."

"I can't think of any reason the storage place worker would have to harm Gina. I'm not even sure she stopped by the storage place when she left Galveston. Besides, we know she went to La Grange after that, so don't even write him down."

"And the security guard at the condos."

I shrugged. "Same. Same. What motive could he have? If I learn of one, we can add him to the list."

"Okay, nine if you count Tom's wife."

She looked at me like she thought I could give her the answer to who it was, but I had no clue.

"I want to narrow that list down. I'm going to rule out the Galveston people right off the bat since Gina was last seen in La Grange. Anyway, Tom loved Gina—as a cousin—according to Conrad. Tom's wife, Susan, would have no motive. And why would Conrad, just because he thought she was a B?"

"Okay, six. Blanche, Nancy, Beth Anne, Arnie, Cora, and Dewey."

"It would have helped if Gina hadn't been found outside her condo and inside her van. I'd love to rule Nancy out."

"What about Arnie's mother? Didn't you say she's ancient?"

"Yes, so that would rule her out, because she couldn't move Gina's body or the chest."

"Without help."

"I'm not sure she could even carry part of the load. So I'm not going to consider her a suspect unless she was an accomplice."

"Five as to the actual killing. And, Mavis, could anyone move the body or the chest without help?"

"Good question. Now that I think about it and having seen the chest, which is the size of a coffin, I don't think so. It took two people to load it up empty on the trailer."

"In Galveston."

"Yes, Gina and Conrad. A woman and a small man, though Conrad looked pretty sturdy."

Margaret's eyes had widened. "So we're looking at two people?"

I hadn't gotten that far in my thoughts the night before as I tried to fall asleep on the sofa. "At least. Two people when the chest was empty."

"Maybe they moved the chest into the van and then put her body in it, otherwise wouldn't it be even harder to move the chest?"

"Yep. And even though Dewey is awfully strong—I saw him in his workout clothes, a wife beater shirt and shorts—the whole scenario doesn't fit."

"So he could move a body, maybe, but a chest from a trailer to a van? And then drop off the van and get rid of the trailer? Sounds too complicated for one person."

"I'll review my notes. He's going to send me his alibis for last weekend. And if he needed help, who would he get to help him? Who could he trust that wouldn't rat him out? He has lots of fans, but does he have any close friends he could trust like that?" Margaret and I exchanged looks. "I have no idea." My brain was racing. "Plus, he would have had to know when she left Galveston, where she was going, and followed her. Then if she was seen in La Grange, he would have had to hang out there until he could get her alone."

"Didn't you say Gina was supposed to deliver that chest to the La Grange store so the couple who bought it could pick it up there? Or was she going to deliver it to their house? Or what?"

"Well, whatever, she never delivered it. I think we should put the idea of Dewey aside. With all his money and his career, I don't see him killing her."

"Or Blanche, either, Mavis. Who would Blanche have gotten to help her? And why? As angry as she was, would she give up her career over $60,000?"

"And she wouldn't be hiring someone to serve Gina with process in a lawsuit if she'd killed her. Back to Nancy. She's harder to fit into the scenario than Dewey. She would have had to go to La Grange to accomplish everything."

"That leaves the La Grange people."

The La Grange people were where I'd have to focus first. I got chills. Goose bumps on my arms. The back of my neck tingled. Margaret and I stared at each other. "Are you thinking what I'm thinking?"

Margaret's eyes flared, and she said, "You need to make another trip to La Grange."

"Yes, I do. I need to talk to that Sheila person to confirm Gina was there on Saturday and whether anything happened during the day that would lead to Gina's demise. After that, I'll reassess the situation and figure out my next move."

"I'm coming with you," Margaret said, hand on hip. "You need someone to have your back."

"No. I need you here in the office. We need to keep this place running, and we can't do it from out of town. I can take care of myself. I'll be fine."

"You do remember you almost got thrown off a roof in Galveston?" Margaret's voice had risen an octave. "You need someone with you, and that someone should be me. Candy can handle the office for one day."

"Tell you what, Margaret. Instead of taking you with me, I'll take my thirty-eight." I got up to go into Candy's office where we'd moved the safe. "And don't you dare tell Ben."

Margaret followed. "Don't be crazy. You don't intend to shoot anyone, do you?"

I stooped over to do the combination to the safe, not answering her. I'd never shot anyone yet, but I had practiced when Ben took me to the firing range. I could hit a target pretty well, though when I'd been in Galveston that had not been the case. Not that I'd shot anyone in Galveston, just shot at them. I retrieved my gun, unzipped the carrying case, and checked for bullets. Ben wasn't past hiding them from me. The thirty-eight was a five-shot revolver. Though the gun wasn't loaded, the five bullets were in a small plastic bag. If I needed more than five rounds, I was in big trouble. Closing and locking the safe, I stood and faced Margaret down. "I need you to do something for me. Make an appointment for me with my mechanic for Monday morning. That'll be one less thing I have to worry about."

Her voice had softened. "Please let me go with you, Mavis. We almost lost you last time."

I patted her cheek. "Tell you what, I'll call you if I need your help. How about that? Now move out of my way, and let me get on the road."

CHAPTER

EIGHTEEN

So here it was, a week since anyone in Galveston had seen Gina. Was it only last Tuesday that Blanche had hired me to serve her petition on Gina? That I had driven up to La Grange? That Beth Anne had told me Sheila had picked up pastries for herself, Gina, and Arnie on Saturday? And coffee, I remembered her saying, though usually they didn't buy coffee, but their coffee maker was on the fritz. When I thought about it, I realized Beth Anne had never told me she'd actually seen Gina.

So, fired by Blanche and hired by Dewey. I wished I could have two clients on the same case at the same time, that being Tom in addition to Dewey. We could use the money. Of course, I couldn't do that. I have my standards, not to mention ethics and all.

Back to the events in La Grange. Arnie had said Gina had been in the store. I was sure of it. I couldn't remember his exact words, though, from when I'd had tea and cookies with him and his mother. Maybe he had implied it. I'd only been trying to serve Gina with the lawsuit then or I'd have made notes.

Sheila would be my starting point. I didn't yet know her last name or I would have asked Margaret to search for her on the Internet. I'd have to contact Sheila through the store. I carried the file with me to my car, escaping Margaret, so I wouldn't have to argue anymore. Flipping through it, I found the number for Fayette Antiques in La Grange and made the call.

"Fayette Antiques," a male voice said. Could have been Arnie. I wasn't sure.

"May I please speak to Sheila?" I wasn't going to identify myself if I could help it.

"She's with a customer. Who may I say is calling?"

"It's a personal matter." My heart pounded in my throat. Until he was in the clear, I didn't want Arnie to know I was going to talk to Sheila, if that was Arnie who answered.

"Hold on," he said in an annoyed-sounding monotone.

A few moments later, I heard, "Sheila, phone call. Says it's personal."

There was a rustling noise, then, "Hello, this is Sheila."

"Sheila, this is Mavis Davis, the PI who was up there a few days ago looking for Gina Collins. You probably heard I was there. Don't say anything. Don't say my name. Sheila, I want to speak with you privately. I'll be up there this afternoon and would like to meet with you."

"Not at this time."

"I guess you're aware Gina was found in her van in Houston?" When she didn't respond, I asked, "Is Arnie nearby?"

"Yes. Yes. I have all the life insurance I'll ever need, thank you. And lady, I don't know how you got this number, but don't call me at my place of business again." The call disconnected.

So did she mean I should call her at home? I couldn't do that if I didn't even know her last name. I couldn't get her last name without going to La Grange or calling Arnie or Beth Anne and asking them. I sure as heck wasn't going to do that.

When I arrived in La Grange and showed up at the antiques

store, Arnie, if he was there, would know I wanted to talk to Sheila. If he wasn't there, I could talk to her unless someone else was there who would tell Arnie. I didn't want to get her in trouble with Arnie in case he was somehow involved in Gina's demise, which I didn't yet know. Seemed to me the best thing would be to interview each person out of the presence of the other people. How could I do that?

I hoped that after interviewing Sheila, Beth Anne, and Arnie separately, I'd have more information to go on, more people to talk with in addition to Arnie's mother, Cora. She might not be strong enough to participate in something like a transferring the chest to the van and putting the body inside, but she still had her wits about her and could easily impart information that could be helpful. She struck me as someone who was in the know.

So much had happened so fast. I'd criss-crossed from Houston to La Grange down to Galveston and up Highway 6 to a storage unit and back down to Galveston via Tiki Island. Now headed back to La Grange again. I could definitely use some money to buy a new or newer car, one with more get up and go—and better gas mileage. I prayed my Mustang would hold out until the following Monday.

A cold front had blown in overnight, so a chill was in the air. Autumn was finally creeping in. I always loved the smell in the air after a cold front came through. I let myself enjoy the drive, the countryside, leaves starting to drop, and the fall colors. By midafternoon, I arrived and parked next to a pickup truck in front of Fayette Antiques. An Open sign hung in the front window.

I climbed out of my car, stretched to get the kinks out, and, ignoring the bakery, which was sending vibes my way, entered the antiques store. A bell rang overhead, though not a cowbell like we had at our office. A strong aroma of coffee filled the air. A dark-haired woman of about forty held a feather duster in one hand. She called out to me.

"Welcome," she said in a light and friendly tone. "Let me know if I can help you find anything in particular." She had wide-set brown eyes and wore a denim jumper over a floral print blouse, real country-looking.

"Thank you." A man and a woman were examining items at the back of the store. The shop was stereotypical of all the antiques stores I'd visited. Lots of good junk, as my mother used to say. I moved from one defined booth to another, examining items until I grew close to the woman who had greeted me. "Are you Sheila?" I whispered even though I couldn't see anyone nearby.

The woman stopped what she was doing and faced me. "Goodness, no. I'm Carol. Sheila and I don't look anything alike. We couldn't be confused with each other."

I thought that was a weird response but refrained from saying so. "Oh. I don't know Sheila. I just wanted to speak with her. Is she here today, maybe in the back?"

"She was here earlier, but she left at lunchtime and hasn't returned. She doesn't usually come in on Fridays, only if she wants, so there was no reason for her to stay."

"What about Arnie? Is he here?"

She shook her head and whispered, "I'm the only one here right now, but I don't want to publicize that. I guess you could say I'm paranoid about being here alone."

I whispered back, "Was Arnie here earlier?"

She nodded. "But he left shortly after Sheila. Is there something I can help you with?"

I picked up and put down a few things, hoping to look casual. After a minute or so, I said, "I wonder if you could tell me Sheila's last name."

The woman looked at me, her eyebrows pulling together into one long fuzzy line. "So you don't know her? What do you want her for?"

"She gave me a card when we met, but I misplaced it. I remembered she worked here. I wanted to talk to her about something personal."

Clearly, Carol wasn't comfortable giving out that information.

She shook her head. "I don't think so." She smiled like she was sorry and shrugged one shoulder. "I know if a customer came in and asked for information about me, I wouldn't be too happy about it being given out."

"I understand. Do you suppose you could call her and ask her to call me or if I could go see her?"

"That, I can do." She pulled a cell phone out of her jumper pocket and scrolled down. When she came to a certain point, she tapped her phone. "What should I tell her you want to see her about?"

"Could you just give her my name and tell her I'd like to speak with her?"

"I'm not getting an answer. It's rung half a dozen times. Wait—" She shook her head. "Voicemail. Hey, Sheila, this is Carol. There's a lady here in the store who wants to speak with you. Give me a call back as soon as you get this. Thanks." She disconnected and put the phone back in her pocket. "You could come back tomorrow. I know she'll be here tomorrow. She's always here on Saturdays."

"Okay, Carol. I'm going to be absolutely straight with you."

She took a step away from me. "What do you mean?"

"Were you here last Saturday?"

She shook her head. "I'm home with my kids on the weekends. Why?"

"I'm really here to ask Sheila about Gina Collins."

Carol's face turned about as white as a human's face could. "I was so sorry to hear that she passed. Arnie told me about it."

I wanted to ask what exactly Arnie had told her, but one thing at a time. "Yes, very sad." I moved around in the general area where she was standing without getting any closer. Clearly, she was uncomfortable. The couple in the back of the store were measuring a chifforobe. A man, who could have been in his sixties, entered and began browsing. "Carol, I'm sorry for the story I told you. I'm a private investigator. I've been hired to look into the circumstances of Gina's demise."

"Oh. So you want to talk to Sheila about Gina?"

"Yes. I wanted to start with her. Do you know anything about what transpired with the chest she was bringing from Galveston last weekend to deliver to some folks who live up here?"

"No. I said I wasn't here on Saturday. Sheila's here on Saturdays and sometimes one or two others. So you need to come back tomorrow."

I hadn't planned on returning on Saturday, though I had packed a small bag in case I needed to spend the night. Dewey would reimburse me for a place to stay. Still, I'd been hoping to go home and see Ben. We tried to spend time together on the weekends, even if we couldn't get together during the week.

Carol started toward the other side of the room. I followed her. "I live in Houston, but I guess I could stay overnight. If you'd give me Sheila's last name and phone number, I could call her myself and maybe meet her this evening."

"You have any identification?"

I flipped out my ID and let her study it. "Are there B & Bs nearby? I don't want to drive as far as Austin."

"Oh sure, a ton of them." She pointed toward the door. "On the other side of the square, you can't see it because the courthouse is in the way, there's a real estate place that handles short term rentals and houses for sale."

I sighed long and hard like I was forlorn and searched her face for any clues she might have an agenda of her own. She appeared guileless. "Okay. I'll check over there. By the way, did Arnie tell you they think Gina may have committed suicide?" I thought that would be a lot better than telling her Gina may have been murdered.

"I don't think he said, and I didn't want to pry especially, because they were cousins. Isn't that sad? And surprising. She didn't seem the type."

"I don't think there are types. Anyway, I've been asked to assist the police in ascertaining if, in fact, that may have been what happened or whether she could have died by other means." Not exactly a lie. Dewey had asked me, even if he hadn't used the words *assist the police.* "We have information Gina was here last weekend and so was Sheila. So if you could give me Sheila's full name and phone number, that would be a big help."

Carol's mocha-colored eyes had grown wider as I spoke, registering what I was communicating to her. "You mean the police are trying to figure out how she died?"

"Among other things. And whether she'd been assisted."

She stepped back from me. "You think someone killed her? The police think someone killed her?"

"I can't say what the police think. I, myself, haven't formed an opinion. I'm merely gathering facts. By the way, did she arrive on Friday evening when you were here?"

She shook her head. "I don't stay late unless someone is trying to make a sale. If Arnie is here, he'll take care of that, so I can get home to my family."

"I guess you weren't here Sunday either."

She shook her head. "Usually Arnie, Gina, and Sheila cover the whole weekend. Sometimes some of the others drop by if they're not running around the Hill Country to estate sales."

"What about Monday or Tuesday?"

"Yes, I cover some Mondays and Fridays, so I was here that Monday. Why are you asking?"

"I'm trying to figure out where Gina was in the last week. When was the last time you saw her?"

"Let me think. I didn't see her last Monday. It would have had to be Monday before last or Friday before last. I'm not sure. And I just thought of something. I have a girlfriend who owns a B & B. It might be available. But you'd still have to go through the people across the square. They handle everything for her."

"Great. What's her name? Or does she have a name for her place?"

"Corrine Horak is her name. Her place is out in the country, toward Austin, but not too far. I'm not sure if she rents just for one night, though."

"I'll check it out, thanks. And your name?"

"Carol Palacky."

"Let me give you my card."

When I handed her a card, she smiled. "I haven't met a lady private detective before."

I got that a lot. "We do other kinds of work in our office as well, like serving court papers and working up lawyer's documents."

"That's so interesting. I've never met a man private detective either."

"Well, it's nice to meet you, Carol. Thanks for answering my questions. I wish you'd reconsider giving me her phone number. I'd like to get in touch with her this afternoon or evening."

"Okay, Mavis. I guess it'll be okay." She pulled her phone back out.

She read Sheila's name and number to me, and I put it in my phone. "Thanks, I appreciate that. I think I'll go next door and say hi to Beth Anne."

"You know her?"

"I met her earlier in the week. Her pastries are yummy."

"Oh, yeah. I have to stay away from that place!"

"By the way, did y'all get the coffee maker fixed?"

"I guess not. There's a new one now, and it's working fine. Sorry I didn't offer you a cup. Usually I do, or a glass of wine. I don't know what got into me."

"That's okay. I'm not a coffee aficionado anyway. I'm a tea drinker."

"Well, I apologize. I should have offered you something."

I shrugged. "You take care now. Thanks for the help. By the way, if you would refrain from mentioning my visit to Arnie, that would be a good thing." I figured my visit might spur a phone call since she was one of his lessees, but it didn't hurt to ask.

Carol gave me a simpering smile and slipped her cell phone into a pocket. "Of course."

I went out onto the sidewalk and glanced at my watch. It was getting late, and I still had people to interview. I'd visit the bakery and then cross the square to the real estate office for a place to stay. Before stepping next door, I glanced over my shoulder through the front window of Fayette Antiques. Carol was punching numbers into her cell phone.

CHAPTER

NINETEEN

I had no way of knowing whether Carol was placing a call to Arnie or her best friend, but I wouldn't wager money that it was her best friend. From where I stood on the sidewalk, I could see into the bakery, as well. Beth Anne was watching me. I might as well go inside and visit with her. And while I was there, I'd indulge and buy one of those ginormous Bear Claws for breakfast.

I was about to open the door when my phone rang. Margaret's name and photo showed up. "Hey, Margaret. What's up?"

"Mavis, I was in the kitchen working on modifying that Bear Claw recipe to get it just right for you, and I thought of something maybe you should know, if you don't already. So, are you in a place where I can tell you?"

I always try to be patient with Margaret when she becomes verbose. "Yes. Out on the sidewalk. Go ahead."

"Okay, then. You know how almond flour was used to make those almond cookies you got from that old lady and at that antiques store in Galveston?"

"Yes, Margaret. Those yummy almond cookies I'm going to try to get the recipe for. What about them?"

"You realize Bear Claws are usually filled with almond paste, right?"

"Yes, Margaret. I tasted it when you made that first recipe." I'd thought she'd overdone it but hadn't said so since I love the taste so much. "What's your point?"

"You know what sometimes smells like almonds?"

Something in the back of my brain niggled at me, but I wasn't sure what it was. I turned my back to the bakery entrance and Beth Anne. "What?"

"Cyanide."

Indigestion attacked my insides with fervor, though I hadn't eaten in several hours.

"If she'd ingested cyanide, Gina could have had bluish fingernails and lips. Did you notice that?"

I almost choked. "To do that, I would have had to see the body."

"How long have we known each other, Mavis?"

"The less you know, the better, Margaret."

She whispered into the phone, which led me to believe Candy wasn't far away. "You can't tell me you didn't search her van and her condo before the police came. I know you found her body."

"Please don't say that. Especially if Ben drops by."

"Don't worry." She continued to whisper. "And I won't tell Candy, either."

I let out the breath I hadn't known I was holding.

"So did you see any evidence of the color blue in her face or her extremities?"

"No, though her body had begun to decompose. How long does that effect last?" I didn't know much about bodies after someone was dead except for *rigor mortis*. Everyone has heard of that.

"What about the color of her skin? Was it pink? Pinker than a normal person's skin would be?"

"I don't know. It was dark, and I only had the light from the flashlight app on my phone. I take it you've been researching poisons on the internet?"

"Once I remembered all the stuff you've been eating with almonds in it."

"I did find a bag of cookies in the van." I had sat on the cookies when I climbed into the vehicle.

"You didn't take any of them or eat any of them, did you?"

"I left everything in the van how I found it."

"Good! You could be dead right now!" Margaret hissed.

"Okay, well I need to go. I'm standing outside the bakery."

"Do me a favor, will you? Don't eat stuff from any of those people you run into who knew Gina."

I would have laughed but instead shivered at the thought I'd eaten cookies at Cora's house and at the antiques store in Galveston and that taste of a Bear Claw when I'd been at the bakery earlier in the week. Of course, we had no way of knowing whether Gina had died from a dose of cyanide. That's what I needed to find out. Or, at least, who gave it to her.

"One more thing," Margaret said before we disconnected. "Not everyone can smell that tell-tale almond scent.

I shivered again. I wanted to end the call and get on with the purpose of my visit. Doing an about-face, my eyes met Beth Anne's, before I spun around again. "Okay, I'll be careful. I really need to go."

"Just don't eat anything when you're around them. It can be put in other stuff, too. Be careful. I know how you are. I know you'll snitch any snacks in bowls in those places."

"We don't know Gina was poisoned, or if she was, that it was cyanide, but okay, Margaret. I get your drift. I won't be purchasing that Bear Claw I was going to have for breakfast tomorrow. I won't buy anything at the bakery. When I have dinner, I'll be sure I'm eating alone." I still stood on the sidewalk in front of the bakery, needing to decide whether I'd go ahead and enter the bakery or leave. If I wasn't going to buy anything, would Beth Anne be friendly?

"Were you planning on having breakfast there?" Margaret's voice had risen an octave.

"Yeah. I was going to call you in a little while. I'm going to see if I can find a place to stay for one night."

"Why?"

"Haven't been able to talk to Sheila Siska yet and kinda want to nose around the town and see if I can find out anything."

"That's her name, Sheila Siska?"

Didn't I just say that? Anyway… "I was going to call you if I couldn't get ahold of her. I was able to get her phone number, but the woman in the antiques store wouldn't give me Sheila's address. I'm going to talk to Beth Anne, the woman in the bakery, and then call Sheila after I drive to the other side of the courthouse square, where I shouldn't be overheard or interrupted."

"What's on the other side of the square?"

"The real estate place where I hope to find accommodations for tonight. So, if I can't get Sheila on the phone, I'll text you and you can try to find her address for me. *Comprende?*"

"I can go ahead and do that anyway, just in case. I don't like it that you're planning to go to her house. I'm nervous about you being alone up there, Mavis. I'll stay in the office until I hear from you again."

"You're sweet, but you don't have to."

"I wish you'd taken me or Candy up there with you. If you want to wait, I'll get Candy to watch the front and drive up there so there will be two of us. You shouldn't be all by yourself in a strange town. If someone thinks you could be on to them, you could be next."

She was making *me* nervous. "I'll be okay. I'll call you in a little while if I need Sheila's address. Hang tight."

"Before you hang up, Mavis, promise me you'll be careful."

"Okay, Margaret. I appreciate your concern."

WHEN I OPENED the door to the bakery, delicious smells engulfed me. My mouth watered, as always, and I regretted I wouldn't be able to buy anything. "Hey, Beth Anne. How're you doing?"

Beth Anne wore an outfit similar to the one she'd worn before except this one had a full-length white apron over the long-sleeved dress. "Great! What brings you up here again, Mavis? Serving more papers?"

"Have you heard the news about Gina Collins?"

She slid down from her perch and came to the cabinet, standing behind the rows of kolaches. She wore the expected sad face, her mouth turning down in a frown, her eyes tearing up. I wondered how authentic her apparent feelings were.

"Arnie told me. That's so sad."

"Could I ask you a few questions? I was looking for Arnie, but apparently he left the store a while ago." I wasn't going to mention everyone I planned to talk to. That information was on a need-to-know-basis.

"Oh? Well, I don't know where he is. I don't keep track of him." She leaned against the cabinet on her forearms. "What can I do for you today?"

How true was that statement? I remembered her telling me she and Arnie had gone to school together. And I think she said Gina had interfered with their relationship. I nodded like I believed her, though I wasn't sure I did. "When I was here trying to serve Gina with that lawsuit, didn't you say Sheila had been in last Saturday to get their usual order of pastries?"

"For Arnie, Gina, and herself. That's right."

"So I got to thinking, did you ever actually see Gina? Or did you think she was here because Sheila picked up Gina's *usual* pastry?"

Beth Anne struck a thinker pose, her chin resting on the heel of her hand. Her eyes peered past me as though she were visualizing the previous Saturday.

"I'm trying to figure out Gina's whereabouts from the time she left Galveston last Friday until the time she was found the other day," I said.

Her eyes shifted to the ceiling. "I don't think I actually saw her come in or out of the store. But she could have parked in the back. I rarely go out my back door except when I come and go unless I'm putting out the garbage. That's where the dumpster is."

Beth Anne wasn't *actually* answering my question. "Did you see her anywhere that day?"

Her eyes flickered to the right, and she blinked several times in quick succession. I wondered whether I should interpret that in some way. Articles, if not books, had been written about eye movement and lying. The Internet had scads of information. When I lied, I always made an effort to look the person in the eye.

Beth Anne shrugged. "I can't say if I remember seeing her that Saturday."

Can't or won't? "Okay." I moved closer to the pastry cabinet and lowered my voice. "What can you tell me about Sheila? Have you known her very long?"

"I'm assuming you're asking about Sheila Siska, right?"

I nodded. "Isn't that the name of the woman who has a booth next door?"

"Yes, the one who came in and got the coffee and pastries that Saturday. That's who we're talking about, right?"

Was her prevaricating designed to confuse me? I wasn't sure, but I did note the sweet smile she'd greeted me with when I entered had now turned sour. "Yes, Sheila Siska."

"If that's who you mean, I haven't known her that long. She didn't go to school with us. She's a lot younger than Arnie and me. In fact, Sheila's not from La Grange. She's originally from Austin and moved here last year. She has a place kind of out in the country, kind of in a forested area."

"Are y'all close friends?"

She shook her head. "Not really. Why, do you think she has

something to do with Gina? Could she have done something to Gina? You are helping the police, right?"

"I'm trying to find out information I can give to them." I stared straight ahead. And I would give it to Ben if I found out anything he needed to know.

"Hmm." Beth Anne put her hands on her hips. "I wonder if she had a run-in with Gina. Gina could be—uh—difficult. At least that's what Arnie has mentioned from time-to-time."

That was a strange answer coming from someone who had known Gina since high school. "Do you know whether Gina had any enemies? I mean, could she have been at odds with Sheila or someone else?" I wondered how much Beth Anne knew of the circumstances of where Gina was found. Did the police officer who was supposed to have come up there told Arnie the details? After all, Arnie was the next of kin. Could Arnie have told Beth Anne? I realized I wasn't going to get much, if any, information from Beth Anne.

"I wouldn't know. She could have. Is there a reason why you think someone from La Grange or even Sheila might have had something to do with Gina dying in Houston?"

"I'm just wondering." Could Sheila and Gina have had some kind of confrontation on that Saturday? What about on Sunday? Had the two of them been at the store both days? "I don't suppose you know who else worked the antiques store that weekend."

"That would be a question for Arnie. I only know who I saw coming and going when I wasn't busy. I don't pay attention to what goes on outside most of the time. And some of the people who have booths park in the back or across the street in a lot, if there's room. If Gina hasn't taken up a lot of space with that trailer of hers."

"Did you see her trailer that Saturday?"

"I believe I did."

Now we were getting somewhere. "So Gina had to have been here, right?"

"I guess so. At least she would have had to come and drop the trailer off sometime."

"If she left Galveston on Friday, she would have had to drop off the trailer sometime between Friday evening and when you saw it."

"Yeah, you're right. I'm trying to remember whether the trailer was there when I arrived on Saturday morning to open up. It may well have been. I didn't have any trouble parking, but my comings and goings and Gina's and Arnie's and some of the other people's are so routine. We don't pay a lot of attention to that kind of thing unless there's something unusual. I don't recall anything unusual."

We? Who is *we?* Was she speaking for Arnie and Gina? "But you would have remembered if the trailer was parked out back on Saturday morning, or even on Sunday?"

"Not necessarily. I have a young woman who works here, too. I could ask her, though I don't know why she'd remember either."

"And her name is?"

"Phyllis. She'll be here tomorrow if you want to talk to her."

"You couldn't give me her phone number now?"

"I'm not real comfortable with that, Mavis. I mean, we're only acquaintances, and I don't give out phone numbers to strangers— mine or my employees."

"So you have more than one employee."

"Some kids in the summers and at Christmas when it's busy."

"Well, I can come back tomorrow morning, or could you call Phyllis and give her my number and ask her to call me?"

"Sure, no problem."

"That sounds good. I'll be in town—not that it matters since I always have my cell phone with me. My number's on the card I gave you the other day."

"By the way, do the police know how she died? Have they said someone killed her? The whole thing's horrible."

"If they do, they haven't told me. But it's early days. The ME would have to do an autopsy first and in Houston, they're always backed up."

The door behind me opened, and the people who had been in the antiques store came in.

"I'll get out of your hair," I said.

Turning her attention to the couple, Beth Anne said in a melodious voice, "May I help you folks? Our kolaches are the best in the La Grange area."

I took a moment to observe Beth Anne's demeanor before I let the door close behind me. Nothing gave off even a hint that she could be the culprit in Gina's demise. Don't know what I expected. Few people have the word GUILTY engraved on their foreheads.

Sliding into my car, I aimed to drive across the square to secure a place to stay. My Mustang, however, chose that moment to give me trouble again. At that time, and at that location, I did not need a car that wouldn't run. Or even one that was unreliable. I turned the key several times, but the engine wouldn't catch. Adrenaline rushed my chest. After sitting quietly for a few minutes—okay, praying for a few minutes—I gave it another try before heading back into either the antiques store or the bakery to get a recommendation for who to call in La Grange, Texas.

Thankfully, she decided to start. I swear I didn't swear at her. I drove across the square to the real estate office. After I parked, I called Sheila's number. It rang about half a dozen times before voicemail came on, so I left a message. "Sheila, my name's Mavis Davis. I'm a private investigator looking into Gina's death. I'd like to meet with you this evening. Please give me a call, and I'll come out to your house." I recited my cell number to be sure she'd be able to call me from whatever kind of phone she had.

Before I went inside the Realtor's office, I received a text from Margaret with Sheila's home address. At least there was progress on that front. After a reasonable period of time that would allow Sheila to arrive home, assuming she was going home, I'd go out to her house if I hadn't heard back from her. In the meantime, I'd find a place to stay and then head over to Cora's. I wanted to find out more about what had transpired the previous weekend. And if Gina had stayed with them, when did she arrive and when did she leave?

CHAPTER
TWENTY

Interviewing people and making conclusions had never gone quickly in the past, so I don't know why I was impatient. Plodding along from one person to the next was part of the job. If anything critical came up, I would, of course, turn everything over to the police and let them finish the case. I wasn't seeking the glory, just earning the fee from my client, Dewey, and the "bonus" Blanche would pay me once I recovered her legal fees.

At least that's what I kept telling myself.

I needed more information than I currently had in order to have a firm list of suspects and to narrow that list down. Once I had the keys to the short-term rental belonging to Carol's friend, interviewing Arnie and his mother was next on my agenda.

When I arrived at Cora's house, I didn't see a vehicle, but one could have been in the garage. Dusk was hovering, so I hoped at least Cora was home. If a caregiver had been with her, that person had probably left, or their car would have been there.

After ringing the doorbell several times, I waited, giving whoever was home plenty of time to get to the door, while I enjoyed the leaves that had changed to autumn colors. Finally, the little woman answered the door. I hadn't realized quite how tiny she was. She peered up at me through her thick glasses, her cornflower blue eyes magnified behind them. She wore a red plaid shirtwaist dress and furry blue and red house shoes. "Hello. You're that lady who was here a few days ago." She pulled the door wider, her leathery face breaking into a smile.

"Yes, ma'am, Mrs. Saxberg. Mavis Davis. How nice of you to remember me. May I come in?"

Humming a toneless and pitchless tune, she glanced behind me, then behind herself, as if mulling over whether to let me inside. "Yes, okay." She stepped back and allowed me to enter.

"I was looking for Arnie. I take it he's not home?"

Cora closed the door behind me. I half expected to be led toward the living room, where we'd had our tea and cookies the last time, but she took a different path. "I haven't seen Sonny since he left this morning."

Okay, so now how should I proceed? "I can stay and visit with you while I wait for him. That is, if you don't mind."

"Come on in." She gestured toward a different room. "Why don't we go into the kitchen? I still have some cookies left from my last batch, and I baked a cake yesterday. We can have a snack before dinner." She snickered. "Our mothers aren't here to tell us we can't."

I sure wished I knew how Gina had died. I wouldn't mind a slice of cake, but no expletive way was I going to have anything not out of a can at Cora's house. And then I'd want to be present when the can was opened. I laughed. "No thank you, Mrs. Saxberg. You're very kind, but you go ahead. If you don't mind, I'll take a few cookies for later." And have them analyzed, which I wasn't going to say. "I'll sit with you while you enjoy your cake. Maybe Arnie will return while I'm here."

"Okay, come on into the kitchen. I'm going to slice the cake and make a cup of decaf coffee."

We entered a functioning kitchen that smelled faintly like pumpkin pie and sugar. Though an ignorant person might consider the kitchen retro, it wouldn't qualify, as the wear and tear showed it must have been furnished in the middle of the previous century. The appliances were a mixture of harvest gold and avocado green with color-coordinated cafe curtains, more than a bit gray around the edges, hanging from a window overlooking the backyard.

She stood at the yellow-gold laminate counter and filled a kettle with water. "I guess you haven't found Gina to give her those papers or you wouldn't be here."

So Arnie hadn't told her about Gina? I sure wasn't going to. Not in my job description. "I've been unable to serve her. I met her cousin Tom and his wife, though, in Galveston when I was down there looking for Gina. Nice people."

"I guess so. I don't know them very well. No reason to." She put a yellow plastic napkin holder with thin, patterned paper napkins on the small, green Formica kitchen table.

"I was wondering, and planning to ask Arnie, did Gina stay here at your house last weekend? I'm trying to find out whether she was at the store, and if she told him where she was going from there. Also, what day she left."

She pointed to a chair and indicated for me to sit. In the center of the table stood an aluminum cake plate and cover, like something my grandmother used to have. "Go ahead and have a seat." Her humming set in again.

I sat, happy the old lady was so hospitable. Maybe she didn't get a lot of company. "Tom told me Gina had an old hope chest she was bringing over here to deliver to a couple who had purchased it in Galveston." I sure wished I could read Cora's mind. I'd pegged her as very clever. I needed to make sure not to underestimate her, not that I suspected she was involved in anything nefarious, but she might suspect my motives. She appeared to be weighing what to tell me.

"If you'd come earlier, you could have met my helper," she said, changing the subject.

"Helper?"

"They call them caregivers, now. They used to call them companions. But she's still my helper. She comes in and helps." Her mouth spread into a smile, which I was unable to read.

"Either you or Arnie mentioned that last time we met. Does she come every day?"

"No, not on Sundays or Mondays. She works for this company that has a minimum of hours, though. We pay for her to come about half a day every day but Sundays or Mondays." She nodded as she spoke and bustled around the small kitchen.

In other words, Cora had someone with her even on Saturdays, because Arnie would be at the store. Sundays, she must fend for herself. "I would have liked to meet her. I have a friend who owns that kind of franchise."

"She's very nice. She helps me bake."

So maybe there was no cyanide in Cora's kitchen, or the helper would know about it. I don't know why she'd have any in her kitchen anyway or where she would get it, though almost every-thing was available through the Internet. I was rather relieved about the helper being with her so much. I liked Cora and didn't want her to be involved. Besides, imagine an old lady like her doing time in prison.

"What else does she do for you, Cora? Is there a senior center in La Grange she takes you to?" I wanted nothing more than to get back to the subject of Gina but didn't want to be too obvious.

"We often have lunch on the square. I enjoy walking around the area. Good exercise."

"And poke into the antiques shop?"

"For a moment sometimes."

"Did you do that last Saturday? Did you see Gina?"

She shook her head. "No, we drove around and looked at the Halloween decorations. Have you seen what people have done? Some are quite elaborate."

"So you didn't see Gina last weekend?"

"Don't think so. I would have remembered if she was here, though my memory is getting worse by the day. Sometimes I get the days confused. You know, at my age and being retired, the days feel the same. Except for Sundays."

"Church?"

"Sonny takes me to church, and then we go out to eat, and then he brings me back and then I take a long nap. He goes to the grocery. That's how I know it's Sunday."

"I look forward to being retired someday," I said and forced a chuckle. "But I guess you would know, at least, whether Gina spent a night or two with y'all, wouldn't you?"

"I suppose so." She leaned toward me. "She hasn't stayed here much since her divorce, Mavis."

"Why's that?"

She whispered, "Sonny and she had an argument." She looked over her shoulder. "I'm not sure exactly when it was. But I know it was after her divorce. She wanted us to buy her out of the store. Of course, we couldn't do that."

Couldn't or wouldn't? "Why not?" An argument between them could mean something. What, I didn't yet know.

"Sonny and I don't have that kind of money—not what she was asking. We've made a living from the store but only a modest living. You can see that, can't you? If we had lots of money, you think we'd still live in this little house where I raised Sonny? He hates it here. People are building big houses in La Grange but not us. Sonny would love to have a newer, bigger place."

"I could see that. These days people seem to like McMansions."

"We've never had that kind of money, and when I got sick, we had even less."

"I'm so sorry. You look so healthy. I never imagined you could have been ill."

"Cancer. I had breast cancer, and our insurance wouldn't pay all the bills. Money got so tight that we sold some of our share of the store to Gina."

"So she owns more than fifty percent?" This story was the opposite of what had happened in Galveston. There, Tom had bought into the store when Gina needed money for her divorce.

"Oh, yes. A lot more. Sonny and I sold her a percentage, so we could pay my bills, but then more bills came and more and more until now she owns eighty percent. How could she expect us to have the money to buy her out?"

"Why did she want to sell?"

"Well, I was in the other room when they were arguing, but I heard her say she was tired of driving back and forth. She wanted to focus on starting a new life and only have the Galveston store. Maybe she had some friends there."

"Well, that makes sense, I guess. So what was—is going to happen to the store?" I sure didn't want to use past tense around her in case she wondered why.

"I'm not sure. I heard Gina tell Sonny she thought she had a buyer, but the buyer wanted the whole thing, not just her part. And then what would we live on? Our twenty percent wouldn't last long."

Arnie would have to find a job, but I wasn't going to say that. Cora was way too old to find a job herself. "Arnie couldn't keep working in the store?"

"I don't know, Mavis. He's stopped talking to me about it lately. He said not to worry, that he'd handle it."

Cora pulled a long, stainless-steel cake knife with what looked like a silver-plated handle from a drawer. She grinned at me as she came back toward me, but she stopped when she reached the table. She removed the metal cover from the cake plate, revealing a dark orange Bundt cake with toffee-colored icing dripping down the sides.

"Pumpkin cake, umm. Sure you don't want some?"

My mouth watered, but I was not going to succumb to temptation. "No, thank you, ma'am, but it does look tasty."

She cut herself a one-inch slice, which she laid on a saucer she'd gotten from a cabinet while the kettle was boiling. Then she poured instant decaf crystals into a cup and made her coffee, dumping sugar in by the spoonfuls. She glanced at me with raised eyebrows as if to see if I'd changed my mind. I shook my head and watched her dig in.

Having already been there longer than I'd intended, I wanted to leave. From my phone map, I knew Sheila's place was in the opposite direction, and Carol's friend's place was in still another direction. My stomach growled, but I wanted to see Sheila before I went to dinner. If Arnie didn't show up in the next couple of minutes, I'd have to catch him in the morning. I didn't want to drive around in the countryside looking for houses in the dark.

Cora said, "I haven't been much help, have I? I could have Sonny call you when he gets home. He might have some idea where you could find Gina. That is, if you can't stay longer. I saw you look at your watch." She scooped another spoonful of cake into her mouth.

"I believe he has my phone number, but I'll leave another card with you, if that's okay." I laid my card on the table. "Before I go, though, do you mind giving me your cookie recipe for those almond cookies? I can't get enough of them."

"I don't mind at all. I'll pack up some for you to take with you, too."

I'd take them, but I sure wasn't going to eat them. "Thank you, that's so sweet. If you don't have many left, just give me a couple. I'll take the recipe to the office. I'll get my assistant to make a batch for us to offer in our office reception area. She loves to bake."

Cora put a few cookies in a sandwich bag before finding a slip of paper in a kitchen drawer. She copied down the recipe and handed it to me. "Lovely to see you again," she said. "You come back any time."

I backed up to let her pass, feeling like a giant next to a gnat. We went out onto the almost-dark landing. "Thank you for the visit."

WHEN I REACHED MY CAR, I was relieved she started right up. Though I wanted to stop and eat, that could wait. I needed to make some progress on the case, so I could report something to Dewey. I had left my cell phone in the car when I went into Cora's, so I checked for messages. Three identical phone numbers I didn't recognize, but from the La Grange area code 979, popped up. I clicked on the little phone icon.

"Miss Davis. I know you've been looking for me. I'm at my house now if you want to come out here." She recited the address. "Oh, this is Sheila Siska."

I didn't look to see what time she'd left that message. The address sounded the same as what Margaret had given me.

The second was also from Sheila. "Miss Davis, I need your help. Please hurry! I need to tell you something." Anxiety gnawed at the bottom of my throat making drawing a breath difficult.

A third one said, "Miss Davis! He's pulling into my yard. I'm scared. I swear all I did was carry the coffee and pastries. I didn't know. I didn't know!" A sound like banging on a door started in the background.

I shivered. My stomach twisted into knots. I needed to get there pronto. "Siri, directions to Sheila Siska's house in La Grange at ..." I looked up the address and recited it to Siri. Trying not to panic, I focused on the dark road under Siri's instructions.

Out in the country, there are no streetlights. I sped along a two-lane blacktop, my headlights lighting up fence posts.

Siri, who I prayed wasn't leading me astray, had me turn by a beer sign onto an unpaved, rocky path bordered by tall grasses and small pine trees. I passed rows of mailboxes. A tennis court appeared. The trail wended and weaved for a while. From nowhere, headed directly at me, came a vehicle looming out of the darkness —a large, white pickup truck. The headlights weren't on. I was unable to see the make though it looked very much like many I'd seen in the countryside. Well, many I'd seen in Texas. Flicking on my brights, I saw the driver, Arnie Saxberg. I would have sworn our eyes met, but I don't believe he could see my face with my headlights on and his not. The truck came straight for me. My Mustang was no match. I swerved off the path to the right, which, fortunately, had a gap between trees, and jammed on my brakes as I plunged through the bushes and tall, thick grasses. The truck powered past me.

Remaining stationary for a few moments, my heart pounding and limbs trembling, I drew in a deep breath and glanced over my shoulder to ascertain whether Arnie was returning. He wasn't. If he'd intended to run me off the road, so I'd get hurt, I was all right with his not stopping. More than ever, I knew I had to hurry to Sheila's. I threw the Mustang into reverse and backed onto the path, continuing to pick my way through the woods with Siri not giving as explicit directions as I would have liked. Finally, another clearing came into view with a car in a less rustic area next to a house. Siri informed me I was at my destination. Another car sat on the other side of the first car, the second one a make and model with which I was very familiar, and which I hoped I was mistaken about. The house stood in complete darkness.

Grabbing my flashlight, I climbed out, careful to survey the area for anyone who might be a threat. I realized, then, the second car was indeed Margaret's. Someone, blocked by the car, moaned. The down on my neck rose. Jogging toward the front door, I found Margaret sitting on the steps, rubbing the back of her head. Tears dripped from her chin.

"What are you doing here? Are you okay?" I crouched in front of her.

"Oh, Mavis. I'm so glad to see you. Someone—someone hit me and knocked me off the porch."

I knew who that someone was. I felt the back of her head. A lump was growing, but when I pulled my hand away, there wasn't any blood. I hugged her shoulders. "Take a couple of deep breaths. Want some water? I have some in my car."

"I—I have some in my car, too. There's a little cooler on the passenger seat. Would you get a bottle for me?"

"Sure." Maybe Sheila would give us an ice pack. I retrieved the water and a handful of tissues.

Margaret took a couple of swallows and kept averting her eyes. "I know you're probably wondering what I'm doing here."

"You think?" I couldn't be angry with my injured friend.

"I had a bad feeling about you being by yourself and so did Candy. We decided I should come help you, and she could watch the office. I drove like a crazy person to get here, thinking you'd be at Sheila's by this time."

I couldn't very well yell at her after she'd been the victim of the violence that would have been directed at me. I had momentarily forgotten Sheila. "Is Sheila here? Have you spoken to her?"

"I waited for you for a few minutes but then thought I should go ahead and talk to her. She must have been wondering who I was. That car and the truck you had to have passed on the road were already in the yard when I arrived."

"Did you see or hear anything?"

"I went to ring the doorbell, even though no lights were on. The front door stood open, but the screen door was closed. It was creepy, Mavis." She blotted her face with the tissues. "When I opened the screen door, pounding footsteps came toward me. Someone knocked into me and pushed me off the porch. Then the truck was racing away."

Bending down to hug her again, I said, "I'm glad he didn't do anything worse to you, my friend. I couldn't stand to lose you."

"Yeah, me, too. Should we go inside and see if Sheila's there? The person who hit me could've been a woman, but I think it was a man."

"I know who it was. I saw his face when he passed me on that little road. Your attacker was Arnie Saxberg."

She sobbed for a moment and smeared the mascara all over her face. "He could have really hurt me."

"Why don't you put the cap on that bottle and hold it to the back of your head. Maybe that will keep the swelling down at least a little. I'm going inside."

"Be careful."

"I will, but I'm betting he was alone."

Opening the screen door, I proceeded through the not-large house, the light from my flashlight leading the way. When I reached the living room, a woman fitting Sheila's general description was lying on the floor with her eyes closed. She didn't appear to be breathing. My stomach clenched as did my teeth. If only I'd arrived sooner.

I checked her pulse but couldn't find one no matter how many different places I tried. I ran outside. "Margaret, we need to call 911! A woman's inside! I think she's dead."

"There's no signal out here. I tried to call you when I arrived."

Instead of searching Sheila's house in hopes of a landline, I raced to my car. On the off chance the woman inside was still alive, that I was inept at checking for a pulse, my time would be better spent finding a signal, so I could call an ambulance. "I'm going back to the bigger road to call. Will you be okay? Could you go inside and see if you can find a landline to call 911?"

"Oh my God. I don't know. I'm so scared!"

I hurried over to give her another reassuring hug. "You'll be okay. No one else is around, or we'd know it by now. You want my gun?"

"What? No. Just come right back."

"I'm going to call for the EMTs and then decide what to do next. I think I know where Arnie may have gone."

"You can't follow a killer, Mavis. You might be next."

"I'll take my gun out of the glove box and keep it within reach. I'll be okay. Don't worry."

Of course my Mustang chose that time to give me trouble. After three tries, I jumped out with my purse and gun and ran back to Margaret. "I need your keys."

She shook her head. "It's not safe."

"Margaret, I have to call the police and an ambulance, at least. "Give me your keys."

She pulled them from her pocket.

"I promise I won't confront him. If I find him, I'll call the police. Just give me your keys."

"I don't like this at all," she said as she handed them over.

"You know I can't let him get away."

"Promise me you'll call the police about him," she yelled. "And Ben, too. He'd want to know."

I waved at her as I backed out onto the path and raced toward the big road.

TWENTY-ONE

I focused on the road, but I couldn't get it out of my mind that Arnie was a killer, that he'd done something to Sheila, which led me to the conclusion that he's the one who killed Gina. Reaching the turnoff onto the blacktop, I tried my cell phone. Still no signal. I continued on, periodically checking until finally I could pull over and make the 911 call. I told the dispatcher what I'd found and gave her Sheila's address. When she asked if I'd be there when the ambulance and police arrived, I told her Margaret would be, that I'd be available by phone. I might have set myself up to get into trouble with the La Grange police, but speaking to a police officer over the phone, much less back at Sheila's house, would definitely delay me. I wanted to find Arnie. I needed to do more than sit around waiting to be interviewed. I needed to be proactive.

Before I could call Ben, my cell phone buzzed. I scrolled past Sheila's messages. If only I'd gone to her house earlier.

The next call was from Ben and must have come in when there was no signal. "Mavis, I'm almost to La Grange. We need to meet up. Margaret told me what's going on. Your victim didn't die of cyanide poisoning. I asked the doc to check after Margaret told me what you thought. Call me back, so we can arrange where to meet."

My victim? Gina wasn't *my* victim. It was pretty clear now she was Arnie's victim. And Beth Anne's victim too, I think, if Beth Anne put something—apparently not cyanide—in Gina's coffee or the Bear Claw Sheila had picked up for her. What the substance was didn't matter. Who it came from, and how it was administered, mattered.

When I reached Cora's house, not even a porch light was on. I went to the front door, wishing they'd had one of those garage doors with windows in it, so I could see if a truck was parked inside. If it wasn't, I might not need to be there. I didn't think Arnie'd had time to exchange the truck for another vehicle.

I knocked and stepped aside in case Arnie wanted to shoot me through the door. I thought it unlikely, but I'd been told to do so when I was a trainee child protective services worker. No one can know what's going on behind a door.

While I waited, I punched Ben's number into my phone. The call went to voicemail, so I left a message. "I would tell you that you didn't need to come to La Grange, Ben, but I think I'm going to need you to intercede with the police up here. Could you contact your friend at the La Grange PD?" A noise came from inside Cora's house, so I disconnected.

No one came to the door, but I continued to wait, giving Cora time to toddle to the front of the house from wherever she'd been. The house wasn't very big, but she was small and took small steps. I knocked again, louder and longer. In the meantime, Arnie was probably headed to Timbuktu. That is, if he wasn't hiding inside.

The third time I knocked, Cora called out something. Her voice sounded far away. Then she said, "Hold your horses."

Finally, she cracked the door, concealing all but one eye. "Oh, it's you." She pulled the door open wider, revealing a shotgun tucked under her arm. I stepped back, my skin tingling.

"Yes, Cora, I'm back," I said in a sweet, melodic tone, hoping she wouldn't shoot me. She wasn't aiming the thing, but one can never be too careful.

"What do you want that couldn't wait until morning?" Her demeanor was not nearly as friendly as it had been a short time earlier. She swallowed a couple of times in quick succession and leaned the shotgun against the door jamb. She wore a fluffy blue robe belted at the waist and no shoes.

"I apologize if I got you out of bed. I'm afraid I'm still looking for Arnie. Have you seen him?" I kept a close eye on her hands in case they moved toward the shotgun.

She shook her head, her eyebrows drawn together. "No, and he usually calls me if he's going to be out late. You want to come in again and wait?"

"No, thank you. Hmmm. It's curious, isn't it? I thought I saw him in a truck that passed me going the other way when I was driving to a friend's house. I waved, but he didn't stop." Not huge lies. "Does he drive a pickup truck?"

"Yep. An old white Chevy. It was his father's, but Sonny has kept it running all these years."

"Are you sure he hasn't come home? I mean, were you asleep? Could he have come in after you went to bed and you didn't hear him?" I wanted to find out where he was and then I really was going to alert the police. They needed to know what I knew about the whole situation.

"I'm a light sleeper. I would have known if he returned. I'm worried."

"He doesn't stay out late much?"

"Sometimes, if he's at Beth Anne's. They're great friends, you know, ever since high school."

I was pretty sure I knew what great friends they were. "Ohhhh, Beth Anne the pastry shop lady. So they're uh—intimate friends?"

A small smile formed on her lips. "Possibly. I don't pry. She's a nice girl, and I can only hope. I'd like to have a grandbaby someday."

Didn't look like that would happen. "They've been involved since high school?"

"On and off. I once thought they'd get married, they'd been together so long. But then Gina came along."

"There wasn't anything between Arnie and Gina, was there?" Somehow, I couldn't picture Gina-the-sorority-girl and Arnie-the-country-cousin together.

"Oh no. She just didn't like Beth Anne. Gina wanted to be in charge of everything, including Sonny and me."

"A control freak?"

"That's what Beth Anne called her once when she and Sonny were here and had a disagreement. It got worse once Gina owned more of the shop than we did."

That certainly gave Beth Anne motive to participate in doing away with Gina. I wondered how they thought they were going to get away with it. Sooner or later, sooner in my case, people were going to find out Arnie's motive, that Gina wanted to sell the shop and leave him and Cora pretty much penniless. A little research would possibly show there was some kind of agreement about what happened to the antiques store in the event one of the owners died. Wouldn't surprise me if the other inherited the decedent's share. They were cousins, after all. That would sure be a nail in Arnie's coffin. Put Arnie's motive and Beth Anne's motive together and what do you get? Murder.

So—my brain working double time—I figured Beth Anne must have put something in Gina's coffee over the weekend or in the Bear Claw that Gina always bought, and that something killed her. Probably she died at the antiques store. Then Arnie and Beth Anne must have moved the chest into the van and put her body in the chest. One of them drove the van and trailer away from La Grange, dropped off the trailer where it wouldn't be found any time soon, and then drove the van to Houston. The other must have followed and picked up the driver.

All that felt like it fit together. In the meantime, what was Sheila doing? Was she part of the planning? Had she covered for them? Did she help load the body into the chest? Had she figured it out somehow, and when Arnie heard I was looking for her, did he decide she knew too much? I hoped it wasn't the latter. Guilt was settling over me like a dust cloud.

So where was Arnie? I looked down at Cora, the poor old thing. She most likely had no idea what had transpired.

"I hate standing here with the door open, Mavis. Sure you don't want to come in?"

"You think Arnie could be at Beth Anne's house? I don't know where she lives. I don't have that address."

"Oh, it's not far from here." She gave me the address and directions. My heart went out to her. Her future would be dim. She'd be heartbroken, lonely. Eventually she would probably have to go into care, paid for by the sale of their house. I wanted to comfort her in some way for something that hadn't happened yet but knew I couldn't tell her what was going on. I thanked her and beat feet to my car.

As I drove away, I got to wondering. If Beth Anne was in on Gina's demise and Sheila was in on it too, and he, or they, killed Gina and now it looked like Arnie did his best to kill Sheila, would he go after Beth Anne next? Was he feeling desperate enough to get rid of the woman who loved and supported him but who might give evidence against him if he, or they, were caught?

Goosebumps rose on my arms. Could I get to her house in time to stop him if that's what he was about? And how exactly would I do that?

I picked up my phone while I drove and clicked on Ben's name again, hoping this time he'd answer. He didn't.

My brain rushed through all the possible scenarios as I sped toward Beth Anne's house. Either she was in mortal danger or not. Arnie was either inside or not. Beth Anne could be packing to join him someplace if he'd contacted her that evening.

Her place was in an old-fashioned subdivision with residences on both sides of the street, white picket fences in most yards, and single car garages. Most houses were similar to Cora's, approximately the same vintage, with a few newly built mansions interspersed on double lots. Beth Anne's house had no porch light on, but faint light glowed from windows in the back.

A car stood in her driveway, so I drove by without stopping. To be on the safe side, I parked several houses down. No reason either of them, assuming Arnie was there, would be looking out the front window. But still...

Holding my thirty-eight in one hand, I crept toward Beth Anne's house. All was quiet until a dog barked. I jumped. My hair rose, and a shiver scrambled across my shoulders. A light breeze had developed, but I was perspiring like crazy. The crisp, dry air smelled of freshly cut grass. Crossing the street to be on the same side as Beth Anne's house, I tried my best to stay in the shadows, thankful for the quarter moon, which helped me stay hidden. A few houses had porch lights on, and one of them was on the side from which I was coming. I crouched down and duck-walked past her front door to get to the garage. The porch light came on. I about jumped out of my skin again. I prayed it was one of those movement-activated lights.

Standing on the side of the house in the dark to catch my breath, I wondered whether the light coming on would have any effect. Would one of them come out to see if anyone was there? My stomach had turned to granite. After a minute or two, when I wasn't so weak-kneed, I peeked around the corner. No one there. The light had gone out. No one was in the area of the house next door or on the street.

Slithering around to the front edge of the garage, I stood on my tiptoes and peered inside, then stepped back around the corner. A vehicle was inside, but the interior of the garage was so dark, I couldn't definitely say whether it could be Arnie's truck. Taking a deep breath, I tapped on the flashlight icon on my phone and put my finger over the light until I again went to the front edge of the garage. I removed my finger, shining my flashlight through the windows and onto an old, white Chevy pickup truck.

Adrenaline rushed through my body again head-to-toe. I slid around to the side of the garage and turned off the flashlight. What were the odds that there were two white, Chevy pickups pretty much of the same vintage in La Grange, Texas? Zero to none? I crouched down, making myself as small as possible, which was no mean feat. I needed to make a plan.

I had my gun, but I didn't want to confront Arnie. I had no authority to do anything. I had options, though. I could ring the doorbell and, when Beth Anne answered, tell her I was looking for Arnie, and did she know where I might find him? That way I'd know if she was alive. If Arnie had harmed her, she wouldn't be answering the door. However, if she was his accomplice, he would have told her I passed him on the way to Sheila's house, and that I had to know what had happened to Sheila. Assuming he'd told her what he'd done to Sheila.

I could keep hiding and call the La Grange police. What would I tell them? They could be looking for me, if Margaret told them about me. Would they come arrest Arnie on my word and ask questions later? And Beth Anne, too, if she was still alive?

I wasn't used to asking for help, but maybe I should leave and go to the police station. They might listen and send some cops to arrest Arnie and maybe Beth Anne, at least take her to the station. Though I could picture a lot of cops being out at Sheila's house, there would still have to be someone at the police station I could speak with.

I remained crouched beside the house, my thirty-eight down by my side, as I considered the possibilities. Should I ring the doorbell or call the police for help? About the time I made my decision, someone grabbed me from behind and murmured into my ear, "You plan on using that thing?" I gasped and jumped and shivered all at the same time. A hand clamped over my mouth.

"Quiet! It's me," Ben whispered in a near hiss.

"What the—" I turned in his arms, our faces within an inch of each other. I might not like asking for help, but boy, was I glad to see him.

He pulled me further around the side of the house and released me. He whispered, "I'm sorry if I frightened you. You looked like a cat getting ready to pounce."

I whispered when I wanted to shout. "Frightened me? I'm going to die ten years younger than I otherwise would have." It took a moment to stop shaking. "What are you doing here? How did you find me? No one knew where I was going except Mrs. Saxberg."

"Do you really want to discuss that now? I'll tell you later."

I definitely wanted to know how he found me, but more than that, I wanted to get Arnie taken into custody, and Beth Anne, too, if she was still alive. "Okay. But you're going to have to explain this. Don't think I'll forget it."

He nodded and shrugged, looking a little like a contrite young boy. "Who lives here?"

I gave Ben a fast rundown. He was quick-witted, so it didn't take much for him to put it together. When I came to the end, I said, "I looked in the garage, and it has to be Arnie's truck inside."

"You think he's in the house?"

"Yes, with Beth Anne, dead or alive. I hope she's alive. I believe she's his accomplice, so there'd be no reason to harm her unless she threatened him in some way."

"All right. I figured it was something like that." He pulled his cell phone from his pocket and placed a call to someone I assumed was his contact at the La Grange PD. He said into the phone, "I found her." He recited the address. "We're around the side of the house now, the garage side. We'll remain out of sight."

A lot must have happened while I was driving to Cora's house, talking with Cora, and then driving to Beth Anne's. I sat on the grass and waited for him to explain.

He sat on the ground beside me. "They'll be here in a few minutes. We need to keep our voices down. I think we're safest if we don't go anywhere. We don't want either of them to come outside."

Looking down the street I'd driven in on, I whispered, "Where did you park?"

"In front of Margaret's car."

"I didn't notice you drive by."

"You must have been too busy hiding in the shadows."

"Doing my best. Have you talked to Margaret?"

"Okay, here's the short version. After I got your message, I made contact with the La Grange PD. Some officers were headed to where you'd directed them. After speaking to Margaret, they called me back. They'd meet me when I found you. If this Arnie person is inside, they're going to take him in for questioning."

"Take him in for questioning until they figure out if there's evidence he murdered Gina?" I guess they wouldn't just take my word for it, even if I'm convinced he did it.

"Right. They can't just charge him. You know that."

"Yeah, I guess. Margaret's okay, isn't she?"

He nodded. "They're going to take her to the station. But you've got a lot to answer for."

"You're going to tell me I should have stayed put, but when I was driving out there only one vehicle passed me headed the other way. I saw the man's face. That's when I figured Arnie Saxberg, Gina's cousin, had to have been involved in all this. When I arrived at Sheila's, well, you know the rest."

"Still, Mavis, you should have called it in. Let their department handle it. Look." He pointed down the street.

With no sirens and no lights, a parade of police cars headed our way. I admitted to being relieved. Once they'd parked, Ben stood, and a man clearly in charge looked our way. The man twirled his forefinger around in the air. Ben said, "Stay where you are. I'm going around back. They'll cover the front."

Before I could say anything, Ben disappeared behind me. I was left with nothing to do but peek out from around the corner of the house. A couple of minutes later, the cops crossed over to the front door. An officer blocked most of my view, but the door opened and moments later, a uniformed cop led Beth Anne away in the opposite direction.

One of the men yelled into the house, "Saxberg, we just want to talk to you. Ask you some questions. Come on out."

About a minute later, a commotion came from behind me. When I turned, a person rushed toward me from the backyard. Aiming a handgun that looked like a cannon in my direction, Arnie Saxberg, his distorted face like a ghoul's, was almost upon me.

Ben hollered, "Get out of the way, Mavis!"

I scrambled backward for the front yard until Arnie was so close all I could do was put my feet and arms up to block him.

Just as Arnie reached me, he hit the ground, "Oof." One hand grasped my ankle and pulled. I jerked my foot away and kicked at his other hand, the one still holding the gun. Ben had tackled him.

I scooted out of the range of their struggle, though not the gun if he had managed to fire it. "Hey! Over here." I called to the cops in the front of the house. They ran toward us, but by the time they got there, Ben had overpowered and disarmed Arnie. Jerking him to his feet, Ben pushed past me and turned Arnie over to the custody of the La Grange PD. He handed over Arnie's cannon, too.

I hated to do it, but before we followed the officers to where the cars were parked in the road, I gave Ben my gun to, basically, hide. I couldn't very well go walking up to the cops with a gun in my hand. I could tuck it in the back of my pants but thought better of it. Ben was a cop. It was okay for him to have a gun. He tucked it into the back of his pants.

As Arnie was taken to a police car, Ben introduced me to Lieutenant Jack Biel who, not smiling, eyeballed me. An older man, with gray at his temples, Lieutenant Biel wore a dark-colored uniform, a badge, and had the beginnings of a beer gut. Overall, though, I concluded he was more than capable. "I want to talk to you when we get to the station, Miss Davis."

"Yes, sir," I said, glancing from his face to Ben's, both of which were grim. I wasn't looking forward to spending the remainder of the evening at the La Grange police station with Lieutenant Biel, but at least I was safe. My heart rate was returning to normal.

CHAPTER
TWENTY-TWO

On the way downtown, I phoned Margaret. She was at the police station and would catch me up with what had been going on with her once I arrived and vice versa. When we reached the police station, each of us under our own steam —not the suspects, but the rest of us—Lieutenant Biel relegated me to a bench in a hallway. He allowed Ben to go into the interrogation rooms with Arnie and Beth Anne, separated, of course. I followed the lieutenant's directions. When I turned the corner to get to the bench, Margaret was already warming it and holding a cold pack to the back of her head.

"Boy, am I glad to see you," she said after a long, tight hug. "I've been so anxious." She released a slow sigh to go with the hug.

We sat down together. "They haven't been giving you a hard time, have they? They must have questioned you at Sheila's and figured out what was going on?"

"I think Ben called them or something before they got to me. Even though I couldn't get a signal to call, I could text. I explained everything as best I could. When the ambulance came, some EMTs went inside. One stayed and checked me out."

"No concussion?"

She put the bag back on her head. "They don't think so. Just this goose egg that's throbbing like a hammer hitting my head."

"I'm so sorry you got hurt." I understood that she and Candy were worried about me, I did, but couldn't condone her behavior. What if something worse had occurred? "What happened with Sheila?"

Margaret's chin trembled. "She didn't make it. They found a faint pulse but couldn't revive her. She passed away before they even got her into the ambulance."

Guilt tugged at me. The illogical side of my brain said my call to Sheila at the antiques store earlier in the day had started a chain of events that caused her death. My logical side said no, Arnie was responsible.

"What are you thinking?" Margaret asked. "You look like something is on your mind. I mean, more than what I've been saying."

"That I'm partly responsible for Arnie killing Sheila. I called her at the antiques store this morning. I'm pretty sure Arnie answered the phone. He probably recognized my voice."

"You didn't know then what you know now, Mavis. You didn't know Arnie would hurt her."

"I just remembered something. Sheila left three messages on my cell this afternoon, but I didn't check my messages until it was too late." I stood. "I need to tell Ben and that lieutenant. They'll want to hear them. I'll be back in a few minutes."

I rushed around the corner to the entryway and down another hall until I was stopped by a uniform.

"You're not supposed to be back here, ma'am."

"I'm looking for the police officer from Houston and Lieutenant Biel. I need to tell them something important."

He raised a skeptical brow. "Stay right here, and I'll see." He passed several doors before going behind one.

Even though I had the distinct impression the La Grange lieutenant didn't care for me, and that possibly Ben might be annoyed with me for having gotten involved with an active Houston murder investigation, I hoped the phone calls Sheila had made would redeem me in their eyes. At least a little bit.

A few minutes later, Ben came out with the officer who'd had me wait in the hall. Neither of them looked all that pleased. Ben said, "What is it? You're not supposed to be on this side of the building."

Being as how I knew I was in the doghouse, I didn't respond with anything like sarcasm, which I sometimes have a tendency to do. "With all that's happened, I forgot to tell y'all I received some messages on my cell phone from Sheila. Unfortunately, I didn't get them when I otherwise would have because I'd left my phone in the car when I went to see Arnie's mother this afternoon."

"All right. Let me hear them." Ben sounded like his patience had grown very thin, or else he was tired, or both. I was fatigued myself and hungry and remembered the cake Cora had offered me.

I put in my password and played the three messages for Ben. The officer stayed nearby. Ben flexed his hands, itchy to get them on my phone.

"All I have to say at this point is that if you'd gone out there earlier, you might be in the same place as Sheila is headed. The morgue." He snatched the phone out of my hand. "Go back to the other side and wait for me. I'll bring this to you when we get the messages off it."

I started to salute but knew he wouldn't appreciate it. I returned to Margaret and sat next to her.

"What did Sheila say when she called you?"

"I never talked to her, but she left messages, the last one saying she was scared of *him*, who by the time I heard the message I knew to be Arnie."

"Oh my," Margaret said, her eyes tearing up. "When I think of what could have happened to all three of us. He could have hurt me a lot worse. And if you'd gone out there earlier…" Same thing Ben had said. Maybe I'd consider safety in numbers in the future, although one time in the past, Candy and I were inadvertently together and experienced a life-threatening incident.

I patted her arm. "Don't dwell on it. We're fine, or at least pretty much fine. You will be when your bump goes down. I wish we could get something to eat. Did you eat on your way over here?" I shouldn't be thinking of food, but my stomach had a mind of its own.

She shook her head. "I'm starving. They probably won't give us anything or let us leave to get something."

"That's the understatement of the century. Have you given a statement yet?"

She shook her head again and winced. A moment after that, a uniformed officer came and said to her, "If you'll come with me, ma'am, I'll take you to a room where you can make your statement." When she stood, he cupped her elbow, but gently. She gave me a frightened look.

I gave her a reassuring smile in return. "You'll be all right."

"Someone will be with you in a few minutes," the cop said to me.

I wished I had my phone back. I wanted to call Dewey and tell him I was ninety-nine-point-nine percent sure he was off the hook and to be ready to write Blanche a check. I sure hoped they'd give my phone back to me before the night was over. I couldn't afford to buy another phone to replace that one unless Blanche followed through with my "bonus" when I took her Dewey's check. I didn't want to use any of the money I was hoping she'd give me for a new phone. I had promised myself I'd do something about either Candy's vehicle situation or my own, which at that point took precedence. Or both.

Remembering my Mustang, I realized I needed to call for a wrecker to haul it to town. I didn't think Dewey would reimburse me for that kind of expense, darn it.

I paced the length of the hall, accompanied by my growling stomach. A couple of times I thought an officer was coming for me, but no. Just passing by to get somewhere else. I searched my shoulder bag for some chewing gum and found an old piece with lint stuck to the wrapper. Still, it was better than nothing.

About half an hour after they came for Margaret, the officer who'd been in the other hallway came for me. He escorted me to where Ben and Lieutenant Biel had been. The room was bare except for a table and several chairs and a one-way mirror in the wall. Were people going to watch me while I was giving my statement? For what purpose? The officer stood near the door. I sat at the table for a few minutes before Ben and the other lieutenant came in and sat down.

"Could I have some water?" I looked from one to the other.

Lieutenant Biel nodded at the officer who made a quick exit. "We got a statement out of Miss Novak right away. She's pretty scared. But Saxberg's not ready to admit to anything yet." He handed over my cell phone.

Ben said, "You can leave after your statement, Mavis. Margaret's already made hers. She wants to wait for you."

"She has to wait for me. I have her keys and will need a ride, remember? My car is still at Sheila's."

"We had it towed," Biel said.

"Oh, really? So where is it?" I asked, concerned for the well-being of my classic car.

"Outside a mechanic's shop. I know the guy. He said he'd take a look at it in the morning." Biel's tone held disdain.

"I wasn't leaving town anyway. I rented a B & B for the night. Margaret can stay with me."

The cop who had been by the door returned with a bottle of water and left again. After a few quick swallows, I launched into my story, sticking to everything I'd previously told Ben. Of course, I'd never admit to getting into Gina's van and condo and didn't see how that information mattered anyway. They asked questions as I went along. I answered them to the best of my ability. Except for the afore-mentioned.

When I finished and someone who I assumed had been on the

other side of that mirror came in with several pages all printed out nice and neat, I read over it and signed it.

Lieutenant Biel stood and didn't offer his hand. I didn't offer mine either. His attitude had been stern and scary, and I was afraid he had one of those bone crushing handshakes so many men had that I dreaded. He started to leave, but before he exited, he said to me, his forefinger pointed at my chest, "I'm going to say one thing, then Lieutenant Sorensen can fill you in on everything else we've talked about if he feels you have a need to know."

"Yes, sir," I said, making my eyes as wide and friendly as I could. "What is it?"

His finger came closer. "I don't appreciate your coming into my town and doing what you did, and especially not checking in with us, not letting us know you were here."

"But, sir, I originally came just to serve papers on someone."

"Doesn't matter," he said, his eyes fierce-looking, communicating his anger to me, as if I couldn't tell from his tone of voice. "Don't you ever do that again, or I'll find something to charge you with."

"Yes, sir," I replied. I didn't salute him, either. I didn't think it would be well-received.

He glanced from me to Ben and shook Ben's hand. "Thanks for your help." He wasn't addressing me, I could tell. Then he left.

Ben and I followed a few moments after. I wanted to give Biel some space between us. We walked to the other side for Margaret, who no longer held the cold pack to her head. "Let's go outside," I said, beckoning to her. "We can decide what to do from there."

The three of us went out into the night to the parking lot where we'd left the cars.

"Margaret, I rented a B & B that sleeps four. Since it's so late, we'll see if we can find someplace open to get something to eat. We can spend the night there, and in the morning, you can take me to find my car."

Margaret's eyes had been darting back and forth between Ben

and me. She'd been around almost forever and knew what our relationship was like. "I'm starving."

"Can you give us a minute?"

She nodded and walked unsteadily to her car to wait, one hand absentmindedly touching the bump on her head."

Ben said, "I'm going to head back to Houston."

"You can stay, too. There's room. At least stay and have something to eat with us."

He shook his head. "I'm tired. If I eat, I'll get sleepy. I need to get back, so I can write this up."

"Are they charging both of them with murder?"

"Yeah. We'll have to work together to figure out exactly what to charge who with." He shook his head. "See how tired I am?"

"It's been a day. Heck, it's been a week. My mind is still racing. So will they be prosecuted here?"

"Looks like it. Gina Collins was killed here, at least that's what that woman, Beth Anne Novak told us. And then there's the phone calls from Sheila Siska to back her up."

"So it wasn't cyanide."

"The ME said there were no signs of cyanide. He thinks she died of drug intoxication—a mixture of street drugs. They'd be easy to get these days."

"Like fentanyl? Or cocaine? Or meth?"

"Or all of the above. Or others. He'll figure it out. The two inside will be charged with conspiracy, as well. And Saxberg with both murders. It doesn't look like Beth Anne Novak had anything to do with Sheila Siska's death. At least, not so far. Biel will find out, I'm sure."

We reached his car. He leaned down and kissed me on the cheek. "We have a lot to talk about Mavis, but this isn't the time or the place."

"Including how you found out where I was. Don't think I've forgotten that."

He opened the door and got in. "I know you better than that. And you know me better than to think I've forgotten my topics for discussion, too. I'll see you at home."

Anxiety fluttered in my chest as he drove away. At least I had some time to figure out what to say to him about the night Gina's body was found.

CHAPTER

TWENTY-THREE

N
ot only did Margaret and I have a hefty late dinner Friday night, but Saturday morning, we ate a hearty breakfast before we went in search of my car. There was no telling how long we'd be stuck in La Grange waiting for the car to be fixed. I didn't want Margaret to leave me and go home before we knew for sure whether I'd get the Mustang back that day. Once it was repaired, Margaret would follow me on the highway back to Houston in case my car broke down again.

Well, as it turned out, he couldn't fix it that day. He wasn't sure when or if he could fix it at all. He'd have to let me know. Not the news I wanted to hear. I might have to hire someone to tow it home. On the way back to Houston, I searched the Internet for a car rental agency, a cheap car rental agency—my definition of cheap—of which there are none. One turned up that had reasonable weekly rates. Their definition of reasonable, not mine. Margaret dropped me there.

Having managed to obtain a nondescript, small SUV that could get lost in the sea of SUVs on the Houston roads, I drove to the office to make some calls that would lead to the conclusion of the Gina Collins case. And get me some *dinero*.

As I thumbed through the messages and small stack of mail on my desk, I made my first call. Dewey picked up after only one ring.

"Mavis!" His voice was so loud I had to hold my cell away from my ear. "Can you hear me okay? I'm down on my dock. The wind's blowing like crazy."

"More to the point, can you hear me? I called to report in—well, more than report in. I have good news for you."

"Let me get back inside." The phone went silent, followed by the sound of a door closing. "Okay. Now. What's the good news?"

"You're in the clear."

He grunted. "That is good news. What happened? What's been going on?"

"It was Arnie and his girlfriend, Beth Anne Novak. But I was wondering, Dewey, I know it's Saturday, but if you're going to be around today, could I come by and conclude our business? I could tell you the details then."

"You mean pick up the check for Blanche?" He snickered. I could imagine his face.

"Yes." No sense being evasive. "If I can get that done, I'll be closer to moving on to something else." Like paying my bills and doing something permanent about a vehicle. The rental costs could bleed me dry. Not that our coffers weren't pretty much dry already.

"I already put a stop payment on the other one."

"I'd expect nothing less. No telling where it's gotten to."

"All right. We had a deal. Bring me your expense report this afternoon, and I'll have Blanche's check ready for you and write you a check for any expenses you incurred."

I wanted to tell him how easy I was finding him to deal with but didn't want to add to his already inflated ego. "One more thing, could you sign a copy of one of your books for my assistant?"

"No problem. Text me when you leave Houston. I'll be sure to be around when you get here."

My next call was to Blanche's cell, rather than her office number. It was Saturday, after all. Big shot lawyers couldn't be expected to be in the office during the weekend. At least, that's what I thought. She answered immediately.

"What have you got for me, Mavis?"

"Good afternoon, Blanche. How are you this lovely Saturday?"

"Whatever. I have a client sitting across from me. What do you want? I need to get back to her."

That blew my stereotype of big shot lawyers not working weekends. "I was going to ask for an appointment for Monday, so we could conclude our business transaction." That should be an attractive subject for continued conversation.

"Hold on a minute." She said to someone, "I'll be right back." Moments later she spoke in a quiet voice, "You have my money? My check?"

"If you're ready to keep to your side of our agreement, I'll have it later this afternoon and can bring it to your office."

Her tone of voice shifted discernibly. "Mavis, you're a complete doll. I'll be here all afternoon."

"I'll be there before dinnertime." I clicked off, euphoria filling me up at the thought that I'd deposit enough money in the bank on Monday to take care of a number of issues.

As soon as I was off the phone, it chimed Ben's special tune. Dragnet. "Hey, Ben. You just caught me."

"You're back in Houston? Did he repair your car?"

"Yes to the first question. No to the second. Margaret took me to rent a car. I'll have to figure out what to do about the Mustang once it's fixed— if it can be fixed."

"You said 'caught me,' where are you going?"

"You want to get together? After all, it's Saturday, right?"

"Right. So where are you going?" Persistence was in his blood.

"If you must know, Tiki Island and then, Galveston."

"Uh huh. When will you be back? Will it be really late?"

"I don't expect so. Shouldn't take me more than a few minutes at each place, but, of course, the drive is more than an hour each way."

"We could have a late dinner. Tell you what, you call or text me when you get on the road back here. I'll pick up Thai and meet you at your place, with the wine this time." The tone of his voice came across as suggestive. We hadn't spent any quality time together in a while, so I hoped I heard him correctly.

I wouldn't be at all surprised if he also wanted to interrogate me about what I'd been doing at Gina's condo the night her body was discovered. Maybe that subject would be delayed to another time, but if it wasn't, I had questions for him, too. I still didn't know how he'd located me in La Grange. He couldn't have affixed something to my car that would indicate where I was, because I was in Margaret's car at Beth Anne's. Inquiring minds wanted—needed—to know how he did that.

After we ended the call, I was almost through the stack of things on my desk that needed my attention, when the cowbell over the front door clanged.

Candy came bopping in, wearing torn jeans and a T-shirt. Her usual weekend attire. "Hey, Mavis! I wondered if you'd be here today. I drove by your house, and your car wasn't there." She stepped toward the side of my desk like she was coming around to hug me and stopped, apparently thinking better of it. "I was worried about you. Margaret told me both of you were okay, but I wanted to see for myself."

"How's your car running?"

She shrugged and made a face. "As usual, like yours."

"Yes, but mine has the distinction of being a classic, whereas yours..."

"Belongs in the junkyard, I know."

"I was thinking. Maybe I could help you get another mode of transportation."

Her eyes lit up. "Really? What does *help* mean?"

"If you were to go out to get a new or newer vehicle for yourself, what would you look for?" I wasn't sure what I'd be able to afford but wanted to get an idea of what she'd like to have.

Candy threw herself into a chair opposite me. "I've already saved some money toward a motor scooter, like a Moped." She held up a stop sign hand. "I know what you're going to say. They're dangerous, etcetera, etcetera, but, Mavis, they're affordable and cheap to drive."

I couldn't help wincing. I wanted to ask what her mother would say, but I didn't want to see her reaction at the mention of her mother. "Yeah, well, I don't know anything about scooters, but I did hear once Mopeds were somehow different."

"I'm studying them, trying to decide what I need."

"You know I don't like the idea of you taking something like that on the highway."

"Me, neither, Mavis. I wouldn't." She pulled the chair up close to the front of my desk. "See, here's what I was thinking..."

I was thinking she was sounding a lot like me...whether that was a good thing or not remained to be seen.

"Are you listening? Because I have a plan." She watched my face, which I kept expressionless as best I could.

"I'm going to use the scooter only on the city streets of Houston, not the highway. I'll keep my car, even get it worked on a little when I have some extra money to make it more reliable, and if I have to go on the highway to get somewhere where I have to serve papers, I'll take the car. Or if it's raining or foggy. I wouldn't want someone to run over me in the fog."

I hoped she was a lot like me. She was so smart. When I'd first met her, with all her colored hair, weird clothes, and multitudes of earrings, I'd had my doubts. But underneath that oppositional defiant demeanor lurked a needy, loving young woman. "If you're determined—"

"I am." She crossed her arms. She knew I knew what that meant.

"I was going to say, today I'm headed south to pick up some

money. If all goes as planned, we can go shopping for your new vehicle next week." I swear I thought she was going to cry. Candy is someone who would never want anyone to see her cry.

She jumped up and actually came around the desk and hugged my neck for a moment. "I'm going to my office to study makes and models on the Internet and find out where they sell them. After that, I'll study my school stuff, if I can concentrate. Thank you so much, Mavis."

For once, everything proceeded as planned. Dewey let me in the gate right away and had the check to Blanche ready for me. He told me to keep whatever was left of the first check he'd written to me. In exchange, I didn't submit an expense bill. He also gave me a signed copy of one of his books for Margaret.

Blanche wasn't wearing her lawyer attire. She actually had on a jacket, a blouse, and jeans, so she'd made a concession for the week-end. She didn't hug my neck like Candy had. That was okay by me. What she did do is have a check written out except for the amount. I'm not sure she trusted me. Or maybe it was Dewey she didn't trust. I showed her his check. She grimaced and wrote out the agreed-upon amount for me.

"At least, Blanche, you didn't have to get me out of jail or represent me in court for free. That's something." I still hadn't talked to Ben but didn't think, no matter what I said, that he'd arrest me.

After leaving Blanche, check secured in my purse, I parked down the street from Beachy Antiques. Beachy Antiques and Blanche's office are both downtown. Tom stood behind the counter and was talking to a customer.

"Just wanted to touch base with you," I told him. "I don't know if you've heard the news."

"Be with you in a minute. Susan's in the storeroom if you want to talk to her."

Susan had her hair tied back and was wearing a T-shirt and jeans. Looked like she was unpacking some boxes. "Hi, Mavis. What's up?"

"Hey. Good to see you. I don't think there's any reason for me to wait to tell both of you at the same time. Gina's cousin, Arnie, and his girlfriend, Beth Anne Novak, have been arrested for Gina's murder. I'm pretty sure they're going to charge Arnie also with the murder of a woman named Sheila Siska."

Tom entered the room and stood in the doorway as Susan, stunned, dropped into an empty chair, her mouth open.

"What's this?" Tom asked. "Arnie killed someone?"

Eager to get back on the road to Houston, I summarized what had happened since I last saw them. Both were wide-eyed, clearly flabbergasted at the news. Neither had much to say. They kept looking from me to each other in disbelief.

"I need to get back to my office," I said when I got to the end of the story. "Once you digest this news, if you have further questions, you can call that police officer who was here or me. I'm going to keep up with the case, out of curiosity. I won't have any further role in it."

Susan shook her head. "Hard to believe."

"I know. I'm out of here, take care."

Tom walked me to the door, not saying much of anything. I had a feeling he was staggered by the news. He opened the door. "Thanks for letting us know. When you get back down here, stop by. I'll give you a cookie." He gave me a faux smile.

I didn't laugh. I thought it inappropriate, though I did smile back.

LATER THAT EVENING, Ben and I were curled up on my sofa after having consumed the Thai meal he'd brought over as well as a bottle of wine. Neither of us had, so far, broached the subjects on our minds. Silence settled over us and the moment of reckoning came.

He had his arm around me, so I moved away to be able to see his face. "So tell me now how you found me."

"Look, Mavis, if we're going to be honest with each other, we need to be completely honest. That applies to you as well as me." He had pulled his arm down and assumed a less friendly demeanor.

I would be honest, answering exactly what he asked me and no more. After all, I didn't have the requisite intent when I'd gotten into Gina's van and condo. That would have been my defense had I been caught *in flagrante*. I knew enough about criminal law to know culpability revolved around intent. I had good intentions.

"You first." I scooted a bit further away, so he'd have room to get comfortable as would I.

"Okay. I put a tracker on your cell phone before I gave it to you for your birthday."

A red haze came over my vision for a few moments. How dare he? What an invasion of my privacy! "Ben! My iPhone?" I slid even further away. "You've been tracking me all these months since my birthday?" My face had grown hot.

He held his palms up and shrugged. "Guilty as charged."

"I can't believe you can be so cavalier about this. I thought that was an awfully nice gift you gave me. Why did you do it? Don't you trust me?" I was having trouble keeping my temper in check. Heck, I was having trouble believing my longtime boyfriend would do something like that. What a betrayal.

"Sure, I trust you, but I did it for just the kind of situation you got into in La Grange. I swear I don't track you every day. I don't have the time."

"You wanted to protect me, is that it? Protect the little woman?"

"It wasn't like that. You do have a way of getting yourself in hot water."

I was bursting with anger. I knew he loved me, but that had nothing to do with it as far as I was concerned. He didn't think I was able to take care of myself. Hadn't I always called on him when I needed help? Well, most of the time, anyway. I shook my head to clear it, trying to cool down.

"I don't see how it has hurt you in any way. In fact, it's helped.

What were you going to do out there at Beth Ann Novak's house by yourself?"

He had a point. "I would have called the police. I know I've been terrible at asking for assistance when I need it, but I'm getting better. I am. Anyway, what do you say to it being an invasion of my privacy?"

"You have something to hide from me? Something you're doing you don't want me to know about?"

"How would you feel if I put a tracker on your phone?"

"If it will make you feel better, I'll let you."

"Oh, sure. Like as a police officer, you'd let someone track you." I slapped him on the arm, having cooled off a little.

"As long as it was only you." He took my hands and moved over to me, kissing me lightly on the lips. "Don't be angry. I'm trying to always be there for you."

I pushed on his chest. "Some people would call you chauvinistic. Get away from me. I'm not sure how I'm feeling about this information." If he could track my phone, he knew I was at Gina's condo complex before he ever arrived. That is, if he'd looked. I wasn't sure whether he'd had a reason to look. Afterall, no one knew whose van it was when the police arrived.

I knew little to nothing about trackers on phones. I didn't know to what extent they could give details about the person's location. I'd thought about putting one on Candy's, since she was the one mostly serving papers and exposed to lots of different people. I would discuss it with her, though, unlike some people. Were trackers able to pinpoint a person's *exact* location, like the room or the vehicle they'd climbed into? I couldn't remember whether I'd had the phone on me when I'd gone into Gina's condo. I'd had it when I spoke to Blanche, when I was inside the van. I possibly left it in the trunk when I took my tools, so I could pick the lock on Gina's door. Could trackers give the history of where you'd been or only the current location?

"You know, you haven't told me what you were doing outside Gina Collins' condo."

"Whatever it was, it's moot now, isn't it?"

"We had a deal. I told you how I found you. Now you have to tell me what was going on when you were outside her condo. More specifically, what you were doing when Lon Tyler saw you come from around back."

"I wasn't doing anything when I came from around back. But, if you want to know what I did when I went around the back of her condo, I checked the back door to see if it was locked and whether the window or windows were locked or unlocked. That's not a crime."

He gave me the police officer's steel stare. If he wanted to know more, he needed to ask specifically. I wasn't volunteering anything. I'd learned long ago not to do that.

"So they weren't unlocked?"

"No."

"And if they had been unlocked?"

"They weren't. Neither was the front door or any of the side windows. I already told you the other day I looked into the van windows."

"We're getting nowhere fast." He exhaled.

I kind of thought he didn't want to know any more than what I'd already told him. If he didn't know, we wouldn't get into an argument. If he found out, he might have to do something, though I couldn't think what. Anyway, the whole incident was practically ancient history. The killers were caught and would be prosecuted. Whatever had happened over the past week, events had worked out well.

And, I was pretty sure both of us had other things on our minds. More intimate things. So, we were at a kind of stalemate. I couldn't very well stay angry about the tracker when I was guilty of things he didn't really want to know about. I reached for him. He reached for me. The rest of the evening is also history.

The issue of the tracker is not moot. Maybe after Thanksgiving and Christmas we'll address it again. In the new year. I would hate to ruin the holidays.

THANK YOU FOR READING

Thank you for reading!

If you enjoyed **NOT MURDER**, I would appreciate it if you would help others to enjoy this book, too.

Share it with a friend.
Recommend it. Please help others find this book by recommending it to friends, readers' groups, and discussion boards.

Please tell other readers why you liked this book by reviewing it at Amazon or Goodreads. If you do write a review, please send me an email at susan@susanpbaker.com so I can thank you with a personal email.

If you'd like to be on my mailing list so you can receive news of events and publications, please sign up at https://www.susanpbaker.com/contact.

READ ON FOR CHAPTER 1 OF DEFENSIBLE MURDER, NO. 5 IN THE MAVIS DAVIS MYSTERY SERIES

CHAPTER 1

I was at my desk in the back of the building when the bell above our front door chimed. No one had an appointment, so I didn't pay any attention to the bell, figuring one of the staff, Margaret or Candy, would handle whatever was up.

A minute or so later, a woman I'd never seen before stuck her head around my door jamb and said "Mavis Davis?" The woman was middle height, plump like she was some months pregnant, and had huge, bruised circles under her bloodshot eyes.

Yes, that's me. Private Investigator. Former social worker. Employer of two women, one my age—thirty-something—and one not yet twenty. Tenant of a repurposed house in an older neighborhood of Houston, Texas. Single woman with a cop for a boyfriend.

Who else would be in my office? I wanted to ask but didn't. My mother raised me to be more polite than that. "Yes, ma'am, that's me." I coughed. "I've tested negative for Covid so don't worry. This cough is left over from some other crud I caught from my assistant, Margaret. Did she send you in here?"

"I couldn't find anyone in the front, so I came on back." Her chin trembling, she said, "I hope you don't mind."

I was going to kill Margaret and/or Candy, whoever was supposed to be staffing the front desk at that time for letting someone come back without notifying me. They were supposed to work out who occupied that space when one of them had other obligations, though the front of the office was mainly Margaret's terrain.

I had slipped in through the back and hadn't checked to see who was handling the front desk. Hadn't paid attention to any vehicles parked behind our little house-office. Not normal for me. Though I was recovering from whatever had ailed me, my focus hadn't returned one-hundred percent.

I hadn't wanted to be bothered with new cases for a few days, until I was better. I was doing some reading and research until I got my energy back. Without visibly sighing and without offering her a chair, I asked, with hope in my heart the pitiful-looking woman didn't want to hire me, "What can I do for you?"

She glanced at one of the chairs positioned in front of my desk. "May I sit down?"

I almost said, *if you must* but refrained. "Please." I'd let her sit, but she wasn't getting a smile out of me. I coughed into my tissue, and by the time I looked up, she was ensconced on the edge of a chair, her oversized handbag resting on the side table.

"Have you tried that stuff you squirt up your nose? It's supposed to really help the cold not be so bad."

"Yep. If I hadn't, I'd probably be home in bed. So, anyway..."

"I heard of you and know you do investigations including kidnappings. Not too long ago I read about that big case where you found that girl and boy whose mother had lied about their father and gotten him thrown in prison."

"You needn't go on. I remember it well." In fact, the money I'd been paid—including a nice bonus—had enabled me to pay some bills and be choosier about what clientele I took, but I wasn't going to tell her that.

Her eyes wide with hope, she said, "I want to hire you."

"Uh-huh." She must have mistaken my grunt for one of interest, because she kept talking.

"Someone has stolen my babies. My twins."

Oh shoot. Twin babies. How low could a person go? I didn't mean the baby-stealers, although that was beyond low, I meant the story—how could anyone resist helping a person whose twin babies had been stolen? I really needed to develop a thicker skin. I blew out a long breath—no cough, yea. She had me. "Tell me more," I said in a raspy voice. My laryngitis had improved over the past week. Any earlier and she wouldn't have been able to hear me.

She grimaced, her face scrunching up, her eyes full of tears. I didn't blame her. If I'd had even one baby stolen, I would have cried for days. Not that I had any babies. I did not now and didn't intend to ever have any. I pushed my almost-empty box of tissues to her and waited for the dam to burst. Instead, she took a lot of short breaths like I've heard women must do when they're going through natural childbirth.

"I promised myself and my husband I wouldn't cry. I've cried a river since last night."

I nodded. No tears. Good. "So, if you want to tell me about it, I'm eager to hear." Hate to admit it, but it was true.

"My babies were born six weeks ago today. Fraternal twins, a boy and a girl. Fred and Frederika."

No comment on the awfulness of the names. Who was I to judge, with the name my mother had given me? I pulled out a yellow legal pad. "Fred and Frederika?"

"They're named after my great-uncle, my German great-uncle Friedrich, who left us some money in his will."

Had she read my opinion of the names in my mind? Or on my face?

"Oh, my goodness, I'm so sorry. You're asking last name. I forgot to introduce myself. I'm Connie Wite. No H." She held out a lavender-smelling hand for me to shake.

"I don't think you want to shake my hand right now. I don't think I am, but I could be contagious. What does that mean, no H?"

She withdrew her hand. "W-I-T-E. Wite with no H. Fred and Frederika Wite are the babies' names. And my husband is Dave."

"Number one, you want to tell me what happened? And number two, have you gone to the police?" Private investigators were not supposed to involve themselves in active cases. Not that I'd ever let that stop me.

She settled back in the chair, but her shoulders were still up around her ears. "Well, I feel so guilty, but the fact is, after six weeks of crying babies, my husband and I were at our wits' end. Last Sunday, we asked Dave's sister, Louise, if she would babysit for us just for a few hours, so we could go out to dinner and a movie on Wednesday, that would be last night. She usually goes to church on

Wednesdays, but she agreed so long as we didn't mind her taking the babies to church with her."

"And you and your husband went out?"

"We loaded her car up with both car seats and two diaper bags full of diapers and several bottles of milk—I nurse the babies, but I express enough for several bottles extra just in case."

My boobs cringed. I did my best to continue keeping a straight face.

"When we returned to our home—Louise was going to go back to our house after church and meet us there when we were through with our date—Louise was pacing up and down the sidewalk outside in the dark. She was near hysteria when we stopped the car and got out. Someone had taken the babies from the church nursery while the little girl who attends them was in the bathroom."

Astounded, I sat back and took a moment to just stare at her. If I were a lawyer, I'd be wondering whether Mrs. Wite could sue the church for negligence for losing her children. But I wasn't. Just a P.I. So now I'm wondering whether my energy is back enough that I can help this lady and, also, what the police were up to. "Y'all did call the police?"

"They did at the church, but no one called us. My husband's own sister. Can you believe that? She thought she should come home first and tell us in person and let us handle it. Sometimes I don't believe her stupidity."

Was she saying she and Louise didn't see eye-to-eye on things? And was that relevant?

"Not long after we arrived home, the police showed up and took a report. I could hardly talk, but my husband told them what they needed to know."

Stating aloud what I'd already reminded myself of, I said, "You know, private investigators aren't supposed to get involved in active police investigations."

"Oh." She collapsed like a deflating balloon, folding in on herself.

"Is there some reason you don't want to let the police handle this? Did they say they wouldn't look for your babies? I can't imagine that."

"The one officer was nice, but his partner looked at us funny and asked a lot of questions that made me feel like I'd done something wrong. We're worried he'll focus on us and not search for them."

"Like how did he behave?"

"Frowned at us. Looked at us with an eyebrow raised, his eyes squinting, just like you see them do sometimes in the police shows on television." Her voice grew higher and louder the more she talked. "Like he didn't believe us. Like maybe we or Louise had done something to our babies."

Nuh-uh, he did not. Not in this day and time. With all the human trafficking that was going on, especially in Houston, Texas? My blood pressure rose. Where was that blood pressure cuff when I needed it? "Since last night, have you heard back from the police?"

"Dave and I went down to the station first thing this morning and confronted them to see what they were doing. We're the kind of people who aren't going to sit around and do nothing even when told to stay by the phone and wait for a ransom call."

"That's what the police said to do?" Not quite a rhetorical question.

"But Miss Davis, we're not stupid. We're educated people. Someone could sell our babies and get more money than we could come up with for ransom even though we're both working and making good money. We read. We know what's going on in the world. We know Houston is practically the capitol of human trafficking."

She could probably read the surprise on my face. "And I suppose you have cell phones, so if there was a ransom call, if anyone could even get your cell phone numbers, you could take the calls on your mobiles."

"Of course. And I think the police are doing exactly nothing."

"They did, at least, put out an Amber Alert?"

"Yes. I must give them credit for that."

"Were other children taken as well?"

She shook her head. "No one else brought kids to church last night."

"Huh, back to Louise. They interviewed her separately?"

"Yes. Apparently first at the church and then again at our house."

"The police went to the church and—"

"Talked to the minister and the little girl who was supposed to be babysitting. They also talked to other parishioners or whatever you call them in that Holy Roller church."

Holy Roller church? "And got nowhere?"

She shook her head. "Got less than nowhere."

"Hmmm. I don't usually mess with investigations where the cops are involved." This time I said it aloud. My legs were crossed under my desk. She would have seen my fingers if I'd crossed them.

"Oh, please, Miss Davis." Her voice squeaked. "If you could just ask questions and look around, maybe they missed someone or something. We would never tell Officer Ryan and Officer Tyler you were helping us."

She couldn't have been more sincere. Her big brown eyes welled up with tears. Then I registered what she'd just said. "Officer *Tyler*? Lon Tyler?" OMG. My arch nemesis.

"I think that was his first name. A kind of piggish cop, if you excuse the pun. You know him? He's the one who acted like he didn't believe us." She covered her mouth in disgust. "Are you friends?" She stood.

"Oh, *please*, sit back down. We are definitely *not* friends." But if it was Lon who was doing the *alleged* investigation, it would not bother me one bit, not one teeny-weeny (again no pun intended) bit to help poor Mrs. Wite.

So, against my better judgment, which some people say can be questionable—but I won't go into that—I decided I'd at least do some inquiring. Okay, to be perfectly honest, I decided to let her hire me. I couldn't let her and Dave be victims of Lon's doltishness, assuming the case wouldn't be handed off to someone more competent. "Tell you what, I'll go over there and look around for you." I wrote a not-small sum on a piece of paper. "Here's my fee, for starters. This amount will cover a couple of days. If my investigation runs longer than that, my fee will be more. You can bring the money back here before five this afternoon and give it to Margaret or Candy, okay?"

"Margaret or Candy?"

"The two women who also work here" (allegedly, I thought, since neither of them was actually in the office), "one of whom was supposed to be sitting at the front desk when you came in."

"Okay, Miss Davis. I'll have to make a trip to the bank, but I'll have it by then. And here's the name of the church and the address and my sister-in-law's name and address." She handed me a pink Post-It Note. "And here's my card. I wrote my husband's cell number on the back." It listed her name, address, phone number and "Freelance Writer. Former Teacher."

"By the way, where is your husband right now? Why isn't he with you?"

Her eyes shifted to the right. I'd have to look up whether that meant something. Or was it eyes shifting to the left that meant something? "He had some business to take care of. He dropped me off at home after we left the police station. I drove my own car over here."

"I'll need to meet him pretty soon." I stood. "I'll do what I can. You don't have to tell me that time is of the essence, Mrs. Wite. I know it is, especially with little babies. By the way, when they took the babies, did they take the milk and diaper bags? I hope they have enough stuff to take care of them."

"No. They just took the babies and their blankets. They must have bought some supplies—diapers and formula." She let out a sob. "They'll have to feed them formula. I wasn't going to ever feed them formula."

A twinge of anger coursed through me at the heartlessness of the situation. "I'm so sorry. I'm sure that's not the way you intended to wean them from the—the—breast. One more question, you said Holy Roller church, and I see from the name that's what it sounds like. Are you and your husband not members of the same church as his sister?"

Her lips stretched thin. "Oh no. No way we could buy into all that —we're atheists."

An atheist brother and an evangelical sister. Interesting, but none of my business. My business was finding those babies as quickly as possible. I walked her to the door. "I'll get back to you this evening. Why don't I come by and meet your husband and report on anything I find today."

She nodded as she walked out the door, wiping her eyes as she went.

After closing the door behind her, I punched Candy's number into my cell phone. I hoped she and Margaret weren't up to any mischief.

END OF CHAPTER 1

ALSO BY SUSAN P. BAKER

Novels:

My First Murder

No. 1 in the Mavis Davis Mystery Series. A cafe owner hires Mavis as a last resort to discover who murdered his mysterious waitress.

The Sweet Scent of Murder

No. 2 in the Mavis Davis Mystery Series. Mavis' search for a missing teenager turns into a murder investigation in Houston's Ritzy River Oaks.

Murder and Madness

No. 3 in the Mavis Davis Mystery Series. Mavis takes on the cold case of a grisly ax murder of a cruise ship captain in Galveston.

Not Murder

No. 4 in the Mavis Davis Mystery Series. Mavis is hired to locate a lawyer's deadbeat client and finds a Pandora's box of problems, including a dead body.

Defensible Murder

No. 5 in the Mavis Davis Mystery Series. Can Houston, Texas P.I. Mavis Davis rescue kidnapped twins and clear their father of murder without becoming a victim herself?

Death of a Prince

No. 1 in the Lady Lawyer Mystery Series. Sandra Salinsky & Erma Townley defend the alleged murderer of a Galveston millionaire plaintiff's attorney who was Erma's best friend.

Death of a Rancher's Daughter

No. 2 in the Lady Lawyer Mystery Series. Sandra & Erma defend a family friend for murder while fighting gender and racial prejudice in a small Texas town.

Ledbetter Street

A Novel of Second Chances: Not just the story of a mother fighting for custody of her disabled son, but one of love, tragedy, and the relationships of the women of Ledbetter Street.

Suggestion of Death

An investigative reporter who can't pay his child support searches for the killer of deadbeat dads, before he becomes the next victim.

UNAWARE

Attorney Dena Armstrong wants to break out from the control of the two men dominating her life, unaware that a stranger has other plans for her.

Texas Style Justice

Judge Victoria Van Fleet aspires to the highest court in the land, but is she willing to pay the price?

Nonfiction:

Heart of Divorce

Divorce advice especially for those who are considering representing themselves.

Murdered Judges of the 20th Century

True stories of judges killed in America.

Fly Catching

An eclectic collection of short pieces.

www.susanpbaker.com

ABOUT THE AUTHOR

Susan P. Baker, a retired Texas family court judge, presided over everything from murder to divorce for 12 years. Afterward, she traveled around Texas as a visiting judge for another 12. Prior to being elected to the bench, she practiced law for nine (9) years, and was a probation officer for two (2) years. Susan's works are derived from her experiences in the justice system or events in and around courts in Texas, *fictionalized*, of course!

She is the author of 11 novels of mystery and suspense set in Texas, two nonfiction books, and an eclectic collection of short pieces. Her novels include five featuring Mavis Davis, a private detective; two Lady Lawyer mysteries starring criminal defense lawyers Sandra Salinsky and Erma Townley (3rd in the works); and four standalones with court participant protagonists (including judges and lawyers).

Her two nonfiction books are Murdered Judges of the 20th Century and Heart of Divorce—Advice from a Judge. The title of her collection is Fly Catching.

Susan is a member of All Author, Alliance of Independent Authors, Sisters in Crime, Authors Guild, Writers League of Texas, Texas Authors, and Galveston Novel and Short Story Writers.

She has two children and eight grandchildren. She loves dark chocolate, raspberries, and traveling the world (and has lost count of the number of countries she's visited). An anglophile, Susan most enjoys visiting her cousins in England and Australia (where she was finally able to visit in September of '22). She hopes to finally drive

Route 66 in 2023. She is at home in Galveston with her rescue kitty, Tudi.

Read more about Susan, find her books at www.susanpbaker.com, sign up for her mailing list here: www.susanpbaker.com/contact. Like her at http://facebook.com/legalwriter. Follow her on http://Twitter/susanpbaker and on Instagram@suewritesandreads.

www.ingramcontent.com/pod-product-compliance
Lightning Source LLC
Chambersburg PA
CBHW060634260626
47161CB00008B/2887

* 9 780999 803903 9 *